THE WORLD ASUNDER

BOOK TWO OF THE PSYCHE OF WAR

Kacey Ezell

Theogony Books
Virginia Beach, VA

Chris Kennedy/Theogony Books
2052 Bierce Dr.
Virginia Beach, VA 23454
http://chriskennedypublishing.com/

Publisher's Note: This is a work of fiction. Names, characters, places, and incidents are a product of the author's imagination. Locales and public names are sometimes used for atmospheric purposes. Any resemblance to actual people, living or dead, or to businesses, companies, events, institutions, or locales is completely coincidental.

Ordering Information:
Quantity sales. Special discounts are available on quantity purchases by corporations, associations, and others. For details, contact the "Special Sales Department" at the address above.

The World Asunder/Kacey Ezell. -- 1st ed.
ISBN 978-1950420292

Acknowledgements

Once again, I could not have brought this book to you without the help and support of an entire cast of characters. First of all, this time, I'd like to thank my father, Lieutenant Colonel Robert E. Coacher, USAF (ret), who first told me the story of the Berlin Airlift and took my nine-year-old self to meet Colonel Gail Halvorsen (aka, The Candy Bomber.) If you don't know Col. Halvorsen's story, I highly recommend you check it out. It's a fantastic one. Secondly, I'd like to thank my publisher, Chris Kennedy, for continuing to believe in my psychics, and for encouraging me to do the same. Even more thanks are due my editor, Tiffany Reynolds, for making my work shine. I couldn't do it without you. Thanks also to my myriad coauthors on all my various projects. Marisa, Mark, Griffin, Chris, John, Speaker, Doc, Josh, Nico, thanks for your patience and willingness to work with me. I'm truly honored and in awe of your talents, all of you. Same with The Badasses and the Cabal. You ladies and gentlemen inspire me daily. I am so thankful that you're my friends...and DONE! :) Special thanks also to the Sunday and Monday crew at Silver Diner in Waldorf, MD. Thanks for giving me a place to write and feeding me delicious food in the process.

I would be remiss if I didn't mention one particular research book this time around: Operation Paperclip: The Secret Intelligence Program That Brought Nazi Scientists to America by Annie Jacobsen. This book is a fascinating and enjoyable read and it takes an unflinching look at one of the murkier chapters of our recent history. I recommend it.

Last, but never least, to my husband and my girls. Thank you for everything. Without you, there is no me.

–Kacey Ezell, April 2019

For EZ. Still the coolest guy I'll ever meet.

Chapter One – Awakening

On a sticky summer day in June of 1948, Adalina Sucherin remembered who she was.

She'd been walking home from work, but she hadn't really been paying close attention to her route. There was no great reason for her to hurry home to her solitary flat. It contained only a creaky bed and the few meager possessions she'd been able to scrounge after the war. Her neighbors, perhaps, might have looked for her, but they knew her habits, and it wasn't unusual for her to walk for hours each night. There was solace in movement, in the illusion of action that exercise provided. Standing still gave the horror an opportunity to creep in, so Lina preferred to walk.

It was the sound that did it. She would remember that, later. That deep rumble, just at the edge of her hearing. It started in her chest and built to an audible roar…but distant. A sudden flash of fear brought her head up from her unseeing study of the broken concrete road. Bombers? An air raid?

No. Stupid, stupid, she chastised herself. The war had been over for three years. Three years since the Reich had fallen, taking with it all her illusions, all her fire. Three years since the Soviet soldiers came ravening through the streets of Berlin, looting and raping everything in their path. Three years since she'd last torn a man's psyche apart, watching him bleed from his eyes and nose as his brain hemorrhaged in response. Three years since she'd killed to keep herself and three little girls safe, then locked her power away behind shields thicker than concrete, stronger than steel. Three long, uncertain, fear-tainted years.

Those weren't bombers at all.

She glanced around, looking for the hand-lettered signs that sometimes indicated the names of streets in this corpse of a once-great city. *Wilhelmstraße*. She hadn't realized she'd come so far south. She was right next to the border of the American zone, just north of the airport. A glance at the sky showed her a line of aircraft darkening the horizon. She watched them as she continued walking.

"I'm sorry, miss. You can't go any further without a pass."

Lina blinked and focused on the man, who spoke in harshly-accented German. She pressed her lips together and fought not to recoil in revulsion. A Soviet soldier, standing next to one of the borderlines the so-called allies had set up when they'd drawn and quartered Berlin after the armistice. She gave him a nod (one must be polite, else one invited more attention!) and started to walk away, when a thought stopped her. These "allies" *did* have men with guns stationed on the borders of their claimed territories. That didn't seem like a particularly warm alliance to her.

"Sir," she asked, "why are there so many aircraft?"

He gave her a smile, a sweet one. It made him look young.

"Do not be frightened, miss," he said. "The war has not begun again. The British and Americans are flying supplies into the other sectors of Berlin in an attempt to bribe the population with their decadence and corruption. But it won't work. No ground transportation from the west is permitted into Berlin at all. No one has ever supplied a city this size by air alone. It cannot be done! The city will be reunited under the rightful rule of the workers soon enough. Have no fear."

"Thank you," she murmured, and stepped away. He touched the fingers of his free hand (the one not holding his rifle) to the brim of his cap and gave her another smile. She barely noticed, as thoughts began to tumble one over the other in her brain while she resumed her walk home.

Berlin was cut off from the west. The Soviets were trying to starve the population of the British and American sectors out.

The British and Americans were airlifting in supplies. Why? Did they know what kind of hell the Soviet occupation of Berlin had been?

If they knew, why had they allied with such monsters?

Lina did not like the British. The Americans were worse. During the war, the Americans had bombed her hometown and killed her family. Then, just when love had ignited in her life amidst the dreariness of war, another American, a woman, had destroyed everything she held dear. Lina had carried the woman's name in her heart as a talisman against fear, and as fuel for the fires of hatred she nurtured inside. One day, she'd promised herself, one day Evelyn Adamsen would pay for what she'd done...

And then the world had ended, and the Soviets had come.

Amid the fires and the screams, Lina had hidden with her neighbor's three daughters in a cellar under a bombed-out building. They'd heard the cries and laughter, the crashing of glass, the sharp coughs of rifle fire, and the distant booming of the field guns. For three nights and days she'd hidden with those girls, drinking water from a leaky pipe, eating the crumbs from an old crust of bread. Until the night a group of soldiers had crashed drunkenly through the hidden cellar door.

For the first time in three years, Lina didn't flinch from the memory. She forced herself, instead, to examine it. To replay it in her head, just as it had happened.

Something heavy hit the door. It cracked near the hinges, along the lock. Something hit it again, and it slammed open, banging against the far wall. The girls screamed and fled for the corner behind Lina. So young, all of them. Nine, seven, and barely three. Mere babies.

Lina interposed her body between the girls and the soldier. He reeked of alcohol, sweat, and gunpowder. He leered at her, craned his neck to see behind her, his pig-like eyes glinting in the light of their single lantern. Behind him two more crowded in, then stopped, drunk and confused.

"Take the woman," the first soldier slurred. Lina was fluent in Russian, and she barely understood him. "I'll take the girls."

"No," Lina said, her voice cracking like a whip.

"Shut up, cunt," he said with a laugh, "You're too old and ugly, especially when there are pretty little girls—"

Lina heard no more. She took two steps forward and jabbed her fingers into the man's throat before he could marshal his drunken reflexes to react. The moment her skin touched his, she reached out with her mind, in the way she'd been taught by the Reich's best scientists and theorists, and she ripped his natural, latent psychic shields away. And then she, the most powerful student to ever graduate from the Reichschule, *stabbed her power deep into his brain.*

His cranial capillaries exploded. All of them. All at once. Blood flowed from his eyes, ears, nose. She watched him stumble toward her for a step, and then crumple to the ground. Then she turned and looked at the other men in the room. One raised his rifle halfway to his shoulder. She stared at him, wondering if he would do it.

He didn't. Neither did his partner. They just turned and left. The corpse of their friend stayed crumpled in a heap on the cellar floor.

Lina blinked away the memory and looked skyward once more. She didn't like the British, or the Americans. But they were crazy enough to try to airlift supplies into her city rather than see it all in the hands of the Soviets. Evelyn Adamsen had been an American aircrewwoman. Perhaps...perhaps there was hope.

For the first time in three years, Lina felt a spark of interest ignite in her mind, and the coals of her burning need for revenge began to smolder once again.

* * *

In the past three years, Lina's neighbors, the Thanhousers, had all but adopted her into the family. Rolland Thanhouser had been a respected chemist during the war, and his wife Isa had been from a well-to-do Berlin family. Their fortunes hadn't survived the war, nor the sack of Berlin that followed. But thanks to Lina, their three daughters had, so Lina found herself an honorary auntie.

After the chaos of the initial occupation, the Thanhousers had joined thousands of Berliners, doing their best to rebuild their homes and lives. Rolland took a job working in a soap factory, while Isa cared for the girls and Lina. After the episode in the cellar, after the pain that reverberated through all of Berlin as it burned, Lina had closed herself off. It had saved her mind, but to be so head-blind had made her basically nonfunctional. Isa and the girls had kept her safe and hidden, made sure she ate and drank water, and basically kept her doing the bare minimum of human tasks necessary to survive until the ravening Soviets had vented all their fury on the broken corpse of the city.

Slowly, Lina had become more and more self-sufficient as she learned to cope without using her gifts. She couldn't feel the world around her, but she was eventually able to care for herself, and then to obtain her own apartment and a job as the whole city struggled to rebuild. The Thanhousers prevented her from retreating back into herself and slowly, Lina realized, despite everything, she'd managed to find herself once again part of a family.

Given her history with families, it was a mixed blessing at best.

Still, Isa and Rolland had been good to her, and the girls, Ginette, Aleda, and Johanna, adored her. They saw her as the powerful auntie who'd kept them safe. Though three years on, only Ginette, now twelve, reliably remembered the horrors of Berlin's fall. At least, so Lina surmised.

It wasn't something they discussed much.

"Isa?" Lina called out as she let herself in to the Thanhousers' apartment. Her voice echoed through the small, scrupulously clean entryway. "Isa? Are you home?"

"In the kitchen!" Isa called, her voice ringing cheerfully down the hallway. Lina admired her for that. Even after everything she'd been through, Isa never lost her sunny outlook. "Come on back, Lina. The girls and I are making Berliners."

"Where did you get jam for the filling?" Lina asked as she walked down the short hallway and into the warm kitchen. The girls, their faces dusted with varying amounts of flour, smiled up at her from their places around the central work table. Isa turned from the stove with a wide grin.

"They had cherries in the market, and I'm stewing them with a bit of honey. It won't be exactly what you remember, but it'll be close. And it's fun to experiment, right girls?"

"Yes, *Mutti*," little Johanna said, her smile impish.

"Will you help us, *Tante*?" asked Ginette, the eldest. A serious twelve years old, she had less flour on her face than her sisters, though she wasn't entirely unsmudged.

"If you like," Lina said and went to pump water into the sink to wash her hands. Getting the running water back a little over a year ago had been a big moment, and Lina never failed to appreciate it after so long without. She wiped her hands on a towel and joined the girls as they stirred and kneaded the dough.

"Did you see the airplanes?" Lina asked softly after a moment. She kept her tone casual, lest she alarm the girls, but Ginette looked sharply up. Lina smiled and shook her head slightly. "Cargo planes only. Flying into Tempelhof."

"I heard them," Isa said, stirring the pot, "but I didn't think anything of it. The Amis are always flying in and out."

"Not in these kinds of numbers," Lina said. "I spoke to one of the Red soldiers guarding the zone crossing point. He said something about no ground transportation being allowed into the western part of the city at all. So the Amis and Tommies are flying supplies in."

"Hah," Isa said, shaking her head with a little laugh. "So first they bomb our city to rubble, and now they feed us from the sky? Irony must be an American."

"I wonder if they'll be able to do it," Lina said. "The soldier seemed to think the west wouldn't be able to hold out, and would give in to the Soviet demands."

"What demands?"

"I don't know. Unification under the communists, maybe? The soldier said something along those lines."

"I'd almost rather starve," Isa said softly, but then shook her head and smiled brightly, taking refuge in her usual positivity. Lina didn't understand it, but she wasn't one to judge another woman's coping mechanisms. Especially not one who'd been as good to her as Isa had.

"Hello, my girls!"

Rolland Thanhouser walked in to the kitchen, his eyes tired in a smiling, careworn face.

"Papa!" Aleda, the middle daughter, shrieked. She launched herself from her chair and flew at her father, who caught both her and her younger sister (who'd followed a breath behind Aleda) into a big, tight hug.

"Hello, my sweet ones!" he said, bestowing kisses on the foreheads of each of his daughters after letting the little ones go. "Mmm. You really are sweet. What are we making?"

"Berliners," Ginette said, "only with honey-stewed cherries instead of proper jam."

"Sounds delicious," Rolland said. "And *Tante* Lina is helping? I didn't know you were a baker, Lina."

"I have many talents," she said, with a smile for the only man she trusted anymore.

"That's certainly true. Hello, my love," he said then, walking over to kiss his wife gently on her offered cheek. "What possessed you to make jelly doughnuts?"

"I saw the cherries in the market, and I just couldn't resist. I know it's an extravagance…"

"But we all need a treat sometimes," Rolland finished for his wife with a smile. "A few cherries won't quite beggar us."

"My thoughts exactly," she said.

"Papa, did you see the airplanes today?" little Johanna asked then, her piping voice innocent and excited to be part of the grown-ups' conversation. Rolland looked down at her and then at Isa and Lina in turn.

"No, darling," he said as he slung his coat over the back of a chair and lowered himself into his seat. "What airplanes?"

"The American and British cargo planes flying into Tempelhof," Lina said. "The communists have blockaded the west of the city, it seems, and the Amis and Tommies are trying to supply the city by air."

"They're trying to starve the west into submission," Rolland said, his voice as tired as his eyes. "I'd heard rumblings of something like that. What an audacious move by the Americans and British, though! To supply a whole city by air. I really don't think it can be done."

"At least they're trying," Isa said softly.

Much as Lina disliked thinking well of anything American, she had to agree. At least they were trying to keep western Berlin supplied.

"Have you been in touch with your sister, Isa?" Rolland asked. "Should we arrange to have her move in here with us? We can get her a ration card…"

"She wouldn't come," Isa said. "I got a note from her the other day. She's fallen in love with an American and fears that she'll never see him again if she comes east."

Lina snorted. "Likely he'll return home, and she'll *still* never see him again."

"You're probably right," Isa said with a sigh. "Still, Emilia will have her own way. Plus she hates the Reds."

Lina looked up and met Isa's eyes, which had gone grim with remembered pain. Whether her own or on her sister's behalf, Lina didn't know. It didn't matter. They all carried it.

"Well," Rolland said, "that's as may be, but you should contact her anyway. Let her know she has a place with us here whenever she needs it."

"Thank you, love," Isa said, her eyes softening into a tender smile for her husband.

"You're a good man, Rolland Thanhouser," Lina said. "We're lucky to have you."

* * *

She felt like a babe with eyes newly opened.

Oh, it wasn't as bad as all that, but as Lina ventured out the next morning, she began to realize just how much she'd missed while she'd been locked in her mind's fog. Berlin still bore the horrific scars of war, with buildings missing or reduced to piles of rubble, but the streets at least were clear, and the sounds of rebuilding and new construction echoed off the cobblestones and brick all around.

The sun had just started to peek over the skyline to the east when Lina approached the barrier she'd found yesterday. Once again, the distant rumble of aircraft engines throbbed through the air. On impulse, she stepped out into the street and walked up to the checkpoint itself. Unlike yesterday, the guard today gave her no smile. He simply stared impassively as she cleared her throat and spoke.

"Ah, excuse me," she said, "do you know why so many airplanes are flying again?"

"No," he said, his voice clipped in heavily-accented German.

"Is the checkpoint closed?" she asked, trying again.

"Do you have your papers and ration card?" he asked. Lina nodded and drew them forth from the handbag she carried on her shoulder. As she looked down, she took a deep breath and very, very carefully stretched out her senses, seeking the guard's surface thoughts.

It had been so long. Her gift leapt free like a puppy unchained, and she had to grasp it with desperate, iron control before it slammed into the man's natural barriers and gave her attempt away. Ugh, but she was rusty! She pulled the papers forth and grasped her seeking gift with all her will before looking back up to meet his eyes.

Just a tendril, Lina thought. *Just a touch...*

There. Clumsier than she would have liked, but she brushed her mind against the guard's surface thoughts. Boredom, fatigue, an edge of hunger. A wish to go home and leave this wreck of a city. The wide cheekbones and broad smile of a brunette girl...

Lina pulled back, the papers rattling as her hand trembled just a little bit. The guard looked at her, his gaze sharpening.

"Are you well, Fräulein?" he asked.

"Y-yes," Lina said. "A bit sleepy perhaps. Are my papers in order?"

"Yes," he said, his eyes snapping down to them and back up to meet her blue gaze. "You may pass. Keep that ration card close, though. People in the West aren't getting them."

"Thank you," she said and tucked her documents away before stepping down into the street and joining the flow of traffic that wound through the barbed-wire maze of the checkpoint.

Lina didn't really have any particular destination in mind. Eventually she'd have to arrive at her job in the typing pool at one of the government buildings back on the east side of the barricades, but she could blame the traffic and the new barriers for making her late. She let the flow of the crowd carry her down along the street.

As she walked, she reached out with her mind, tentatively at first, then with growing confidence. She let her awareness skim over the surface emotions of the people around her, like a hummingbird taking a sip from a forest of flowers.

A shiver ran from her scalp down the length of her spine as fear and uncertainty flooded in through her open barriers. Anxiety rose all around her in the hearts and throats of the people. Nervous glances dominated as they passed one another, then looked with desperate hope to the airplanes thrumming through the skies overhead.

Lina dragged in a deep breath and slammed her barriers back into place. Her hands trembled, and she made her way to a nearby bench before her unsteady legs collapsed under her. Damn it all! She hadn't been ready for that. Maybe if she hadn't been hiding behind airtight barriers for the last three years…

No, she thought, forcing her spine straight. *Self-recrimination does nothing. It's a mark of the weak. What's done is done. You're here now. You must move forward from this moment.*

"Fräulein?" someone asked. Lina looked up to see an older woman with a bright green head scarf and a kindly smile. "Are you all right?"

"I'm fine," Lina said, trying to return the smile. "I just got a little dizzy."

"Eh," the woman clucked, sympathy in her eyes. "Not enough food. You must eat more." She sat down beside Lina and began rummaging in the large shopping bag she carried.

"No," Lina said, "really, Oma. I'm fine, thank you."

"No, I insist," the old woman said. "Aha! Here you go. Sweet honey candy. It will give you a little boost, enough to get to where you're going, yes? I love them so much. My sweet Gus, he would buy bags and bags of them for me before the war. Take it, take it!" She pressed a small, hard lump wrapped in waxy paper into Lina's hand with surprising strength.

"Thank you," Lina said as she took the candy and unwrapped it. She put it in her mouth and let the sweet-sticky flavor of honey dissolve over her tongue. To her surprise, she actually did feel a little better.

"There," the old woman said, her face crinkling in another smile. "No pain is so large that it can blot out all sweetness, yes? Good girl. Get to where you're going, now. And try to get more food to eat, if you can. I know it's difficult."

"I'll be fine now," Lina said. "Thank you again."

"This is what we do," the woman replied. She reached out a hand for Lina's, then pushed herself slowly to her feet. "We help one another. That's how we survive."

Lina didn't know what to say to that, so she just nodded. The woman patted her cheek, and then started humming an old tune as she continued her interrupted journey. Lina watched her go while she continued sucking on the hard, sticky candy.

* * *

Eventually, Lina got up and walked to her job. Navigating the checkpoint proved to be a slow and frustrating process, since traffic flow increased as the morning wound on. The guards inspected her ration card and waved her through without ever looking at her face. She didn't try to touch their surface minds again, though she did drop her barriers slightly to continue letting in the feel of the crowd around her.

It was like someone had turned on the lights when she'd become used to existing in a dark room. The emotional sensations flowed in and threatened once again to overwhelm her, but she steeled her nerves and fought for the control she'd learned at the *Reichschule* so many years ago. Slowly, bit by bit, Lina began to parse the incoming impressions as she walked, until she arrived at the door to the government building where she worked.

For the first time, she looked, really *looked* around as she pulled the door open and walked down the short grey hallway toward the clickety-clacking sound of the typing pool. On the surface, it didn't appear much different from any other day. Women sat at their small desks, quietly hunched over their typewriters as the cacophony of keys filled the air. Light from the tiny windows high in the far wall streamed in, spilling over the floor in elongated rectangles.

It should have been beautiful and soothing: the neat lines of desks, the almost-musical hum of thousands of keys, the picture of honest labor as these women worked to recover their lives, their livelihoods, and their nation from the chaos of the war. After a war, few things are as beautiful as order.

So why, then, did Lina feel a discordant note in the air, like an electric buzz just under her skin? Why were the faces of some of the women pinched and pale? It could have been hunger, of course. Resources were still scarce, after all. But Lina didn't think so. Her gut instinct said something else was in play here.

Slowly, carefully, building on what she'd learned while walking, Lina lowered her barriers and reached out, skimming over the surface of the ladies' thoughts. As ever, it was harder to get clear impressions from women than it had been for the men outside, but she managed.

It wasn't anything specific that flowed in along her channels from the room, more an overriding sense of dread. The women typically didn't read the memos they typed, but it was impossible not to pick up the gist of things. A piece here and a piece there, and Lina found she had a pretty good sense of what was happening...and the reason for the overall sense of bad times to come.

It seemed the government of the Democratic German Republic was doing more than just locking down the western half of Berlin. Lina felt a shiver of fear run up her spine as the picture became clearer: they were creating a national secret police force whose purpose would be to root out dissenters and "criminals"...basically anyone who had supported the Reich. She couldn't tell what would happen to these individuals, not from what the ladies were typing, but based on her previous career as an interrogator, she could certainly make an educated guess. During the war, she'd interrogated and given testimony against actual criminals who were fighting against their legitimate government. In this case, the "government" was merely a collection of puppets manipulated by the communist Soviets in Moscow.

Fury began to simmer deep in Lina's belly, and she raised her shields once more before it spilled out into the room. Odds were none of the other women in the typing pool were psychic, but one couldn't be too careful. Especially with what she'd just learned. She absolutely could not afford to be labeled a dissenter, no matter how much she hated the Soviet occupiers and their complicit German mouthpieces.

"Lina!"

The voice behind her made her jump, and she turned to meet her supervisor's disapproving glare with wide, startled eyes.

"Why are you late?"

"I am sorry, Frau Hoffmann," Lina said, allowing her voice to sound breathy, as if she'd just arrived. "They had my street barricaded, and I had to find a way around. Then I ended up on the west side and had to make my way through the checkpoint..."

"Hmmm," Frau Hoffman said, but her glare softened, and she gave a slight nod. She took a sheaf of papers from the folder she held in the crook of her arm and held them out to Lina with a rattle. "These memoranda must be typed up, in triplicate, by the end of the day. If you don't have any questions, you'll want to get to work right away."

"Yes, Frau Hoffmann," Lina said, taking the papers and turning away. Her workstation was down the aisle of women, toward the back of the room. As she walked, Lina paid attention to the facial expressions of her coworkers. Most merely held concentration, as they tried to produce an accurate document in the minimum amount of time. But here and there, Lina could see a furtive glance, a widened eye, a pinched lip as the import of the words their fingers produced hit home.

The war might be over, but it seemed the fear was here to stay.

* * *

Fortunately, or unfortunately, Lina's memoranda held no titillating tidbits for her to add to the collection in her brain. She spent the rest of the workday typing up the results of building surveys undertaken in one of Berlin's housing districts that had been damaged in the war. The government had taken responsibility for the area, and had broken ground to create new, modern housing designed to meet the needs of the local workers. Lina had to admit that it sounded positive, but the survey results indicated some irregularities in the quality control of the new construction. She knew next to nothing about construction, but if she had to guess, someone in the builder supply chain was substituting inferior building materials and pocketing the difference.

Times were hard all over, after all. Everyone was looking for a way to get ahead. The survey mentioned the irregularities, but didn't draw attention to them, which probably meant whoever was skimming had bribed the surveyor to look the other way.

Everyone was looking for a way to get ahead.

Not my business, Lina reminded herself, though the thought of government corruption repulsed her on an instinctive level. It offended her sense of right and order. People had a duty, and they should do it. *But my duty is to myself and my friends. Any higher duty I had died when Berlin fell.*

She lost herself in the clickety-clack of the typing and the smell of warmed ink and paper until she'd worked through the entirety of the survey. By that time, the sunlit rectangles had traveled the length of the room, and the women around her were covering up their typewriters and pushing in their chairs. Lina lifted her arms overhead and stretched, feeling her spine pop, then rose to her feet and followed suit.

Outside, the summer sun lingered in the sky, and the balmy warmth teased at her as she started the walk home.

It really is a beautiful day, she thought, *despite my dark thoughts this morning. Perhaps I'll go around by the market and bring Isa some fresh flowers. I know she'll enjoy them.*

By the time she got to the market, Lina had all but forgotten about the foreboding with which she'd started the day. The route to the market took her east, away from the barricades, so she didn't have to see and be reminded of the Soviet military occupation of her city. The airplanes still droned overhead, of course, but it was off to the west, and created such a constant droning buzz that it was easy to tune out. Especially since the air rang with the sounds of construction crews closing up for the evening, shutting down the myriad worksites where they labored to rebuild Berlin. The scents of frying meat and woodsmoke teased at her, as someone somewhere began to prepare their dinner.

The market, too, was close to shutting down for the day, but there were still a few hardy souls out peddling their wares. Lina found the flower-seller and purchased an only-slightly-bedraggled bouquet with some of the newly-issued money. She thanked the flower-seller and turned down the street for home, just as the first star winked into view in the east.

"Isa?" Lina called out as she opened the unlocked door to her neighbors' apartment and stepped through. Only silence answered, which was strange. They should all be home by now, even Rolland. She supposed they could have gone out somewhere as a family on this lovely summer evening, though for the life of her she couldn't imagine where they would go.

Or why they wouldn't have invited her. They always had before...

No. There's nothing wrong here, Lina told herself, shaking her head. *There's a logical explanation, and you getting paranoid about either circumstances or your relationship with them will only make things worse. Find a vase and leave the flowers where Isa will see them! You have an apartment of your own to go to.*

She squared her shoulders and continued into the kitchen, where a chipped water tumbler served as a makeshift vase. The area was clean and tidy, as Isa always left it, which lent credence to her theory that they'd simply gone out. Well enough. She probably had something she could heat up to eat in her own seldom-used kitchen.

Lina fussed with the flowers for a bit, then turned and headed back to her own apartment across the hall, locking the door behind herself. Her own apartment was locked, of course, just as it always was. She placed the key in the lock and turned the handle.

Only to have the door snatched out of her hand as someone inside flung it open.

"Oh, Lina!" Isa Thanhouser sobbed, throwing her arms around Lina's neck and nearly collapsing on her. Lina staggered slightly and fought to keep her balance. Isa wasn't a particularly large woman, but Lina hadn't expected to be tackled by her, either. "He's gone! They've taken him!"

"Isa, Isa!" Lina gasped as she got her arms around the other woman. "Slow down! I'm here, I'm right here. Slow down and breathe. What happened?"

Isa's voice broke on another wracking cry, and she slumped as her legs gave out. Lina let out a short curse and fought to keep the other woman upright.

"*Mutti*, here," Ginette said, her voice empty. "You must sit...can you get her here to the chair, *Tante?*"

"Yes," Lina grunted, and she felt some of Isa's weight lift as the twelve-year-old supported her mother and helped Lina maneuver her to the chair.

"Aleda, make some tea for *Mutti*," Ginette ordered as she arranged her mother's weeping form in the seat. "*Tante* Lina has a kettle in the kitchen. Take Johanna with you."

"Do you know what happened?" Lina asked, straightening.

"Men came. They said they were police. State police, though they were wearing suits instead of a uniform. Aleda heard them coming, and told *Mutti*. We came over here while *Vati* stayed behind to talk to them. They arrested him and took him away." Ginette spoke in the same empty, clipped tone as she gave this report.

"What do you mean she heard them coming? How did she know who they were if they weren't wearing uniforms?" Lina asked.

Ginette looked up at her with eyes far too wise for one of her tender years.

"*Tante*," she said, her empty voice taking on an urgency that throbbed just under the words, "she *heard* them. Like you heard the men in the cellar."

Lina froze, ice forming deep in her belly. None of the girls had manifested talent before. Most psychic talents developed during a woman's adolescence, maturing along with her mind and body; however, it wasn't unheard of in a child. Lina's own talent had begun to show when she was around eleven. Generally speaking, there seemed to be a loose correlation between the onset of psychic manifestation and the eventual strength of the psychic. In her heyday, Lina had only ever met one psychic with more power than she had, but she hadn't asked when her power had started to develop.

"She's only nine," Lina said softly. "That's early. Has she done things like this before?"

Ginette gave a little shrug and made a noncommittal noise, then turned back to her hysterically sobbing mother.

Right. One problem at a time.

The kettle in the kitchen began to shriek and was quickly cut off. A moment later, Aleda reappeared, holding a tray with several mugs. The delicate fragrance of Lina's hoarded tea twisted upward from the mugs as she set the tray down on Lina's little table.

"Thank you, Aleda," Ginette said, taking one of the mugs. "*Mutti*, here. Drink some tea. It will help calm you…"

But Isa just continued to slump in the chair and wail, her fists clenched and pressed to her chest. Lina shook herself and stepped forward.

"I'm going to use my gifts to calm her. It'll be faster than anything else," she said to Ginette. Then she turned and looked at Aleda, standing nearby with a mug of tea in her hand. "Put that down and watch me, follow along if you can."

Aleda nodded and set the mug on the table, then stepped forward. Little Johanna followed after, her eyes wide and frightened. Ginette reached out and gathered her youngest sister in her arms, then sat down on the sole remaining chair to watch Lina and Aleda tend to Isa.

On impulse, Lina reached her hand out to Aleda.

"If you allow me, I'll link with you. Then you may feel how I soothe her. I warn you, though, it may be rough for you to feel her distress at first."

"I already feel it," Aleda whispered. "She's so frightened. It spills out everywhere and engulfs me."

"I'll teach you to better shield yourself," Lina said. "For now, I'll do it for you. Take my hand and trust me."

"Yes, *Tante*," Aleda said and put her small, chubby fingers into Lina's.

Lina opened her shields and reached her power out toward the little girl. Aleda's mind opened to her touch, and a connection snapped into place between them.

Can you hear me? Lina asked mentally. She worked quickly to construct a shield that would keep their sensory inputs separate, and hopefully keep Aleda from the worst of her mother's hysteria.

*I...yes...*Aleda replied. *I can feel you, too. Your mind is... slick, but welcoming.*

It's because I'm both female and like family to you, and because I'm psychic as well. I'll teach you more soon, but for now, let us help your mother. When I say, reach out and take her right hand. I'll take her left, and then I'll pull her into our network. I'll do my best to keep you shielded, but you'll feel some of what she's feeling.

I'm ready, Aleda said stoutly, and Lina felt a surge of admiration for the girl's quiet bravery.

Take her hand, Lina directed, and did the same herself. Since her outer shields were down, the touch itself was enough to allow Isa's torrential fear and grief to come roaring down the lines of instant connection. Lina hastily threw more of her power into the shield that protected Aleda, and hurtled one word at Isa's grief-spasming mind.

Calm!

She didn't. Not exactly. Not fully, but the raging current faltered just a bit, stuttered, like a river encountering a natural dam. Lina seized the advantage and pressed forward.

Isa, you must calm yourself! You must protect your girls. I cannot do it without you. I'll get Rolland back for you, I swear it, but you must care for the girls first!

As she sent these thoughts to her friend, Lina willed the seething water of Isa's emotions to slow, and eddy, and still. It felt like powering up a whitewater stream, but leaving glassy stillness in one's wake.

My...my girls? Isa's thought came haltingly...but coherently.

Yes. Lina said. *Your girls are safe for the moment, but we must plan and act quickly to keep them so. Then I'll find Rolland for you.*

You will?

I swear it, Lina said, and meant every word. Never mind that she had no idea how to go about doing such a thing. She would find a way, for this family who had given her so much. *But you must care for the girls.*

Yes. My girls, yes. Lina felt Isa begin to pull herself together, to take over the work of calming her rivers of emotion. The flow receded, and her mental landscape regained a semblance of her usual calm serenity. *My...girls? Aleda?*

Yes, Aleda is here in the net I've created. There's much we must discuss, Lina said, *but first, perhaps we could all use some tea.*

* * * * *

Chapter Two – Fugitive

Lina disconnected the net and took a moment to compose herself while little Johanna handed out mugs of tea to everyone.

"Thank you," she murmured to the wide-eyed blonde child as she accepted her mug, cradling its warmth in her suddenly cold hands. A streetlamp flickered on outside her window, and Lina blinked in the realization that less than an hour ago, she'd been cheerfully buying flowers.

Strange how quickly things could change.

But then, she'd seen that before, during the war.

"All right," she said, shaking herself loose from her woolgathering and sitting forward in her chair. Isa looked up from her own tea, as did the three girls who sat, facing them, on the floor. Ginette had insisted that Lina take her seat, and she'd gone to drag the table over to the middle of the floor to give them something to put their mugs upon.

"Is it?" Isa said softly, her voice sad. Little Johanna reached out and took her mother's hand, then let herself be gathered in to snuggle on Isa's lap. Lina felt a surge of gratitude toward the little one for the timely distraction. Cuddling her children was better than anything else for Isa right now, especially if it helped her focus on what needed to be done. Isa buried her face in Johanna's blonde hair for a moment, then squared her shoulders and straightened up with a sniff.

"No," she answered herself, "but it will be."

"That's right," Lina said, letting herself smile all the way through her eyes to show how proud she was of Isa. "It will be. We must simply keep our heads and act decisively. First of all, we must get you and the girls to safety. Especially if Aleda is showing psychic talent. I don't know for certain, but I suspect the Red Army has rounded up as many of us as they can find. At least, I don't know of any of my former colleagues who are still surviving in Berlin. And now with Rolland..." she trailed off, unwilling to send Isa back into that spiraling, hysterical grief storm.

Johanna reached up and placed a kiss on her mother's cheek, then snuggled her little head harder into Isa's shoulder, and Isa's hand came up to cradle her youngest child's face. The mother blinked, took a deep breath, and nodded.

"I think you're right," Isa said. "It isn't safe for us to remain here any longer. I think...I think we should go to my sister's."

"On the West side?" Lina asked, her eyebrows rising up. "They're being blockaded, Isa. You may all starve."

"No," Isa said. "You've seen the airplanes. The Americans and British are flying supplies in."

"You cannot supply an entire city by air alone, Isa."

"You don't know that," Isa said. "And anyway, it's not an entire city, it's only the Western half. R-Rolland always said the Amis somehow managed to work miracles time and again during the war. Maybe they'll do it again now."

Lina opened her mouth to tell Isa to be sensible, but froze as a memory flashed into her mind—a snow-dusted camp, a tent reeking of blood, pain in her throat from an attack that should never have been possible...

Old bitterness and pain rose up inside her, along with the grudg-ing acknowledgment of the truth. The Americans *had* performed a miracle, and in so doing, had destroyed her world.

"Anyway," Isa said, and her voice brought Lina back to the pre-sent, "it's better than waiting here for the police to return and lock my girls up as well. You know they always take the families, too. If Rolland is guilty in their minds, we're guilty, too, by association."

"You're right," Lina murmured, because that was exactly how she'd thought when she'd hunted enemies of the Reich. "They'll come back, so we must go somewhere. Perhaps your sister is a good idea, at least at first. We can make further plans once we're there."

"*Tante* Emilia has a big house," Ginette put in, speaking for the first time during the conference. "I think she'd be happy to see us and have us stay."

"Excellent," Lina said. "I think we must go quickly, perhaps first thing tomorrow. I walked through one of the new checkpoints this morning. It's bothersome, but they're letting people through. We can leave at first light."

"Should we go pack our things, *Mutti*?" Ginette asked, but Lina held up a hand to stop her.

"No," she said, "I'm sorry. I don't think it's safe for any of us to go back to your apartment tonight. I think it's likely your home is being watched, and I was probably seen when I went there first. It's too risky."

"But our things…" little Johanna started to protest, but her mother shushed her and held her close. Aleda just nodded and looked at her big sister.

"We've lost everything before," Ginette said. "We can do it again."

Lina gave the quiet, eldest girl a smile and a nod. Ginette's strength and iron will might very well be what saved their family. All the girls had their talents, but Ginette led them with a firm, loving hand that made everything easier for the adults.

"You can sleep here," Lina said. "I gather Aleda's warning came soon enough that you weren't seen coming in, otherwise they'd likely have come here directly after arresting Rolland. I have only the one bed, but you're welcome to it—"

"*Mutti* will sleep there with Johanna," Ginette said, pushing her hair back from her face. "Aleda and I will take turns with you, staying up and listening to be sure they don't come back in the night. Can we get out if they do?"

"Of course," Lina said, impressed all over again. "There's a fire escape from my bedroom window. It leads down to an alley too narrow for vehicles, though it still may be watched. But if they come, I think that's our only option."

"Then that'll be our plan."

"Ginette," Lina asked, allowing some of her urgency to creep into her voice, "do you have the talent, too?"

"No," the girl said, "but I suspected Aleda did, and I've been helping her focus. We'll have better warning if I stay up with her."

* * *

In truth, they all stayed up for a while. Isa took Ginette and Johanna into the kitchen to see what she could concoct for a meal. Lina wished her luck, because she'd need it. She spent most evenings with the Thanhousers in their well-stocked and welcoming kitchen, and therefore her own cupboards were mostly bare. Still, Isa was a survivor of the late war and all the privation that had gone with it, and she'd taught her girls well. Before long, the tantalizing scent of a warm, spiced porridge began to waft into the small front parlor, where Lina sat with Aleda.

"That smells good," Aleda said, sniffing the air.

"It does," Lina said. "Your mother will call us when it's ready. For now, I'd like to work with you for a few moments, to teach you to shield your mind better."

"All right," Aleda said, shifting in her seat. "I'm ready."

"Good. Let's link again, and I'll show you what I want you to do." Lina reached out and once again felt Aleda's trust as the girl readily put her hand in Lina's. The connection followed close behind, with only a little push from Lina—and just like that, they were linked.

Good, Lina said. *Now watch and follow along. I'm going to build a barrier between us. Some psychics prefer to visualize building a wall or blowing a bubble. I just decide I want the barrier to exist, and I sort of push it into place with that wanting.*

Like when I really want a new toy?

If you like. Watch me first. Then you'll try.

Slowly and gently, Lina erected a barrier that cut off communication between the two of them, though she didn't sever the connection entirely. This was a delicate business, because if she pushed too hard, she could hurt young Aleda's developing mind and power. But on the other hand, if she didn't use enough of her own force, the barrier wouldn't take, and Aleda wouldn't learn how to protect herself.

I shouldn't have cut myself off for so long, Lina thought, some of her frustration leaking through as she gently willed the barrier into being. *I'm out of practice and lack control and finesse.*

Why did you cut yourself off? Aleda asked.

Because...because... Lina found herself searching for an explanation that didn't involve the horrific truth. Aleda had been only six in that cellar. Who knew what she remembered?

Is it because of what happened in the cellar? How you killed those men? Can you teach me to do that?

No! Lina said, and her mind barrier slammed home in a panic. Aleda gasped, then broke the connection on her own as tears filled her eyes.

"Oh, sweetheart," Lina said, her own head throbbing, instant remorse flowing through her. "Did that hurt you? I'm so sorry!"

Aleda pressed her lips together and gave a mighty sniff as she fought to keep the tears back, but then her face crumpled, and she began to sob.

"I'm so sorry, dear one," Lina said again, reaching out to stroke the child's silky ash-blonde hair. Aleda let out another sob and then threw herself into Lina's arms. Lina held her close and closed her own eyes against the tears that began to burn their way down her cheeks. "I'm so very sorry! I would never willingly hurt you. Please believe that!"

"I do," Aleda said, her voice small and broken through her sobs. "I'm sorry! I didn't mean to make you angry."

"Sweet girl, I'm not angry at you! It's just...what I did to those men was a terrible, terrible thing. Yes, they would have hurt us and probably killed us. Yes, I would do it again if I had to do so, but I cannot teach you to do that. You're so young and innocent...I won't destroy that in you. I cannot."

"What happened?" Isa asked, her gentle voice startling Lina enough to make her jump. She looked up to see the woman standing in the doorway between the living area and the kitchen. "Is she all right?"

"She will be," Lina said. "I scared her, hurt her a little bit, but nothing permanent. But I...I can't teach her, Isa. I'm too long out of practice. Her mind is both incredibly powerful and incredibly fragile, and it's still developing. She *must* be taught, but I can't do it. Not right now."

Isa nodded solemnly.

"All right," she said. "We'll find another way. One problem at a time. Come and eat something, both of you."

Lina gave Aleda a squeeze, then let go of her to wipe her cheeks free of tears.

"I'm sorry, sweetheart," she said again.

"Me too, *Tante*," Aleda said, giving her a watery smile. "I'm glad you're not angry at me."

"Never, dear one. Never."

"Not ever?" Aleda asked, letting a mischievous lilt enter her voice. Lina blinked rapidly, and then began to laugh. In the doorway, Aleda's mother joined in, shaking her head.

"Spirited minx," Lina said, not without affection. "You know what I mean. Go to your mother and sisters. I'll wash my face and join you directly."

* * *

Despite her misgivings, Lina continued to work with Aleda after their filling meal of porridge and a little fried sausage Isa had found in Lina's icebox. She did not again attempt to demonstrate anything while connected with the girl, but she did have Aleda build a barrier and demonstrate that she could both shield from Lina and forcibly sever a connection if she must. It wouldn't hold long against a concentrated psychic attack, but it should keep the girl safe from the overspill of others' emotions out in the world. If that was all Lina could do for the moment, she would have to be happy with that.

Another aspect of her plan changed, as well. Shortly after dinner, the electricity in the apartment flickered and went out. Such things weren't unusual. The government had restored electrical power to large portions of the city in the years since the war, but the service was precarious, and outages were common. Lina had candles and matches stored in one of her kitchen cupboards, so they were well prepared.

"There," Isa said, her hand cupped around the half-burnt taper she'd just lit. "Now we can see again. Let me get a saucer to hold this…goodness! Look out the window, it's gotten completely foggy!"

"Has it?" Lina asked, her head snapping up from where she'd been looking for a second taper.

"Yes," Isa said, her voice holding the same forced cheer she'd had since she pulled herself together before dinner. It wasn't healthy, but it was functional, so for the moment Lina let it go. "It looks like that really thick, heavy fog, too."

"Isa, I have an idea," Lina said, excitement threading through her voice. "How well do you and the girls know your apartment?"

"Very well, I'd say," Isa said, "but why? I don't—"

"Listen," Lina said, beckoning her over. The girls crowded close, too, interested to see what had their *Tante* so animated. "We decided not to risk going to the apartment because it might be watched, right? But with the fog and the power out, maybe you and Ginette could sneak over and gather a few things. Like food and…"

"Warm clothes," Isa said, nodding, "and boots. I know it's summer, but I've been wishing we could have packed those things, just in case."

"Yes, exactly. And one other thing. Do you know where Rolland kept any of his papers? I know he had some records he saved from during the war."

Isa paused, her face going pale in the flickering candlelight. "Do you think…" she whispered. "Do you think that's why they…took him? For his work during the war?"

"I don't know," Lina said, "but it stands to reason that he'll be safer if those papers are safe with us, instead of in the hands of those who might see them as proof of wartime guilt or some such nonsense."

"Yes, you're right. I know where he kept one thing: a notebook. It's in a safe in our bedroom, hidden behind a false panel he put into our wall after we moved in. I can get it."

"Can you move silently and get it? In the dark? They might have planted listening devices, and I wouldn't dare risk a candle over there. Can you open the safe without light?"

"Yes, I have a key," she said. "It's really just a lockbox, not a safe, I suppose. The key is in my jewelry box."

"Excellent," Lina said. "This is what we're going to do. Ginette, you stay here with Johanna. Aleda will stay and 'listen' as she did before. I'll link with her, and she can warn us if we need to get out of there. You get the key and the lockbox. I'll gather your clothes, food, and boots. Yes?"

"Yes," Isa said, her eyes shining with excitement.

"Yes," Aleda said, squaring her shoulders.

"No," Ginette said, and Lina turned and looked sharply at her.

"Ginette?" she asked. "What's wrong?"

"Two things; Johanna's not a baby who needs minding, and you don't know our house quite as well as we do. I think you should link us *all* into a network, and Johanna and I will gather clothing while you get food, and *Mutti* gets the lockbox. Aleda will still stand guard here and listen."

Lina looked to Isa, whose face had gone even paler than before. The mother pressed her lips together and closed her eyes for a moment, then nodded her head in the affirmative.

"Ginette is right," she said. "She and Johanna can help. We can all move silently if we must."

"In the dark?" Lina asked.

"If we must," Isa said firmly.

"Very well," Lina said. "Let's go now, before the power comes back on. It probably won't before the morning, but I'd rather do this while they're still adjusting to the loss of their capabilities. Give me your hands, and I'll link us together."

They all, even little Johanna, put out their hands. Lina touched them one by one, starting first with Aleda, and gently wove a psychic network between them all.

Think to them, Lina urged Isa when it was complete. It would have been better if they'd had time to practice working with the net, but if wishes were horses, the lowliest beggar would ride. They had what time they had. Which was none.

Johanna, Ginette, Aleda…my darlings, can you hear me?

Yes, Mutti, the girls chorused back, their answers colored by their own individual thoughts and personalities. It wasn't the same as each person having a different vocal timbre, but it was easy to tell who was whom, simply because their minds were unique…no matter that they were sisters.

Good enough, Lina said. *Let's get this done, so we can get back safely. Everyone knows their part, yes?*

Once again each of them responded affirmatively, and Lina gave a sharp nod and turned toward the front door.

She took great care to ease it open, lest it creak and betray her activity to anyone investigating the hallway. She reached out with her mind and sensed no other thoughts, so she stepped out into the inky blackness of the hall.

Fortunately for her, the Thanhousers' door faced hers. She had her key ready and took care to open the lock as smoothly and silently as possible. She didn't think the tiny *click* of the tumblers would betray her, but she paused and waited for three heartbeats, just in case. Then she eased the door open and stepped inside.

It's clear, she told Isa and the girls. *Come one by one, quietly. I'll be in the kitchen. Let me know when you have all you can carry.*

One by one, they slipped across the hallway and went to work. Isa was right, Lina realized. She and the girls could move silently when they had to. Surviving a war and the sack of a city taught one a lot of skills, it seemed, costly though the lessons had been.

She took herself to the kitchen and began gathering what travel-friendly items she could. The Thanhousers had some dried meat and fruit that Isa liked to use in her cooking, and a good amount of baking staples. Lina regretted leaving behind the flour and the lard, but she honestly couldn't see a way to conceal the large containers while crossing through the checkpoint. She did take the precious, paper-wrapped fresh pork Isa had gotten as the family's weekly ration. That would be welcome, surely.

I have boots for everyone, little Johanna sent though the network, her tone steady and lacking any hint of her usual playful silliness.

Good work, little one, Lina told her. *Return to Aleda in my apartment. Quietly now. We'll be close behind you.*

Lina felt her moving, slowly but confidently, through the darkened home and out across the hallway to her sister's waiting arms.

My arms are full, too, Ginette said a moment later. *I have clothing for us all, and some knapsacks. I'm going back.* Tante Lina, *don't forget the salt and tea. Those will travel well.*

Good idea, Lina thought back approvingly. *When you get back, split up the clothing and boots, and make up the knapsacks.*

I will, Ginette said, and Lina felt her moving back to safety as well.

Before too long, Lina's own arms were full, and she wished she'd thought to bring a bag to put the provisions in.

Isa? she asked, reaching out to the other woman down the lines of the network. *Have you found the papers?*

*Y-yes…*Isa replied, but her mind-tone was shaky and unsure.

Isa, I need you to hold it together and get back to the girls, Lina said, closing down the channels so none of the children could hear her speak to their mother. *We can't afford for you to fall apart right now. I give you permission to fall apart once we're safe, but for now, get the notebook and get back to my apartment!*

I—yes. All right, Isa sent back. Lina followed along in the back of her mind as the grieving woman put down the shirt of her husband's she'd been cradling and picked up the notebook with the records of his work.

Lina stepped out into the short hallway and waited for Isa.

She was still waiting there when the electric streetlight outside the window flickered on.

Scheisse! Isa, get down below the level of the windows! Lina said, taking her own advice and crouching in the hallway. *The power's back on. We need to go!*

I'm here! Isa replied, and Lina could make out the shape of her, crawling on hands and knees as she emerged from the bedroom and came forward.

The notebook?

I put it in my skirt waistband, Isa replied. *And I got our ration cards. I'm sorry I took so long. Let's go!*

Crossing the hallway was much more dangerous now, with the lights on. Lina reached as far as she could down both sides and found no one, but there was no guarantee one of their other neighbors might not step out or look out and catch them. Still, it had to be done, so Lina steeled her nerve and urged Isa across, then followed immediately after.

We made it! Johanna exulted as the two women flung themselves in through the door, locked it, then turned and leaned on it while they caught their breath. *What a fun adventure!*

Lina looked over at Isa, and despite everything, both women began to laugh.

* * *

The excitement of their adventure in the dark kept them all awake later than Lina would have liked, but eventually everyone else settled down, leaving her alone to watch and listen. She went through and checked each of the knapsacks Ginette had found, and made sure the food was well-concealed at the bottom. Then she made herself comfortable in one of her chairs with another mug of strong tea, and began to flip through Rolland Thanhouser's hidden notebook.

No revelations waited within. Not for her, at least. The slim volume contained pages of complex chemical formulas and notes about them in Rolland's precise, tiny script. She could read the words of the notes, of course, but without advanced training in chemistry, Lina had no idea how to make sense of any of it. Disappointment twinged through her. She'd been hoping for something she could use to bargain with the Americans. It was possible that the notebook would be valuable to them…but without understanding it, she had no way of knowing.

She'd never liked uncertainty.

With a sigh, she returned the notebook to her knapsack and stood up to refresh her tea. As she poured, her mind drifted back to the problem of little Aleda. The girl *must* have training. An untrained psychic was a danger to herself and everyone around her. But Lina herself couldn't do the job, and she couldn't exactly ask around to see if anyone might be hiding psychic talent…

Oh.

Lina's mind landed on the idea like an insect alighting on a hot rock, then immediately skittered away in instinctive rejection. Anger and revulsion swelled within her, threatening to make her choke on her tea.

No, she told herself. *That's not an option. I'll find another way to train her…*

But she *couldn't* train the girl. Not in her current weakened state. Frustration and self-recrimination churned in her belly, and Lina put the tea down and leaned forward in her chair, fighting not to be sick.

There has to be another way!

But try as she might, she could come up with nothing. Facts were facts. Aleda was psychic and needed training. Lina couldn't give it to her. Nor could she safely find another teacher for her here, or even in the west. Most likely, any German psychic who'd been in Berlin during the city's fall hadn't survived. She wouldn't have herself if not for the Thanhousers. As far as she knew, the Soviets killed any woman showing psychic power.

No, if there were any psychics left in Berlin, they had to be British or American.

Lina listened until shortly after midnight, when Ginette and Aleda woke and joined her. At first Lina tried to persuade the girls to go back to bed, but she reckoned without Ginette's implacable will. The young teenager gently but firmly informed Lina that she and Aleda would wait up together for the next few hours, until just before dawn. Then they would make breakfast and wake everyone up so they could leave as planned. She also informed Lina that, as the only trained, adult psychic in the group, it was her responsibility to remain rested so she could safely see them all across the checkpoint the next day.

Perhaps precisely because she *was* so tired, Lina couldn't think of a good argument, and found herself being tucked into bed on the little sofa where the girls had slept earlier. She drifted off to the sounds of the girls chatting quietly.

It felt like no time at all had passed when Aleda shook her shoulder.

"*Tante*," the young girl whispered. "Please wake up. Someone's coming."

Lina sat up, letting the knitted afghan she'd used fall to the floor. "How far away?" she asked.

"I can't tell," Aleda said. "I don't know how to judge."

"It's all right," Lina said. "Go get your mother and sisters."

"Ginette is waking *Mutti*," Aleda replied. "I'm to wake you and bring you to the bedroom. The bags are all ready to go."

Lina shook her head and blinked her eyes as she tried to establish some situational awareness. She glanced over at the clock on the wall, but she couldn't read it in the darkness. The sun hadn't risen, so it wasn't yet five, and based on the diffusion of the streetlight shining through her window, it was still quite foggy.

Perfect.

Lina stood and stretched, then took a deep breath and reached out with her power. She focused as she had while in training at the *Reichschule*, working to make her touch as feather-light and hard to notice as possible. She wanted to see who was coming, how close they were, and how much time she and the Thanhouser women had to escape.

She didn't want to alert them.

Her control was faulty, and Lina could feel beads of sweat breaking out along her hairline as she concentrated. As she stretched her power outward, her grip on it was more and more tentative, until she held on by the barest thread.

I can't, she realized. *I can't reach any further. They're close, that much I know. Maybe not inside the building yet...maybe.*

"*Tante?*" Aleda asked. Lina blinked and came back to herself, throwing her barriers into place.

"They're nearby," she said. "You're right. We should go now."

She reached out to take the girl's hand and walked with her into the bedroom. Isa stood silhouetted by the window, a sleepy Johanna in her arms. Ginette waited next to her, one knapsack on her back and another in her hands. She held this up, offering it to Lina, who took it with a nod of thanks.

"Be very quiet going down the fire escape," Lina said as she shrugged the bag onto her shoulders. She stepped over to the window and grunted lightly as she pushed it up. The wet, misty night air flowed in, bringing the scent of rain with it. "Ginette, you first. Wait at the bottom; stay next to the building, in the shadows, if you can."

The teenager stepped forward, wrapping her hands around the shoulder straps of her knapsack. Her green eyes looked resolute, her face set and calm. At Lina's gesture, Ginette stepped up to the window and put one of her long, coltish legs out. Then she ducked under and stepped all the way out. Lina watched as she darted down the metal stairs, stepping carefully to minimize any noise.

"Good, she's at the bottom. Aleda next, then Isa and Johanna," Lina said.

"Then you," Isa said, an undercurrent of fear in her voice. Lina didn't have to establish a link to realize that Isa was terrified of being left alone with no one else to help her defend the girls.

"Then me," Lina confirmed, giving the other woman a smile. "I won't leave you until you and the girls are safe, Isa. I promise." She raised her hand and touched the other woman's cheek lightly. It was meant to be a reassurance, and it seemed to have worked, because Isa nodded and urged her middle daughter forward to the window.

Privately, Lina wondered if her promises were really only empty comfort. Unease snaked through her as she thought of her lack of control earlier. She'd invested so much of her time and energy into honing her psychic skill—was it all now gone? Simply because she'd been too weak and cowardly to lower her barriers for three years?

"See you at the bottom," Isa said, and the softly-whispered words pulled Lina from her reverie. She nodded and attempted once more to reach out as she watched her friend maneuver through the window while holding a sleeping child. Lina waited until Isa was halfway down, then she followed her out.

"All right," Lina said as her feet touched down on the wet concrete of the alley. She kept her voice pitched low, but didn't whisper. Whispered words tended to carry farther than murmured ones. Another thing she'd learned from the war. "Here's what we'll do. Stay close, and we'll head over to the train station. It's mostly rebuilt, and we can take the train around and across to the west side of the city. It won't be as direct, but that may throw them off, if whoever's coming to the house is looking for us."

Lina looked around at their shadowed faces as they nodded assent. Each of them, even sleepy little Johanna, showed strong determination in the set of their expressions. The tiny girl knuckled her eyes once, then pushed at her mother's shoulder lightly.

"Put me down, *Mutti*," she said in a hushed tone. "I can walk, and you will need your strength."

Lina flashed a quick smile at her, then turned and began to step carefully down the alleyway toward the back of the building.

"This way," she murmured. "Quickly but quietly. And when we reach the street, join hands. We'll want to appear as just another group of sisters and nieces beginning our day with an outing by train."

Then Lina took a deep breath and led the small group out onto the street, while the fog swirled in their wake.

* * *

Fortunately for all of them, the streets of Berlin were filling up with people as the sun rose and the summer heat began to burn the fog away. Lina felt something in her chest ease as they smoothly integrated into the larger crowd of office workers, housewives, and laborers headed to the train station. For once, she didn't mind the press of people as they herded together to board the passenger train.

"Why is the train so short, *Mutti*?" Aleda asked. "We studied trains in school, and teacher said there were twenty cars or more. This one has only six."

"This is a passenger train only, dearest," Isa said, glancing quickly around to see if anyone had noticed Aleda's precocious interest. "There are no cargo cars on this train, so they don't need as many cars."

"Here we are," Lina said, happy to change the subject as the queue finally brought them to the train car's entrance. She guided Ginette and Aleda forward by hand, and followed Isa, who had once again picked Johanna up and carried her in her arms. They wound their way along the narrow aisle between the seats to the rear, where several open rows awaited them. Once they were seated, Lina let out a breath and eased back in her chair.

"Get some rest if you can," she said to Isa and the girls. "It'll be awhile before we get to our stop." Isa nodded and cuddled Johanna close. Aleda sat next to her mother and leaned on Isa's shoulder, leaving Ginette to sit next to Lina across the aisle.

The train filled up with passengers, and before long, the conductor came through, checking everyone's ticket and identification.

"Where are you headed?" he asked them. Isa glanced over at Lina, then gestured to the whole group.

"To visit our other sister," she said, "on the west side of the city."

"Hmmph," the conductor said, but he handed Isa's ticket stub back and continued down the aisle. Isa let her breath out slowly, then looked at Lina again, her face pale.

Lina swallowed hard and opened her shields just enough to reach out toward the other woman's mind. She found Isa's surface thoughts a whirl of nerves and fear, but she was able to hook in to the other woman's slippery mental landscape and create a connection.

Well done, Lina said. *Simple explanation, mostly true. The best kind of lie.*

Thank you, Isa replied silently. She closed her eyes and laid her cheek on top of Johanna's head. The little girl appeared to have fallen back asleep, safe and comfortable in her mother's arms. Lina envied her. *I feel as if my nerves are on fire. I only hope we can get there soon!*

Lina sent her a pulse of agreement before disconnecting and withdrawing back into her own mind. Each use of her power was tiring, and discouraging, but Lina understood enough to grasp that if she were ever going to return to her proficiency of old, she had to practice and push herself. Still, it wouldn't do to overextend while they were so exposed.

Let me get them safe, she promised herself, *and I'll practice until I drop. I will return to my former abilities!*

Despite Isa's wishes, the train ride took the better part of an hour and a half to navigate its slow route with multiple stops. The route looped around toward the east and north before turning back to the west, with the result that it took them about forty-five minutes to come to the place where the railroad tracks crossed the dividing line between Soviet occupied Berlin and the American zone.

Lina had expected a stop and search, but there was nothing. The train rolled right past the coils of barbed-wire fencing that split the perpendicular street in two and kept going. Shock and suspicion ricocheted through her body, and Lina had to fight not to sit up straight and draw attention to herself by looking around.

Instead, she closed her eyes, put her head against the window, and forced herself through some of the calming breath exercises she'd learned before the war. As the motion of the train rocked her from side to side, Lina slowly brought her mind back to tranquility.

A few minutes later, they started to slow. Only Lina's iron will kept her blood pressure from spiking again. She opened her eyes and forced herself to move slowly, calmly as she looked over at Isa and nodded. This would be their stop. One last hurdle to pass before the relative safety of Isa's sister's home.

At least, Lina hoped it would be safety. But she'd deal with that question later. For now, she just had to get them off the train.

The car rocked to a stop with the usual hissing sound. Lina tapped Ginette lightly and stood up, stretching. She retrieved the knapsack she'd stowed at her feet and looked over to see that Isa and the two younger girls were also ready to go. She pressed her lips together and made a decision.

"Aleda," she said softly, "give me your hand, let me help you out into the aisle."

Aleda raised her eyebrows in surprise. She certainly didn't need help getting out of her seat into the aisle, but she obediently held her hand out. Lina took it, and when their fingers touched, she reached out to re-establish the network that had drained her so much the night before.

Tante, are you sure? Aleda asked as their minds linked. *I don't think you should overextend yourself—*

I'll be fine, Lina said, unable to keep the sharp edge off of her words. *I suspect there will be a checkpoint ahead, and if there's a crowd, we may be separated. It'll be safer for all of us if we're linked together.*

But—

Enough, Aleda, Isa said, her tone firm. Like wise children the world over, Aleda let the matter drop in the face of her mother's warning, though she did look over to her elder sister. Ginette gave her a slow nod, and Lina realized, whether she willed it or no, she *would* be fussed over by her small charges.

She didn't know whether to be infuriated or touched.

Either way, it didn't much matter, because the aisle cleared out ahead of them. If they were getting off the train here as planned, the time was now. Lina gestured for Aleda, Isa, and Johanna to go first, then she followed, with Ginette close behind her. They filed down the length of the car and out onto the platform beyond, where Lina was certain they'd be herded to a checkpoint.

But there was nothing. Only the open platform, and people hurrying to and fro in the usual workday bustle.

Behind her, the train whistle gave an ear-splitting shriek, and the noise ratcheted up as the locomotive started moving once again. Lina jumped, then blinked, and realized that she'd paused there in the middle of the traffic.

Tante? Aleda asked.

I'm fine, Lina said, sending the reassuring message down all lines of the net. *Just surprised is all. They're letting anyone into this part of the city? No identification checks at all?*

I'm surprised, too, Ginette said, *but maybe we want to get moving before we draw too much attention?*

The teenager had a point. Lina reached out and gripped her hand, then gestured for Isa to lead the way with the younger girls. Isa took a long look at Lina, as if trying to assure herself that Lina really was all right, then nodded and began walking toward the terminal on the other side of the platform.

Once through the tiny train station, they had a short walk of about five blocks to get to Isa's sister's home. Lina had been expecting a small, cramped apartment similar to her own, but instead found herself looking at a three-story, well-appointed brick house that was obviously one of the few to have survived the war. They stood outside the wrought-iron gate while Isa rang the bell.

You didn't tell me your sister was wealthy! Lina thought, trying to make her tone sound teasing and fun instead of accusatory. She didn't like surprises, and this day had already held too many of them.

I didn't know she was! Our family lost everything in the war! Isa thought back, her own mind full of wonder and confusion as she looked at the well-groomed lawn and flowerbeds that overflowed with color. *But this is the address she gave me...*

She let the thought trail off as the front door opened, and a uniformed soldier stepped out. He looked out at them with a friendly expression, then turned to say something over his shoulder to whoever waited inside. He let out a little laugh, then shook his head and stepped down the front steps, letting the door close behind him as he approached.

"Good morning!" he called out to them in German. His voice carried just a hint of an accent, but he was obviously comfortable with the language. His expression stretched in a wide, friendly grin as he came down the walkway to the gate where they waited. "I heard you ring the bell as I was leaving for work. May I help you?"

"I—" Isa said, confusion deep in her voice. "I am sorry to trouble you. We are looking for my sister's home, but I must have the wrong address somehow."

"Who's your sister?" the American asked. Lina realized with a start that he was an officer, a colonel, unless she'd forgotten her insignia lessons. "Perhaps she lives nearby."

"Emilia Langner," Isa said. "I was certain I'd copied it down correctly…" she trailed off as the officer reached out and grabbed both of her shoulders. Lina felt tension flash through her friend's mind at the strange man's touch.

Johanna, Aleda, step back, Lina ordered, *back with me and Ginette!*

"Isa?" the American asked, his voice flooding with wonder as the two younger girls let go of their mother's hands and hurried back to stand behind Lina and Ginette.

Isa blinked, surprise replacing the horrible tension in her mind.

"Do I know you, sir?" she asked, her voice carefully formal.

"No!" the American said, then he let out a delighted laugh and firmly planted a kiss on both of her cheeks. "But I've been dying to meet you! I'm Russel Connor, your brother-in-law!"

* * *

Families are an interesting thing.

The thought wouldn't leave Lina alone. She'd dropped the network, figuring Isa would want some privacy for what was coming. Lina had never met Emilia, who was several years younger than her elder sister. Isa had often spoken warmly of her sister, but the fact that Emilia had married without her sister's knowledge was not lost on Lina. Something was—or had been—strained in this relationship, and as they followed the American colonel up the wide front steps of the stately townhouse, Lina wondered if that strain would mean more danger for Isa and the girls.

"Emilia is just upstairs," Colonel Connor said as he pushed the heavy, carved wooden door open and gestured for them to precede him into the foyer of the house. "Have a seat in the parlor to your left, and I'll let her know you've come!" His slightly-accented German was loud, but seemed to carry genuine joy, as far as Lina could tell without reaching out with her abilities. He gave her a wide smile as she followed the girls across the threshold, then let the door close behind him and nearly bounded toward the stairs.

"Emilia, darling!" he called out. "You have visitors!"

"Russel, you'll be late for work!"

The voice that floated down the central stairwell was light, and sounded very similar to Isa's. Lina glanced over at her friend, whose face had gone pale. She reached out and caught Isa's fingers in her own, giving them a squeeze.

"Are you all right?" Lina asked in an undertone.

"Yes," Isa said quickly. "Yes, of course. I'm just…surprised."

Lina squeezed her hand one more time before letting go, then reached out to beckon the children to come close to her. From what she could tell, they hadn't seen their aunt in a while, since before the end of the war, and it seemed right to let the two sisters have their reunion first. Little Johanna let go of her mother's hand and took Lina's, and Aleda and Ginette crowded close as well.

"Darling, you must come down!" Connor called out again, laughter threading through his voice. "You really must!"

"Russel, what *are* you on about?" Softly tapping footsteps accompanied the voice that sounded so much like Isa's, and Lina couldn't resist angling her body so she could see the foot of the stairwell, where the Ami colonel stood with his hand extended and his grin stretching from ear to ear.

The woman who descended to take his hand looked less like a younger version of Isa, and more like an older version of Ginette. Her blonde hair lay coiled in a smooth chignon at the base of her skull, and her green eyes echoed her husband's smile as she wove her fingers in with his. She wore a blue dress with a full skirt and modern silhouette that swirled about her legs when she walked. It looked well-made and expensive.

She leaned forward and kissed the colonel's cheek, then backed up and tilted her head to the side, as if waiting for an explanation.

"Darling," Connor said, "your sister has come."

He stepped to the side, leaving his wife with an unobstructed view of Isa, standing in the doorway to the parlor. Emilia let out a little cry and lifted her fingertips to her mouth, then ran forward, heels tapping on the hardwood floor of the foyer, to catch her sister up in a tight embrace. Isa seemed to freeze for a moment, then made a suspiciously sob-like sound and wrapped her arms around Emilia's shoulders.

"Isa," Emilia murmured. "Oh, Isa! I've missed you so much! I've been so worried!"

"I've been worried about you!" Isa said, her voice broken by something that was as much laugh as cry. "I got your note about your new American beau, but…Emilia, you're married?"

Emilia's cheeks turned pink in a blush. She let go of her sister and stepped backward, reaching a hand behind her. Connor was instantly there, wrapping her hand in his large fingers, stepping up to stand beside his wife. Lina didn't like Americans, but she had to admit it was something a good husband would do.

"I am," Emilia said, lifting her chin in a gesture that reminded Lina of Ginette in her rare moments of adolescent defiance. "Russel and I were married by the Army chaplain a few days ago. I am sorry I didn't tell you, but there wasn't time."

"I'm happy for you, little sister," Isa said, smiling and reaching out to brush her fingertips against Emilia's cheek. "You must know that. If he's good to you, I'm happy. But...why the rush?"

Emilia took a deep breath and looked over at her husband. He gave her a soft smile and a nod, and she looked back at her sister and squared her shoulders.

"Russel's being transferred back to America. We just found out about his assignment last week, so we had to act quickly, otherwise I couldn't accompany him."

"Wait...you're going to America?" Isa asked, and Lina recognized the edge of panic in her words.

"I am," Emilia said.

"Emilia!" Isa cried, then clapped her hands over her mouth. She turned away, her eyes filling with tears, and took a stumbling step toward Lina and the girls.

"Mama!" Johanna cried out. Ginette shushed her and took her by the hand while Lina reached out to draw Isa into a hug.

"Isa—" Emilia said, her voice soaked in misery. She looked pleadingly at Lina over the bowed head of her grieving sister.

"Give us a few moments," Lina said. "Please."

"That's a good idea," Connor said. "Come, darling. We'll wait out here. I'll phone the office and tell them I won't be in until noon.

Take as much time as you need," he added, then tugged his wife back out into the hallway before pulling a sliding pocket door shut with a click.

Isa sagged in Lina's arms, and for the second time in as many days, Lina struggled to get her friend to a chair before she fell as the sobs began to issue forth.

"I'm sorry, I'm so sorry," Isa said over and over again through her tears. "It's just...with Rolland gone, and now Emilia's leaving too!"

"*Mutti*," Ginette said, her voice soft as she came to stand beside her mother's chair. She reached up and stroked Isa's hair back from her brow, as Lina had seen Isa herself do when the girls weren't feeling well. "It'll be all right."

"It's just...I always meant to see her more, you know. Things were so chaotic during the war, and then afterward...it was always just such a struggle, and I always, always wanted to find her and have her come be with us, where she would be safe." Isa's words tumbled out, one over the other, punctuated by sobs as she hunched in over herself and cried. "But Emilia was always so strong and independent, and then she had a good job with the Americans that she wouldn't leave...and then she fell in love...and now—now—"

"Ginette's right, Isa," Lina said, kneeling beside her friend's chair, still holding her by the hand. Johanna took the opportunity to climb up into her mother's lap, and Aleda stepped up close on the side opposite her big sister. "It'll be all right."

"But if she's gone, where will we go? What will we do?"

"Leave it to me," Lina said. "I have a thought. The colonel was wearing aviator's wings on his uniform and...well...I have an idea. But you must trust me."

Isa swiped at her cheeks with her free hand.

"Lina, you're as much my sister as Emilia is. I trust you with the lives of my girls."

"Good," Lina said, her face grave and her eyes serious, "because that's exactly what hangs in the balance."

* * *

As ever, Isa proved herself remarkably resilient, even under extreme stress. She hugged Lina and each of the girls, cuddled Johanna close, and pulled herself together within a few minutes. She wiped her eyes one more time and then told Lina softly that she wanted to speak to her little sister.

Lina nodded and got to her feet. The girls stayed glued to their mother's side while Lina opened the door enough to see Emilia and her husband waiting outside with worried expressions on their faces.

"Isa's fine," Lina said, giving them a tiny smile of reassurance. "She's faced a lot in these last two days. She'd like to speak with you, Emilia. Just you, for the moment, if you please."

"Oh! Of course," Emilia said, looking apologetically up at her husband. Again, to his credit, the American colonel smiled at his wife and gestured for her to go ahead as Lina pushed the door wider. Emilia half-ran through, and Lina could hear the woman's voice thick with tears of her own as she started to apologize before Lina closed the door behind her.

"Colonel Connor," Lina said, switching to the English she hadn't spoken in years. "I must speak with you, privately, please. Do you have an office or somewhere we can talk?"

Connor blinked rapidly, obviously nonplussed, but then he nodded and gestured toward the stairs.

"Up and to the right," he said. "I have a small library…if you're sure Isa won't need you?"

"She'll be fine with Emilia and the girls," Lina said, her smile returning. "She's one of the strongest women I know."

"Then by all means, Fräulein, after you."

"Thank you," Lina said, and stepped forward to begin climbing the large, curving wooden staircase. *This really is a beautiful home*, she thought as she ran her hand along the silky-smooth bannister. The wood had been polished until it gleamed with that translucent inner light that highlighted the intricate grain of the old wood. *I wonder which German family yearns for this place they lost to the fortunes of war?*

The library was, as the colonel had said, up the stairs and to the right. It wasn't an overly large room, but it held a respectable-sized wooden desk and several shelves full of books. The leather armchairs and faint smell of tobacco gave the room a cozy, masculine feel, even with the bright sunlight streaming in through the east-facing windows.

"I love this room," the colonel said. "I'll be sad to leave it behind."

"The books aren't yours?" Lina asked as she bent to sit in one of the armchairs. She had to fight to keep it from pulling her into its leather embrace as the cushion sank under her weight. She perched on the edge of the seat cushion and crossed her ankles primly.

"Sadly, no. They're a magnificent collection, but they belong to the house. Property of the U. S. Army," he said with a half-smile. He walked around the desk and sat down, facing her across the polished wood desktop.

Ah, so he's a player, despite the 'hail-fellow-well-met' demeanor, Lina thought with an inward smile. *He realizes this is a negotiation, and that I want something from him. Fair enough. Let's play.*

"Thank you for your warm welcome," Lina said, making her opening gambit. "As I said downstairs, Isa's been through a lot lately. The news of her sister's marriage and imminent departure has come as one more shock among many, but it could have been much worse. So for her sake, I thank you."

"She's kin to my wife," Connor said, "it's the least I can do. But...forgive me. What's your relationship to Isa and her daughters?"

"I'm their neighbor," Lina said. "We've become close since the end of the war and the Soviet occupation. I—we cared for one another, and the girls, and Rolland."

"Rolland?"

"Doctor Rolland Thanhouser," Lina said, reaching into her jacket to pull out the small journal Isa had rescued from her apartment, "once one of the leading chemical scientists in the Reich. Now the manager of a soap factory...and Isa's husband. He was arrested yesterday and taken from their home. Isa and the girls fled to my apartment, and I helped get them here."

She set the book down on the desk, and Connor leaned forward to take it. Lina gave him a moment to flip through and see Rolland's notes before she spoke again.

"As you can see," she said, "Rolland kept meticulous notes of some of his most important work. Isa feared this notebook might be exactly what the Soviets were after when they arrested him."

"It's possible," Connor said, his voice carefully neutral as his eyes continued to skim over the formulas and notations in the book. "When was he taken?"

"Yesterday," Lina said. "Isa and the girls fled to my apartment, and we crossed the barricades to come here this morning. I'm certain our apartment building is being watched, and I fear what will happen to Isa and her daughters if they're taken."

Connor closed the book with a snap and laid it down on the desk in front of him.

"That is indeed worrisome, Fräulein," he said, "but I'm not sure what you want me to do with this information. Emilia's family is, of course, welcome to visit as long as they like while we remain, but I'm scheduled to leave in a few weeks."

"I understand that you cannot be responsible for the welfare of every one of your wife's relations," Lina said, leaning forward as she spoke, "but Colonel Connor, you must understand, it's imperative that Isa and her daughters be protected."

"And why is that?" the colonel asked, his polite, neutral tone never slipping.

Ah. So he loves his wife, but he's a practical man, this American. I should've expected that.

"Because they're precious," Lina said. She wanted to scream at the man, but she kept her own voice level and even. "Because they don't deserve to die or become slaves to the Soviets."

"No one deserves that," Connor said, "yet many will die, and I fear many more will, indeed, become slaves, just as you say."

Lina sucked in a deep breath and took a moment to hope against hope that her gamble wasn't about to backfire and destroy everyone for whom she cared in this world.

"Yes," Lina said, "but it's in your interest, and the interest of your nation, to protect these girls. Aleda, at least, is psychic, and shows remarkable talent for one so young. She'll become very powerful as an adult. The other two show hints of talent as well, and it often runs in families. Without training, these girls will be a danger to themselves and others. With training, they could become incredible assets. The question is, assets to whom? The United States of America? Or the Soviet Union?"

Connor looked at her for a long moment, then leaned forward and spoke in a low tone.

"Fräulein, I'm a soldier and a patriot. I don't want to kill children, but sometimes they die in a war. What's to stop me from simply having these girls eliminated?"

A bluff, Lina thought. She smiled a tiny smile.

"We're no longer at war," she said. "You're a practical man, and yes, a patriotic one, but you're not evil, I think. These girls are kin to you by marriage, and your wife would grieve. But beyond that, you know I'm right about them being assets. You wear flyer's wings. I know your army had psychics flying during the war, so you're aware of the potential psychic power holds for military applications. Take these girls to your Army psychics. Train them to control their abilities, and to love your country as you do. Save their lives and their sanity, Colonel, and see what miracles they'll perform for you…and for America…then."

Connor sat back in his chair and looked at her for a long moment. She studied him back, using the pause to memorize his facial features, in case she should need to remember him someday. He had hazel eyes that fell somewhere between brown and green, and they stared at her through wire-rimmed spectacles. His dark blond or light brown hair was cut short, but he could have as easily passed for a businessman as a military officer, if not for the uniform. His height and build were medium, though his face was handsome enough, with a chiseled jaw. Other than that, though, he seemed designed to be unremarkable...forgettable. Someone who could easily slip into social situations, gather what information was to be had, and slip out again.

"And what about you?" he said, bringing their polite staring contest to an end. "Am I to bring you along to America too?"

"I? No," Lina said. She reached out and tapped the notebook on the desk between them. "I'll stay and find Rolland. Once Isa and the girls are safe, I'll do what I can to rescue him, as well."

Connor's eyebrows went up, and he let out a snort, as if he were holding back a laugh.

"You're going to take on the Soviet state authorities? By yourself?"

"I am not without resources," Lina said, ignoring the cold fear that she was no longer the psychic she used to be. Another long moment stretched between them, until Connor moved quite suddenly, and Lina had to hold herself quite still to avoid a startled jump.

"You've given me much to think about," he said, pushing up to his feet. He reached out and grabbed the notebook, tucking it inside his uniform coat. "Emilia's family is, as I said, welcome to stay with us for as long as we're here. I have to speak with some of my colleagues. Please remain here in this office until I return. I'll have someone bring you something to drink."

"Thank you," Lina said. "If it's not too much trouble, please let Isa know that I'm well, but simply engaged with you and your...colleagues, you called them. She'll worry."

"Of course," Connor said, nodding as he walked to the door of the room. He slipped out and quietly closed the door behind him, leaving Lina alone in the silence of the book-filled room.

Lina exhaled and slumped in the armchair, closing her eyes. Her hands started to tremble from reaction, and she badly wanted to curl into a ball until the shakes had run their course. But she couldn't, not just yet.

Isa, Lina thought, reaching out toward the woman downstairs. The link connected, though it felt stretched, tenuous and thin.

Lina?

Yes. Isa...I may have made a terrible mistake. I gambled with your lives...This colonel, Emilia's husband. I told him about Aleda, and hinted that the other girls might have powers manifesting, too. I asked him to take you all to America, to have one of their Ami psychics train Aleda. I don't know...I don't think he would hurt you, but...

Lina, it'll be fine, Isa sent, her mind soothing. *He's my brother-in-law. I'm sure he won't hurt us, even if he cannot take us with him. You did right.*

But I don't know if I should have trusted him.

I trust Emilia, Isa replied, *and she trusts him. I told her about Aleda as well, and she's thrilled. Shall I have her convince her husband to take us with them?*

Perhaps, Lina said, *if she can be subtle about it. Don't mention this conversation to her, nor my powers, if you can help it. Let's keep that card a secret for now. But you might be able to express some worry about finding Aleda a teacher before she grows powerful enough to be a danger. Perhaps your sister will fill in the rest herself.*

Yes! Excellent plan...where are you?

Still upstairs in the colonel's library. He asked me to wait here while he speaks with some of his colleagues. He promised to let you know.

He's speaking with Emilia now…are you all right?

I am, Lina said. *I'm just terrified I've endangered you and the girls.*

The world has been mad since before the war, Isa said. *We're always in danger. You've kept us safer than anyone, Lina. Don't fret. All will be well.*

I hope you're right, Lina said and severed the connection before the cold, grinding fear she felt leaked down and into Isa's mind.

* * *

True to the colonel's word, someone knocked on the door of the library within a few minutes. Lina called permission to enter, and an older woman with grey hair caught up in a bun and a grandmotherly smile walked in, carrying a tray with a teapot and a mug. She set the tray down on the desk and nodded her reply at Lina's thanks, then left without saying a word.

Lina stood up to pour for herself, and had just lifted the steaming mug to her lips when the door behind her opened again, this time with no knock of warning. She turned to see Connor return, followed by a man who fit the stereotype of tall, dark, and handsome. He wore his dark brown hair short, as befit his US Army uniform. Like Connor, this newcomer sported flyer's wings on his chest, as well as several ribbons and devices. Once, Lina might have even remembered what they meant. Now, however, she found she just couldn't care.

"Fräulein," the newcomer said, giving her a tiny smile that did nothing to touch the empty blackness of his dark eyes, "or should I say, *Oberhelfer?*"

Lina froze. No one had called her by that title since before the war had ended. She said nothing, merely watched the newcomer as he sauntered over and took the remaining armchair. As before, Connor sat behind the desk.

"Perhaps you would like to sit down?" Emilia's husband suggested. His words were mild, the tone friendly, but Lina knew very well what was happening. She'd conducted enough interrogations to recognize one when she saw it.

"Yes, thank you," she said, and took the moment to sip her tea and try to gather up her scattered thoughts. *As long as the girls are safe,* she said to herself, *that's what matters. Only that!*

The newcomer removed a file from a briefcase she hadn't noticed before and flipped it open on the desk. A few photographs lay inside, along with a paper marked with neatly typed lines. He picked it up and began to read.

"Oberhelfer Adalina Sucherin. Born 1924, in Hamburg. No known family living—" He broke off and looked over the edge of the paper at her, and she realized he intended it to be a question.

"My parents and sisters were killed in a bombing raid," she said, her voice careful and even. "I was off at school by then."

"Ah, yes. Graduate of the infamous *Reichschule*, and thus entitled to the rank of SS-Oberhelfer. Doing your part for your Reich, eh?"

"As you did your part for your country when you bombed our cities," Lina said, unable to keep the tartness from her voice. It may have been a trick of the light, but it almost looked like the newcomer's smile grew a tiny bit before he looked back down at the paper.

"It says here you were detailed to Warsaw, and then Paris, as an interrogator?"

Lina said nothing, merely raised her mug to her lips and took another sip. He was working up to something. She'd let him get there before making her next move.

"It also says you had a stellar record of getting results from the hardest cases. What made you so good, Oberhelfer?"

"Please," she said, "the SS hasn't existed for a number of years. That's no longer my title. Fräulein will do. Or Lina, if you prefer."

"Fräulein," the newcomer said, his smile falling away from his face. *So much for being friendly.* "What made you so good at your job? What did you learn at the *Reichschule?*"

Lina settled back in the armchair, cradling the mug between her hands. Her natural caution urged her to deflect and keep quiet, but deep in her gut lay the iron certainty that if she was going to guarantee the girls' safety, she had to push this gamble a little bit further.

"I learned the art of conducting interrogations," she said, "as well as how to use and control my own psychic abilities, and how to integrate them with conventional questioning techniques. Like Aleda, I came into my power early, which is a reasonable indicator of the eventual strength of a psychic's talent. I was very strong and very skilled with my abilities. That's why I was so effective."

"Was?" the newcomer asked, lowering the paper slightly. A tiny crease formed between the dark slashes of his brows. "Are you not any longer?"

Lina swallowed hard and shook her head in the negative.

"After Berlin fell...I had to lock my power down. It remained locked down for several years. I'm only now able to do the simplest of psychic tasks, which is why I haven't yet attempted to read either of you." She looked down to see that her hands had begun to tremble around the mug of tea. She set the mug on the desk and folded her hands in her lap, then raised her eyes to meet the newcomer's dark gaze.

"Plus," he added, that ghost of a smile returning to his mouth, "it would be rude."

"Yes," she said.

Silence descended on the room after that, broken only by the chirping of birds in the tree outside the window, and the ever-present drone of airplanes overhead. Lina sipped her tea and waited while the two men looked at each other. Finally the newcomer gave a small nod, and Colonel Connor leaned forward in his chair with his easy smile.

"Speaking of being rude," he said, "I've failed to introduce you two. Lina, may I present Major Paul Rutherford, US Army Counter-intelligence Corps."

"Not the Air Corps?" Lina asked. "I noticed your wings when you walked in."

"Not anymore," Rutherford said. "I busted an eardrum; can't fly anymore. Had to find another job."

Lina smiled again, her own version of the American's barely-there expression. "We all have our war wounds, it seems."

"Indeed," Connor said. He reached into his uniform and pulled out the notebook she'd given him earlier. "Let's speak plainly, Lina. Earlier you proposed to me that I arrange for the Thanhouser girls and Isa to be taken to the United States in safety, in exchange for this notebook and the information therein, correct?"

"Yes," Lina said, "and that the girls be taught by trained psychics, who can help them control their powers and become an asset to your government, if you choose."

"Lina," Connor said, giving her a smile. Clearly, he was taking the role of the sympathetic one in this exchange. "Do you know what's in this notebook?"

"Formulas and notes," she said. "I flipped through it, but I didn't understand most of the language. Chemistry was never my field."

"Even if it was your field, I'm not sure you'd understand it. It seems Dr. Thanhouser wrote in a personal shorthand of sorts. The entire thing is encoded. Our boys could decipher it, given enough time, but there's a much easier way, one that might allow us all to get what we want."

Here it comes, she thought.

"And what's that?" she asked out loud.

"You want the Thanhouser girls safe, preferably in America, right? And we...we want Rolland Thanhouser." Connor leaned forward in his chair as he said this, his smile wide and friendly. Lina met his eyes, with their lying smile, and considered while quiet stretched between the three of them.

Rutherford broke the silence first.

"You'd be detailed to me," he said, "as a contact and operative. I would accompany you back to the east side and assist you in investigating Dr. Thanhouser's disappearance. Once we find out who's taken him, and where, you'll assist me in retrieving him. In exchange, Isa Thanhouser and her three daughters will accompany the colonel's wife when she immigrates to the United States. Once there, Mrs. Thanhouser and her daughters will be taken to a safe place, where a psychic tutor will be procured for them."

"'A safe place?'" Lina asked, skepticism dripping from her tone. Rutherford lifted the corner of his mouth in reply.

"A *nice* place," Connor put in. "We're not monsters, Lina. They're just kids, and my nieces. We aren't the Soviets, and we aren't your enemy."

You were, she thought, but didn't say. Because he was right. As much as Lina hated Americans, she had to admit they'd treated their sectors of Berlin far better than the Soviets had.

"One more condition," Rutherford said. Lina snapped her eyes back to his darkly handsome face and waited for the other shoe to drop. "If you agree to this, you must create and maintain a psychic connection with me. If the connection fails at any point in our operations, we'll consider this agreement null and void, and all assistance to the Thanhouser family will cease."

"You'll use them as hostages," Lina said softly. "And you tell me you're not monsters?"

"We've been very generous with you," Rutherford said. "Help us retrieve Thanhouser, and you can join the girls in America, where you'll all be safe. Or refuse, and the five of you can take the train back to your apartment tonight."

And there it was—both better and worse than she'd hoped. If she was able to find Rolland and help him get free, she could win safety for all of them. She'd promised Isa to do that very thing…only it was an impossible task. She knew it, deep in her heart of hearts. Finding information about him would be difficult enough. Actually effecting a rescue? Unheard of.

But she didn't have a choice. She couldn't let them take Isa and the girls back to be arrested by the shadowy figures who had kidnapped their father. So Lina did the only thing she could do.

She lifted her chin and stared deep into Rutherford's inky black eyes.

"I accept," she said.

* * * * *

Chapter Three –
Operation Confiscate

It was, all in all, a beautiful summer day; one that Lina would remember for a very long time. After she accepted the Americans' offer, the colonel and Rutherford accompanied her downstairs, to where Isa and the girls sat laughing with Emilia.

"Russel?" Isa's sister said, looking up at her husband as he slid the pocket door open and gestured for Lina to precede him inside.

"Yes, darling," Connor said, all smiles. He clapped Rutherford on the back, then followed the taller man in. "I've gotten in touch with the office and rearranged my schedule, so I can spend the day with you and your sister, and our lovely nieces. And I've asked Paul here to join us for lunch."

"Wonderful!" Emilia said, clapping her hands together. She got to her feet and walked in a sort of grand, sweeping motion that made Lina wonder if she'd watched many American films and tried to emulate the female leads. "Paul, you're always welcome here!"

"Thank you, Mrs. Connor," Paul said. His German was very good, Lina noticed all of a sudden. He didn't have the trace of an American accent that threaded through the colonel's words. *But then,* she thought wryly, *he is a spy...or whatever.*

"Well, that's perfect, then," Emilia said, turning her smiling face to look at all of them in turn, "because I believe it's just time for lunch now! Let's go out on the terrace, and I'll have Marta serve us out there." She made another film starlet-style gesture toward the French doors at the back of the parlor, and Lina could see the corner of a table on a flagstone terrace, surrounded by pots and planters overflowing with blooms of color.

Little Johanna clapped her hands together and ran to be first to open the door. When her mother called her name in gentle warning, though, the child stepped aside and held the door open while the rest of the group filed through.

"What a beautiful garden!" Isa said, tucking her arm through Emilia's. "I love all the flowers! Did you do this yourself, Emilia?"

"I? No." The younger of the two sisters laughed. "I have no talent for gardening, as you might remember, Isa. This is Marta's handiwork. She's our housekeeper, and just as talented a cook as she is a floral designer! I wish we could keep her with us." She turned to make a pouty moue at her husband.

"She stays with the house," Connor said, giving his wife a chuckle. "You know that, darling. Marta's cooking is one of the perks of my position here, and when I leave the position, I leave the perks for my replacement, as well."

"I know," Emilia said. "You've told me. I just hope we'll be able to find someone as clever in your home country!"

Connor and Rutherford shared a look, and for just a moment, Lina was deeply tempted to try to eavesdrop on their thoughts. If she didn't know better, she'd have said that the look was one of affectionate indulgence, as if they were both thinking that the colonel's silly wife had no idea what life was like back in America.

Well, that's fair. I doubt she's ever been there, Lina thought tartly, ignoring her own rising irritation with Emilia's performance. She walked across the flagstones to one of several white wrought-iron chairs arranged around a cloth-covered table. Lina watched the light summer breeze ruffle the edges of the light blue table cloth as she sat down, but the plain white china on top kept everything in place.

The others followed Lina's lead, and she found herself flanked by Isa on her left and Aleda on her right as the much-appreciated Marta brought out a tray of drinks.

"I know it's indulgent of me, but I had Marta open our last bottle of champagne," Emilia said. "We haven't got many bottles of any kind of wine left, but I couldn't think of a better reason to use up the bubbly than to celebrate seeing my sister and nieces again! There's juice for the girls, as well, so they can join us in a toast—to family!"

Lina thanked Marta with a nod and lifted her glass toward the others'. "To Family," she echoed, as did all the others. Then she took a sip, and had to fight not to let her eyes roll back in her head at the pleasure of that ephemeral wash of bubbly, slightly acidic crispness over her tongue. It had been so long since she'd tasted anything of the sort. It had been so long since she could *afford* anything of the sort.

"Heavens, this is marvelous." Isa sighed next to her. "I haven't tasted champagne in *ages*. Rolland would..." She stopped suddenly and put her free hand to her lips. She closed her eyes, as if trying to hold back the tears that suddenly threatened to flood through. Lina reached out and touched her shoulder lightly, just to let her friend know that she was there. Across the table, Johanna's iron chair scraped against the flagstones as she pushed back enough to wriggle her way out and run to her mother's side.

"*Mutti,*" she said, reaching her arms up, her little eyes soft with worry.

Isa put her champagne glass down with a shaking hand and reached out to pull her baby over the arm of the chair and into her lap. Johanna wrapped her arms around her mother's neck and buried her face in her shoulder. Because she was sitting so close, Lina could hear the little girl murmuring words of reassurance as Isa cuddled her tightly.

"Oh, Isa," Emilia said, her own eyes bright with tears. To the woman's credit, the worry on her face looked genuine, and she seemed to have dropped the 'starlet hostess' pretense in the face of her sister's very real distress.

"Mrs. Thanhouser," Colonel Connor said softly, "I wasn't going to say anything, but…Isa, we'll find him."

"What?" Isa asked, lifting her head.

"Your husband. We'll find him for you. Your friend Lina, here, had a tremendous idea. She's going to return home and help one of our people pick up the trail, and we'll see if we can't find your husband and return him to you…in America."

"America?" Isa asked again, bewilderment in her tone.

"Russel? This is true?" Emilia cried out, her eyes wide. "We can bring them?"

"Yes, Darling. I wasn't sure at first, which is why I had to go to work and speak with Paul here, but I knew you wouldn't want to leave your family behind, and you know your happiness means everything to me. So we pulled some strings, and Isa and her daughters will accompany us home."

"And they can stay with us at your new assignment in Washington?" Emilia asked, clapping her hands together in delight.

"As to that, Darling, I cannot say. But they may certainly accompany us when we go to meet my family in Richmond."

"Oh, Isa! Did you hear?" Emilia squealed. "You get to come with me to America!"

Isa stared at her sister with wide, wet eyes for a long moment, then turned to look at Lina over Johanna's bent head.

Lina met her gaze with steady, clear eyes. "I'll find him," she promised, though she still had no idea how. "I'll find him, and we'll get him back for you, Isa. I swear it." *Because if I don't, you and the girls are at risk.*

Isa unwrapped her right hand from around her daughter's small form and reached out for Lina. Lina took her friend's hand and squeezed it gently. Isa returned the squeeze, though not nearly so softly.

"I know you will," she said, and a dark shadow in her eyes showed that she clearly understood something else was going on under the surface here. "You must be careful. Be safe, Lina."

"I will," Lina said. "I swear to that, too."

* * *

That evening, Lina prepared to leave.

She stood in the bedroom Isa was to share with the girls and repacked her knapsack. She removed all the pilfered food items, but kept her warm clothing and boots. The colonel's home was comfortable to the point of luxurious, but the west side of the city *was* under a blockade. Despite the incalculable luxury of the champagne, Lina could see that Emilia's household was feeling the pinch. Their luncheon had consisted mainly of salad grown by the talented Marta, garnished with small bits of meat and cheese. Supper had been a bit more substantial, but not much. Colonel Connor was the commander of the airfield operations at

Tempelhof, where the British and American planes flew day and night to bring in supplies. The US Army supplied him with adequate rations for his family, but that was about it.

Lina feared it would get worse before it got better.

But Isa and the girls would be safe, and they would have plenty to eat in America. Lina didn't entirely trust Colonel Russel Connor, but she didn't exactly have much choice in the matter. She would do her part, and trust Isa and the girls to take care of themselves.

"You'll be careful, won't you?" Isa said then, breaking Lina out of her reverie. Lina looked up from the cans of meat she'd placed on the bed and smiled.

"Of course I will," she said. "And you must be careful, too. I know Emilia's your sister, and her husband seems to be a good man…but he's not telling you everything."

"I know," Isa said. "His offer to take us to America was such a sudden reversal…it's too good to be true."

"It *is* true, as far as I can tell," Lina said, "but he's not doing it just to keep his wife happy. The American government wants to recover Rolland for his research."

"I expected as much," Isa said.

"You must take care," Lina said again. "As soon as you get to America, you must find a job. Get a steady income. Become as independent of Emilia as possible, as quickly as you can. Connor said he would arrange for a psychic to tutor Aleda. Use your judgment about the woman he finds. Trust your instincts, Isa. A mother's intuition is rarely wrong."

Isa nodded solemnly, then reached out to touch Lina's cheek.

"And you," Isa said, "you must take care as well. I know what you did to protect yourself and my girls in that cellar scared you. You must not let that fear hinder you. If it comes to it, you have to choose between your life and the life of the person trying to hurt you. Please, my sister. Choose yours."

Lina swallowed hard and nodded, then threw her arms around the other woman. She wasn't a demonstrative person, but Isa had cared for her when she couldn't care for herself. She'd loved her, protected her, given her a family once again.

And once again, that family was being ripped away.

Isa hugged Lina back, hard, and the two women held each other for a few moments while the drone of the airplanes overhead continued to whine through the air. Finally, Isa sniffed and let go.

"Promise," she said, her voice insistent.

"I promise," Lina said.

"Good," Isa replied. "Then let me bring the girls in. They want to say goodbye."

Lina nodded and waited as Isa crossed the bedroom to open the door. Ginette came first, leading Johanna by the hand, with Aleda bringing up the rear. Johanna looked up and saw Lina dressed to leave and dropped her sister's hand. She ran toward Lina and launched herself up at her, so that Lina was forced to catch her up in an embrace.

"I'll miss you so much, *Tante!*" Johanna said, sniffing mightily. "Please be safe."

"I will, sweetling," Lina said, cuddling her close. "You be safe, too, and listen to your mother and sisters, all right?"

"I will, I promise," the little one said. Then she leaned in close to whisper in Lina's ear. "And I'll keep taking care of *Mutti's* feelings when she's sad, so she doesn't collapse again." She placed a loud, smacking kiss on Lina's cheek, then let go of her. Lina, stunned by the revelation of Johanna's awareness, let the girl slide down to the ground and blinked at the knowing smile the child gave her before stepping away.

"*Tante*," Ginette said, drawing Lina's attention away from the littlest sister.

"Ginette. Take care of them. Please. Help your mother, and…"

"I know," Ginette said, with her own smile that had always been too old for her years. "I will. Come back to us when you can."

"Yes," Lina said and opened her arms to welcome the girl—young woman, really—into an embrace. Like her, Ginette had never been particularly physically demonstrative, but Lina felt the whipcord strength in her young body as she clung, for just a moment, before letting go and stepping aside.

"I remember what you taught me," Aleda said as she stepped forward. "I remember how to shield and how to listen. I'll keep them safe."

"See that you do," Lina said, speaking through a throat thick with tears she hadn't shed in over five years. "Your uncle has said he'll find a teacher for you. Keep your abilities secret from everyone else, do you understand?"

"Yes, *Tante*."

"And study hard. You'll be very powerful one day, Aleda. It's important that you learn control early."

"Yes, *Tante*."

Once again, Lina opened her arms, and once again, found them instantly filled.

"I love you, *Tante*," Aleda whispered.

"I love you too, sweetling. I love you all. Please, please be careful."

"We will. You, too."

"Yes. I will," Lina said, and her eyes began to burn. She blinked quickly, but they still felt like coals glowing in their sockets.

"Come, girls," Isa said. "Let's give *Tante* Lina a moment to finish packing, then we'll see her off at the front door."

Aleda, too, placed a kiss on Lina's cheek, then stepped back. Lina tried to focus on her, on all of them, but she suddenly found she couldn't see. Her vision wavered in a spiky, burning blur.

Lina heard the door close as, for the first time since one snowy, hellish night in the Belgian forest, tears began to fall from her eyes.

* * *

Major Paul Rutherford met her outside the colonel's front door after she'd said goodbye to everyone one more time. It had been easier the second time, after the storm of tears had passed. The icy lump of fear still sat in Lina's belly, but she felt lighter than she had in...well...for as long as she could remember, anyway. She was able to square her shoulders and hold her head high as she descended the brick stairs to the walkway where Rutherford waited.

"I have a car," he said, gesturing to the street where a low, black sedan waited.

"I see that," she replied. "Are we going far?"

"Just to the office at first," he said. "You need to be briefed in. After you." He reached out and opened the rear door of the car, stepping to the side so she could climb in.

The interior of the car was not quite luxurious, but it wasn't far off. Lina hadn't ridden in a car since the war. She'd almost forgotten what it felt like.

"How far is your office?" she asked, once he'd joined her in the back seat and pulled the door closed behind himself. The driver started the engine, and Lina felt the car's vibration like a big cat purring somewhere close behind her.

"Just down at the airfield," Rutherford said. "A few minutes away, no more." His tone was blank and clipped, back to the practical operative she'd first met, with no trace of Emilia's smiling houseguest.

Fair enough, she thought. *I can be professional, too.*

Lina sat back on the car's upholstered seats and let the silence descend around them while she watched the streetlights go by. No power interruptions here, it seemed. Not at this time, anyway. Their route turned and twisted through the darkened city, but before long, they came to a gate structure blazing with light. The driver slowed down, rolled down a window, and presented something to the uniformed soldier waiting there. The soldier waved them through, and the long metal pole barring the way rose up before he handed the credentials back to the driver.

"Welcome to Tempelhof airfield," Rutherford said as the car rolled forward again.

"Thank you," Lina said, then said nothing more until they came to a stop a few minutes later. Rutherford got out first, then offered a hand to help her out. She thought about refusing, but in the end decided to play nice and let him be chivalrous, if he felt like it. It cost her nothing, after all, and didn't interfere with the job she was here to do.

Rutherford said goodbye to the driver, who was apparently not going in with them, and led Lina through the front doors of a building marked "Operations." The building itself was a utilitarian structure, lacking all the grace and comfort of the colonel's home. Once inside, Rutherford took a sharp right turn and led Lina down a hallway to a large room holding a wide conference table. He flipped a sign on the door from "Unclassified" to "Classified," and shut and locked it behind himself.

Lina inhaled through her nose and pushed her fear away.

"Have a seat," he invited, as he reached into his briefcase and pulled out another manila file folder. He placed it on the table in front of her and waited while Lina sat down. "Take a look."

Lina glanced up at him, then pulled the file folder close before flipping open the cover. A glossy photograph stared back at her, showing a tunnel with exposed pipes stretching into a darkened, distant background.

"That's a picture of one of the cross tunnels at a place called Mittelwerk. Are you familiar with it?" Rutherford asked, seating himself to her right.

"No," Lina said, squinting slightly and lifting the photograph out of the glare from the overhead light.

"It was a Nazi research and assembly facility during the war. It was where your people built the V2 rocket. Only it wasn't 'your people' exactly, was it?"

"What do you mean?" Lina asked, looking up at the major, who stared down at her with dark, empty eyes.

"Look at the next photograph."

Lina slid the top photo to the side and picked up the one beneath. It took a moment for her mind to register what her eyes were seeing. Inside another tunnel, similar to the first picture but much larger, a large crane stretched over a rocket assembly line. Twelve bodies hung from the crane, dangling over the heads of the line and the emaciated men who worked it. The camera angle was such that Lina could see the closest body's face, darkened and distorted, with a piece of wood tied into the mouth as a gag, and dead, filmy eyes bulging from the sockets.

"What horror is this?" Lina whispered, not really meaning to.

"That's one of about five executions carried out at Mittelwerk, that we know of. These particular unfortunates took part in an attempted riot against the SS guards, and were hanged, their bodies left to dangle above their fellow prisoners as a deterrent. We found this photograph in the Mittelwerk archives the Nazis kept." Rutherford leaned forward and flipped the second photograph over, revealing a third.

More tunnels, but this time the floor was filled with skeletal human corpses. Bodies lay in haphazard clumps, their spindly limbs tangled and sticking out at odd angles. In the foreground of the shot, three men sat slumped against the tunnel wall, and they looked barely more alive than the remains that surrounded them.

"That photograph was taken by a U. S. Army private when our soldiers liberated the facility. This was the northernmost facility of the Mittelwerk plant. They were all like this. Thousands of men, worked to death."

Lina felt her stomach roil. "Why are you showing me this?" she asked, her voice barely a whisper.

"Because the notebook you gave us was written at Mittelwerk. Your Dr. Thanhouser is a war criminal," Rutherford said.

"No," Lina said, shaking her head. "Impossible. He's a scientist, and the kindest of men. He would never be part of something so horrible."

In answer, Rutherford flipped the photograph over and tapped a typewritten piece of paper. Lina didn't want to look. She didn't want to hear or learn any more. The war had been horrible for everyone. Couldn't they leave the past in the past?

"Read it, Oberhelfer. Or our deal is off."

Rutherford's use of her SS title sent a spike of fear through Lina's mind. She swallowed hard and forced herself to lean forward and focus on the words.

It was a labor requisition requesting twelve more men to work in the chemical synthesis portion of the facility. It was addressed to the leadership of the nearby Dora concentration camp, and it was signed by Rolland Thanhouser, Chief Chemist, V2 Rocket Production, Mittelwerk.

"Look at the third paragraph," Rutherford said, his voice soft, yet cold as iron, "where he states his reason for needing more men. Read it out loud."

Lina licked her lips and forced the words to come. Her voice cracked with equal parts of fear and anger.

"I regret to contact you again so soon," she read, "but I fear the last batch you sent me were in quite bad shape, and could not produce the required output before succumbing to their frailties. Please do try to select hardier specimens this time, so they might survive longer than a few weeks."

"Specimens," Rutherford repeated in that same soft, icy tone. "He didn't even acknowledge them as human."

"We were at war!" Lina cried, shoving the folder and its contents away from her. The photographs slid out of the manila envelope and lay spread across the table like a collage of accusation. "Germany was fighting for her life! You're a soldier, you understand that people die in a war."

"Yes," he said, "but these men didn't die in a *war*. They died in a *slave camp*, starving, freezing, being beaten and worked to death. And your friend, Dr. Thanhouser, was complicit."

"So what does that mean now?" Lina asked, the fear and anger in her gut finally igniting into a passion that poured into her words. "What does this mean for you and me? Rolland may have done this, but his wife, his daughters—they're innocent!"

"So they are," Rutherford said, "and we made a deal. I just thought you should know what we know about Thanhouser. He's a war criminal, and will very possibly face charges for it…but there are other alternatives."

"What do you mean?"

"There is…precedent, we'll call it, for scientists like your Dr. Thanhouser to work for the United States of America. As we told you before, his research and expertise will be quite valuable in the coming war."

Lina's head snapped up. "What war?" she asked.

Rutherford reached out and began gathering the photographs together, stacking them neatly and putting them back into their manila folder.

"The war that's coming, whether we like it or not. This blockade of Berlin is but the opening salvo. The war between the United States and the Soviet Union, which will decide the fate of the rest of the world's people. Will they be free to pursue their own dreams and desires? Or will they become slaves to the communist machine?" he asked, delivering these dramatic words in a calm, almost eerily matter-of-fact tone. He sat back in his chair and folded his arms, staring at her. "That war."

Lina's mind raced. She stared back at Rutherford's dark, measuring gaze and fought to keep her breathing even and calm.

"You're telling me to choose a side," she said, her voice low.

"Everyone must," he replied. "I know you don't like me, Lina. It's pretty obvious you don't like Americans in general. But if we're going to be successful in going after Thanhouser, I need to know I can trust you. Because if we fail, we just might give the Soviet Union what they need to win...and we'll be seeing a lot more scenes like this." He held up the picture of the dead workers.

"That wasn't the Soviets," she couldn't help but point out.

"No," he said with a tight smile, "that was *your* side. Until we defeated you. But then, you know all about being defeated, don't you? You were in Berlin when it fell. Tell me, Lina, based on that experience, do you think the Soviets will be any more lenient than your own Reich?"

Lina jerked backward, her back slapping against the upright back of her chair. "Why do you say these things if you want me to like you?" she asked, letting some of her hatred creep into her tone.

"I don't want you to *like* me," Rutherford replied. "I don't like *you*; you're a war criminal too. But if I have to work with you to protect my country from scenes like this," he raised the photograph again and shook it so the paper rattled in his hand, "I need to know you're all in. The enemy of my enemy is my friend, right? What do you say, Lina? Who's the greater enemy? Me? Or the Soviet Union?"

Lina felt her face grow hot as the rage built within her. The urge to reach out and tear this man's mind to shreds pulsed against her shields. She held herself very still and used every bit of her will to impose an iron calm on her unruly and unpredictable emotions…and power.

"I hate you," she said, making her voice as blank and empty as she could. "I hate your country and what you did to my family. I hate how you think you can sit there in smug superiority and claim the side of right and good when your bombs burned innocent children to death. We need not pretend your vaunted American 'liberators,' as you called them, weren't guilty of plenty of atrocities in their own right…I've seen some of them with my own eyes."

She took a deep breath and closed her eyes for a moment. The memory of a blood-soaked tent rose up in her mind's eye, and she gritted her teeth and forced herself to picture Ginette's face, and Aleda's, and little Johanna's instead. *If it will keep them safe…I can make the enemy of my enemy my friend.*

"But I hate the Soviets more," she whispered. She opened her eyes and allowed Rutherford to see the vitriol burning in her own gaze. "Is that what you wanted to hear, Major?"

Rutherford stared back for a long moment before his lips curled in another one of his small, dry smiles.

"Close enough," he said. He held out a hand to her as if they were being introduced for the first time. "Welcome to Operation Confiscate."

* * *

The next order of business was to establish a link between the two of them.

After the intensity of the previous conversation, however, Lina needed a break and some time to prepare herself, so she asked Rutherford if there was coffee or tea available. He took the hint and left her alone in the conference room while he went to get something. He did leave the manila file, though, and locked the door behind himself.

The enemy of my enemy is my friend, Lina reminded herself as she heard the tumblers turn in the lock. Then she took a deep breath and unclenched her hands, which she'd balled into fists to keep from shaking. Trembles shuddered through her body, starting from deep in her belly and radiating outward, and she fought hard not to start gulping at the air in reaction.

I can do this, she told herself sternly. *I'm a graduate of the Reichschule! I was taught by some of Germany's finest, and I was the strongest student they'd ever seen. I can create a link with this man, and I can maintain it long enough to find Rolland! I can and I will!*

One of the fundamental truths Lina had learned at a very young age came roaring to the forefront of her mind—confidence was absolutely necessary. If a psychic doubted her ability to do something…well…she was right. Doubt was a poison, and it would drain her of power if she let it get any more of a foothold than it already had.

Lina pushed up to her feet and paced away from the table, shaking her hands out in agitation.

I will do this, she said to herself once more. *I did what I had to do to survive Berlin's fall, but I'm still me. I'm still Lina Sucherin, the psychic who tracked Evelyn Adamsen across Europe! My control is degraded, and my power rusty as an old saw, but it's still mine! I can do this!*

Rutherford opened the door, interrupting Lina's mental pep talk. She swung around to watch as he entered the room, holding two mugs of steaming liquid. He held one out to her and she took it, while he closed and locked the door behind himself. It was coffee, not tea, and without milk or sugar, it was quite bitter. Still, she sipped at it, grateful for both the distraction and the kick of caffeine.

"Will that work?" he asked. "I didn't know how you take it."

"This is fine," she said, blowing on the liquid and taking another sip. "Thank you."

"You're welcome," he said. He sipped his own coffee and watched her over the rim of his mug. "Are you ready to link up now?" he asked as he set the beverage on the table.

"If you like," she said. She took one more fortifying sip, then put her mug down as well. "Would you like to take my hand?"

"Do you need to touch to make a connection?" he asked, but he reached out for her hand.

"No," she said, "it just makes it easier the first time. And since you'll need me to maintain this connection indefinitely, it'll need to be a strong, full link. Touch helps with that."

"Ah," he said. "Fair enough."

"You're ready, then?" she asked. Her stomach churned with nerves.

"Yes. Go ahead."

Lina laid her palm atop his offered hand. His skin felt warm and smooth, surprisingly soft, though she could feel the promise of steely strength underneath. She closed her eyes, took a deep breath, and reached out with her power toward that steady, iron warmth.

Ah...

It had been years since Lina's mind had touched a man's psyche. She'd forgotten the delicious feeling of her power flowing into a man's mind. It felt like satin sliding along the underside of her skin, enveloping her in silky warmth as she wove in and out of his mental landscape.

She opened her eyes and saw her own face, her green eyes soft with pleasure, her lips parted as she exhaled. Lina blinked, and her own vision came to the fore, showing her their joined hands. She hadn't realized she'd threaded her fingers through Paul's, but apparently she had.

Lina.

His thought was strong and clear, but had a probing, testing feel. His touch was extremely good, the best she'd ever felt from a man, and she realized abruptly that Paul Rutherford must have extensive experience working with psychic women.

Yes, he thought in answer to the question she hadn't actually asked, *both of my sisters. My twin died when we were young, and my other sister is a very strong psychic.*

I see, she said. *She taught you well.* Unlike her link with Aleda, this connection felt easy, rejuvenating, as if her mind were designed to fit with Paul's. She didn't feel the drain she'd experienced back in her apartment. The link seemed to maintain itself, giving her the opportunity to test her limits a bit.

She flowed through his consciousness, letting his thoughts brush against her. It felt something like swimming, though instead of water, she felt enveloped in the essence of Paul; his strength, his iron convictions, his memories…

No.

Lina blinked hard and actually stumbled backward as her mind hit an immovable, impenetrable barrier. Her eyes flicked up to Paul's, and he shook his head as he met her gaze.

You shield very well, Lina thought to him, letting him feel the dryness of her statement. *I thought we were supposed to trust each other?*

Trust does not mean a complete lack of privacy. You don't like me, I don't like you, remember?

How could I forget? she asked, but she let it go. He was right, after all. They might have to work together, but she certainly didn't like him any more than she had that morning.

Besides, he thought, dropping his hand from hers and stepping back to take the seat he'd vacated earlier, *we have better things to do with our time, which is limited. You mentioned your abilities are somewhat degraded from being locked down so long. What, exactly, does that mean?*

I don't actually know, she said, *only that when I linked with Aleda—the middle Thanhouser girl, the one whose abilities are manifesting already—it was harder than it should have been, and it drained me of energy faster than I expected.*

And do you feel such a drain now?

No, but linking with men is always easier. It's possible that I may become fatigued sooner than I would have before—

Before the war?

Before the end *of the war,* she said firmly. Her powers had been at their height during the war. *Before the ravaging of Berlin.*

Ah, he thought, and she felt his attention receding as he elected not to ask any more questions on that topic. He took up another line of questioning instead. *How's your range?*

At my strongest, I could maintain a connection over kilometers, and catch a trace of an individual over a hundred kilometers away...but that was a particular case. With you? I suspect I could hold our link for a kilometer with no problem, though, again, I cannot say for how long. Much depends, too, on the circumstances. She took his lead and returned to her chair, cradling the coffee in her hands.

Yes, I know you need extra food if at all possible. I'll do what I can to ensure you're supplied, but it may be difficult. I'm not sure exactly what we'll be facing. That's a large part of the reason why you're here, to help me figure that out.

What do you propose? she asked.

For now, we need more information. I think tomorrow morning you should return to your apartment. I don't doubt that someone will come and question you. You'll say you've taken a new lover and you spent today and tonight with me. And then…we shall see. He eyed her over his mug and took a drink.

She nodded her assent and did the same. The coffee's bitter, caffeine-laced bite zinged through her nerves and made her focus feel sharp and ready.

Ready as she could be, in any case.

* * *

They took a circuitous route back to the east side of the city, but eventually, they got back on the train and ended up at the station nearest Lina's apartment building.

Paul dropped easily into the role of her paramour, being solicitous, but not overly so. He would take her hand or offer his arm as they walked, and spoke to her in that perfect German with an easy, unaffected air.

"I hate to leave you, my darling," he said, smiling down at her as they walked up the stairs to the front door of her apartment. "Are you certain you wouldn't rather I stay?"

"I'm certain I would," she said, her smile coming more naturally than she would've expected, simply because he played the part of the teasing, pleading lover so well, "but people will talk, and we have no chaperone here, as we did at your friends' house."

Will the people watching care about such things? he asked, raising an eyebrow at her in mock pleading.

They might. It's hard to tell. Certainly some will expect me to resist such an overt ploy.

"Ah," he said, lifting her right hand to his lips while covering his heart with his left hand. "Then I am bereft until I see you again."

"You're silly." She laughed, unable to help herself. "I'll see you again tomorrow."

"I'll count the minutes."

"Go home, mooncalf," she laughed again. *You're excellent at acting!*

"Good night, Lina," he said, his smile softening as he bent to kiss her on the cheek. *It's my job to be excellent at it. There are two men in the sedan half a block to your right. Don't look at them when you turn. Keep a small smile on your face as you enter your building, and don't be surprised if they come to visit you tonight. I'll be nearby. Notify me immediately if they come, or if you feel the link weakening because of the distance.*

"Good night, Paul," she said and stepped away, giving him the soft smile he'd requested. *All right,* she said unable to stop a thread of fear from winding down the lines of the net.

I'll be nearby, he said again, as if that was supposed to reassure her, and lifted his hand to wave as she turned and entered the front door of the building.

The link between them stayed strong and steady all the way up the inner stairs and into her cold, lonely apartment. She closed the door behind herself and locked it, then let out a sigh of relief.

I'm home, she sent, though it probably wasn't strictly necessary. She knew he could feel her emotions, and she'd left her sensory channels open if he chose to accept them.

Good, he said. *Get what sleep you can. I'm keeping an eye on our friends in the sedan. I don't know how long it'll be until someone contacts you.*

Easy for you to say, she thought, but then sent a pulse of agreement down the lines. She felt his answering burst of wry amusement at her discomfort.

You wanted to be a spy, he said. *Here's your chance.*

I never wanted to be a spy, she flung the thought back, hotly. *I only wanted to keep the Thanhouser girls safe.*

And in order to do that, you must become a spy. I thought that was clear.

It was, she thought, her quick defiance dying under the weight of her fatigue from the long day and the stress of creeping fear. *It is. You've backed me into a corner, and I'll do what you want; you needn't worry.*

I thought rescuing Rolland Thanhouser was something we both wanted, Paul thought, his tone taunting her.

'Rescuing,' what a pretty word for 'executing like a war criminal,' Lina returned. *It's almost as pretty as 'coercion by holding his children hostage.'*

You offered up the Thanhouser girls, Lina, remember that, Paul's bright anger threaded through the words, *and I told you there are other choices. If Thanhouser cooperates, we're prepared to be very generous with him. Far more generous than the Soviets will be, I can assure you of that.*

I don't doubt you're right, Lina thought, her defiance wilting away to nothing once more.

Then quit arguing with me and get some sleep. I have a feeling you'll need it, soon.

I hate to agree with you, but I have a feeling you're right.

They didn't say goodnight, they just stopped communicating. Lina could feel the link still there, strong and full in her mind, but Paul had turned his mind away. He wasn't blocking her, and she could have his full attention again in an instant, but he wasn't right there in the forefront of her psyche anymore.

Interesting trick. She would've liked to question him about it, but he was right. It was late, and it had been a long, stressful day. She walked back into her bedroom, thankful for the modicum of privacy Paul's trick afforded, and dressed for bed. As she climbed in between her sheets, she shivered. Not from the coolness of the fabric against her skin, but more from the strange intensity of the loneliness she felt. Her mind drifted to Isa and the girls, and she fell asleep, reliving the memory of this last, perfect day with them.

* * *

Lina woke with the summer sun streaming onto her face. She blinked, then turned and squinted at the window, whose curtains she'd forgotten to close the night before. *What time is it?* she wondered.

It's just six, Paul answered, his words moving smoothly through her consciousness like a silky balm. *You're a deep sleeper.*

I was tired; it's been a long couple of days, Lina replied, pushing herself up to a seated position. It felt surreal to be sitting in her bed, calmly bantering down her psychic link with an American, of all things, while Isa and the girls were far away, and Rolland was missing. She looked around her bedroom, trying to anchor herself in the familiarity of the spartan surroundings.

Well, you're awake now, so get up and get dressed. The men in the car have swapped out, but they're still watching your building. I suppose you should probably keep to your routine. What would you normally do on a day like today? Go to work?

Yes. It's a Wednesday, after all. I'll have to concoct some reason to have missed yesterday, too, Lina said, sighing as the thought occurred to her. She rolled her head on her neck and squared her shoulders before swinging her feet down to the floor and standing up.

Tell them you were ill. I can get you a doctor's note if you need it, he said. Once again, she felt him turn his attention away as she began to dress in her work clothes.

A bribe would be more useful, she said. *The supervisors are like the rest of us, no one has very much. If I can slip them a few extra marks, they'll look the other way.*

I can get you that, too, he said. *Stop by the trash bins on your way out the front door. There will be a wrapped package between them and the wall.*

Don't be seen delivering it, she warned him as she pulled a brush through her hair.

Don't worry about me, Lina. I know how to do my job. Paul's tone went flat and stiff, much as it had when she'd encountered the privacy block he held so tightly in his mind.

Right, I don't like you and you don't like me, she said.

Exactly.

He didn't say anything else as she finished getting ready for work. She didn't bother eating, especially since they'd cleaned out what little she had in her own kitchen the night before last. She would have to go to the market on the way home and get some actual food, now that she couldn't rely on the Thanhousers to care for her.

A little less than an hour after she'd awakened, Lina stepped out the front door of her apartment building, a half-full bucket of kitchen trash swinging from her hand. She carried it over to the bins and dumped it in, then bent as if to tie her shoe. Sure enough, there was a small envelope that looked as if it had been wedged in between the bin and the concrete outer wall of the building. Only this envelope was too clean to have been there for more than a few minutes. Lina took it and stuffed it inside the neck of her day-dress, then tucked her bucket down next to the bin. If it was still there when she came home, she'd retrieve it. If not…well…she'd find another refuse container.

She didn't see Paul on her walk to work, though she felt him nearby. She could have called up his vision and figured out his location that way, but she figured it was better if she didn't see him, for then she'd have to act like he was her new lover, and things would get complicated.

Best to keep it simple.

Without wandering through checkpoints and testing her abilities to cross over into the west side of the city, it took her only about half an hour to walk to work. Sure enough, as soon as she sat down at her desk, Frau Hoffman approached with a face like a storm cloud.

Lina shot back up to her feet and met the stout woman with a smile.

"Frau Hoffman!" she said, reaching into her dress for the envelope. "I got those papers you sent me for yesterday, but the lazy clerks took so long getting them to me, I wasn't able to make it back before you'd left for the day. Please accept my apologies, but here they are! If you wouldn't mind opening the envelope to check that everything is in order?"

Puzzlement passed over Isabel Hoffman's brutish features, but she took the envelope and opened it enough to look inside. Lina watched as the woman's porcine eyes widened, then narrowed, before looking back up at Lina.

"I don't have time to look them over now, Fräulein Sucherin, but they appear to be correct. Thank you for running that errand for me. I'll be sure to come to you the next time I need some…ah…papers delivered," she said, her face stretching into a grimace that was probably supposed to be a smile. Lina gave her a tiny, wintry smile in return, and sat back down to begin her work as the supervisor turned and walked away, carefully tucking the envelope into a pocket.

Greedy sow, Lina thought. *Your bribe worked beautifully. How much was it?*

Better if you don't know, Paul thought back. *What time do you finish there?*

Five, but I thought of something that might help, if we can get a little lucky, Lina thought, drawing in a deep breath as she loaded the first blank sheet into her typewriter and uncovered the handwritten memo she was to type. *See how this memo is from the ration department? We get correspondence from all over the government flowing through here. Sometimes I can listen to what the women are thinking, and get a sense of what they're typing. If you give me some time, maybe I can find something that might lead us to Rolland.*

It's worth a shot, Paul said. *Your new boyfriend will arrive at five to pick you up. See what you can gather until then.*

Lina sent him a wordless pulse of acquiescence and bent her head to her typing. As she did, she reached out with the lightest touch she could summon and began to skim the surface minds of the women bent over their clacking typewriters.

It still wasn't as easy as it should've been. Her control was still not what it should be, and more than once one of the women shivered, shifted, or looked up as if someone had called her name. Lina found she had to fall back upon her early training at the *Reichschule,* where she'd first learned to keep her touch light and skim the surface minds of those she questioned.

As before, there was a growing sense of unease in the minds of the typing pool women. They worried, one and all, about how hard it was to get things, even ordinary things like food. At one point, when she looked up to change the paper in her machine, Lina noticed that the clothing the women wore was almost universally ragged and patched. She'd never thought about it before, but it stood in stark contrast to the beauty and color she'd seen on the other side of the barricades. Here, everything was scavenged. No wonder there was a general feeling of growing desperation all around.

Lina worked and listened until mid-afternoon before she hit upon something. Even then, she didn't realize at first what she'd found. It was just a requisition reply, like so many others. The thing that caught her attention was, unlike most of the requests for money or other resources, the typist wasn't copying out the terse words of the canned refusal statement. This requisition was actually being approved. Lina drew in a deep breath and made her thoughts light and thin, like a net so finely woven as to be near-invisible, and dipped a little further into the woman's consciousness. She wanted to see what was so important it had actually been approved for purchase.

Desks. A flutter of disappointment rippled through Lina's mind. Such a mundane item! Why…

Oh.

They were for a new state office, she realized as the woman typed out the words. A state *security* office, staffed by Soviet advisors. An organization designed to protect the will of the people from dissidents and enemies of the state

Bitter recognition filled her mind. She knew those phrases, and what they really meant. In the Reich, they'd been called Gestapo. She wondered what term the Soviets would use.

I think I know who took Rolland, Lina thought in Paul's direction. She felt his attention perk up in response. *The Soviet security advisors must have decided he's a threat or dissident of some kind.*

Or maybe they found out about his scientific credentials, Paul replied. *You said he worked in a soap factory?*

Yes, something like that. I never paid very close attention.

Well, pay attention now, and see if you can find anything else.

But that was it for discoveries that day. If there was anything else of value to find, Lina missed it, and before long, five o'clock arrived and the typists began rising to their feet, stretching their weary backs and rotating their heads to work the kinks out of necks spent bent over their machines. Lina followed suit, putting on her own ragged, patched coat, and merged into the gaggle of women as they headed out into the street.

Sure enough, Paul waited there, dressed in ragged clothes and scuffed boots, with a shadow of a beard on his cheeks and chin. He leaned against the grey bricks of the government building and took a long drag from the cigarette hanging from his lips as their eyes met. Lina changed her course and walked toward him.

Smile, he said. *You're supposed to be infatuated with me, remember?*

She blinked, then let her eyes go soft, imagining he was really some new, exciting lover, not just the enemy of her enemy. He blew out his smoke, then smiled back and flicked his cigarette to the cracked sidewalk as he pushed away from the wall.

"Surprise," he said, opening his arms in invitation.

"Have you been waiting long?" she asked, walking close enough that he could wrap her into an embrace. His arms felt steely and warm through the fabric of her thin outer coat.

"No," he said. He squeezed her once and let go, then caught the fingers of her right hand with his. "I took a gamble that you'd be finished soon and thought I'd walk you home."

"Well," she said, smiling up at him, "this is a nice treat. Thank you."

They set off amid the muted chatter of the other women's voices. By the time they'd gone half a block, they were alone enough that no one else was in earshot.

Keep talking about inconsequential things, Paul cautioned her. *It's not safe to let the cover slip outside of a safe area. Not even when you think you're alone.*

What safe area? Lina thought back, tartly. Paul lifted her hand to his lips and brushed a kiss across her knuckles. His lips were warm and dry.

Exactly. Nowhere is safe on this side of the barricade, and since we can communicate like this, there's no reason to invite suspicion.

Lina tried to relax as they walked hand in hand down the street toward her apartment building. They talked of inconsequential matters, like the bright summer weather and how her day had gone. In the course of the conversation, Lina found herself once again admiring Paul's skill as an actor and spy. He managed to fill her in on various details of his cover story by casually mentioning them in conversation. She learned that his assumed persona lived in another apartment building—one assigned to bachelors—a few blocks south of hers. She learned that he worked as a construction laborer, helping to rebuild the city from the ruins left by the war. He spoke brightly of cousins on the other side of the barricades, and cleverly wished aloud that they would join him here in the workers' paradise on the eastern side of the city.

"I don't know how they'll survive the coming shortages," he said. "My family has never been wealthy, and the corrupt upper classes will certainly ensure the poorest starve first."

"Perhaps they can be persuaded to move?" Lina suggested, fighting off a feeling of disorientation. She had no doubt that deprivation was certainly coming for West Berlin; the blockade alone would see to that. But Paul's parroted phrases about "class warfare" and "capitalist corruption" seemed so distant from the bustling, hope-filled city she'd experienced for those few brief hours.

"I'm trying," he said, smiling down at her. "Perhaps together we can make them see reason, eh?"

She smiled back, but didn't answer out loud, since they'd come to her building.

"I would invite you in for supper," she said, "but I haven't gotten to the market yet."

"Oh! That's part of the surprise. I almost forgot," Paul replied, grinning down at her and letting go of her hand to remove the knapsack she'd barely noticed he was carrying. He opened it and showed her the paper-wrapped packages inside. "I stopped on my way to your workplace. I wasn't able to get much, but I've got some bread and cheese. It should do for something to share, at least."

"Sounds wonderful," Lina said and her stomach gurgled in agreement. Scanning the minds of the women in the typing pool had burned through her energy, and she bitterly regretted not packing something to eat at midday. Paul sent a pulse of acknowledgment down the lines of their link, which showed her that he understood her increased need for food based on her psychic activity.

"Well, then," he said, closing the knapsack and swinging it back up onto his shoulder, "let's go in!"

"A moment," she said, remembering something. "I want to get my trash receptacle first…"

Lina stepped quickly over to the refuse bins, which hadn't been emptied yet that day. Despite the sickly-sweet stench of garbage rising in the late-afternoon heat, she crouched and bent close.

What's wrong? Paul asked.

Oh, nothing really. It's just, I have an old tin can I use to collect kitchen trash. I left it out here this morning, and now it's gone. I was foolish to leave it, I guess. I just couldn't believe anyone would swipe it!

Times are hard, Lina. People can and will use anything of value.

It was just an old tin can!

To you, maybe. To someone else, it might be a pot to cook in or something like. People are struggling, remember that. You actually have it pretty good, all things considered.

Lina rose slowly, turning this thought over in her mind, placing it alongside the images of worn clothing, patched in odd fabric scraps, and people hoarding warm coats even in the midst of the summer.

What have we done to deserve this? she thought quietly. *First the war, then the occupation, and now this privation? If there were a God, I would ask him what, exactly, we've done to earn such never-ending punishment.*

Do you really want me to answer that question? Paul asked, his mind's tone going just a bit sharp.

No, Lina said, turning to look at him with serious eyes for a moment before she walked up the steps to the front door of her building. *You're no God.*

* * *

Even when they'd reached the privacy of her apartment, Paul didn't drop the romantic façade. He went right to her tiny kitchen and began pulling items out of his bag. Lina hung her coat up on the hook beside the door and followed him, unsure what else to do. He'd already turned on the stove and begun heating water for tea, so she slowly lowered herself into a seat at the tiny table.

I can do that, she said, feeling a vague sense of displaced discomfort.

You sit and rest. I can tell you worked your talent hard today, Paul thought back in a tone that permitted no argument. *Our link feels stretched and thin. You sit there, and I'll bring you a plate. You need to eat every bite, and then we'll decide what to do going forward.*

Lina wanted to protest, but she found she just didn't have the energy. Which meant, of course, that he was right. She was still not fully back to her fighting strength, and food and rest was the best way to get there. She sat and let him bring her first a mug of tea, and then a plate of sliced bread and cheese, and even some dried strips of what looked like beef.

Don't say anything about the meat, he cautioned her. *I smuggled that in from home. You need the iron, and red meat is too dear at the market right now.*

How did you know I'd need it? she thought as she picked up a piece and put it, experimentally, into her mouth. It was salty and tough, and she had a hard time biting through it.

You have to rip it, Paul said, lifting a piece from the small pile remaining on the wrapping paper atop her counter. He put it between his teeth and yanked his head back sharply, tearing the piece of meat into a small enough bite to fit in his mouth. *Then I recommend letting it sit on your tongue for a while to soften. You can chew it once it gets a little more tender. That's when the flavor really comes out. And I didn't know you would need it, obviously, since I had no idea I would meet you. It's just one of my favorite things to eat.*

You actually like *this?* Lina asked, her mind incredulous. Paul gave her a brief, dry grin in response.

Yes, he said. *Just give it a chance. The company in Sturgis uses really good beef for their jerky. I know it's tough at first, but it's non-perishable, light, and will give you the nutrition you need.*

As you say, Lina said, doubtful. But she did as he said and found, to her surprise, within a few moments the hard little dry stick had softened enough to be a tender, flavorful bite of deliciousness. *Oh! This* is *good!*

Yes, he replied, humor shading his thoughts. *I know. Eat it all, and make sure you're drinking that tea with it.*

What's Sturgis? she asked a few moments later, as he sat down to join her with his own plate.

What? Oh, it's the town where my sister lives. It's in the western part of America.

Is it nice there?

Nice enough, he said, and the flat tone of his thoughts indicated he didn't feel inclined to elaborate further. Lina felt a brief stab of regret, but quickly stifled it before the feeling could resonate down the lines of their connection. He was right, after all. They didn't like each other, so it was better to focus on business. The enemy of her enemy, and all that.

So they ate and kept up the charade of their romantic relationship in case anyone was listening in. Once Lina had cleaned up their dishes, Paul stood up and prepared to go.

"I don't want to leave you," he said in a soft, tender voice. *Tomorrow, we'll have to see if you can glean anything else from the typing pool. Is there any way to predict or influence which memos you type up?*

"What would people think?" Lina said. *None of which I'm aware.*

Well, you'll have to try. Otherwise we may need more drastic action, he said, reaching out and caressing her cheekbone with his fingertips. She fought the urge to shiver from the lightness of his touch.

Drastic?

Yes, like presenting yourself at this new security office and requesting to be hired as an interrogator, he said, his thoughts grim.

That...seems ill advised, Lina thought. Fear fluttered within her, making her swallow hard to retain control. *I don't believe they know who I am, and certainly they don't know of my psychic abilities. The Red Army executed every psychic they could find after Berlin fell. Only the Thanhousers kept me safe.*

But you're still a trained interrogator, he thought as he took a step toward her and bent his face toward hers. His lips hovered just above hers, close enough she could feel the warmth of his breath. *That's a useful skill.*

It seems dangerous, she insisted, refusing to lean toward him and complete the kiss. She didn't like him, after all.

This entire thing is dangerous. It's not my first choice of a plan, but it may be what's left to us. But let's see what tomorrow brings. His lips curved in a smile and he closed the gap, giving her a soft, breathy kiss before stepping back.

"I'll see myself out," he said, backing toward the front door of her apartment. "Goodnight, sweet Lina."

"Goodnight," she replied as the door closed behind him.

* * *

Once again the night passed uneventfully. No burly men showed up at her door in the middle of the night to snatch her from her bed and drive her away to some unknown interrogation center. When the summer sun woke Lina the next morning, she felt a moment of startled surprise.

As she had the day before, she checked in with Paul and readied herself for work. She took extra care to arrive a few minutes early, lest Frau Hoffman come to expect another bribe. But the formidable supervisor was nowhere in evidence for most of the morning, so Lina quietly slipped into her seat and began clacking away as she translated the hurried script of government officials into clean, readable text.

The puddle of sunlight had traveled halfway across the room when Frau Hoffman finally entered the room. Lina didn't notice at first, for she had her head down and was busy scanning the surface thoughts of the other typists as her fingers automatically punched the keys of her own machine. But Hoffman's appearance sent a widening ripple of fear and unease through the group, and Lina finally looked up and blinked to focus her eyes on the woman's severe face.

"Fräulein Sucherin," Hoffman said, her voice harsh as she came to a stop beside Lina's workstation. Men in dark suits flanked her on either side—one of slight build, and one heavyset and muscular. "Come with me."

Lina swallowed hard and nodded silently.

Something's happening! she sent down the link to Paul. She pulled the half-typed document from her machine and set it neatly on top of the stack of work she'd completed, then pushed her chair back and stood up. *Frau Hoffman is here with some men I've never seen before. They're taking me somewhere.*

Stay in contact, Paul ordered her, as if she had much of a choice in the matter. *This might be an opportunity.*

Lina stepped away from the desk and pushed her chair in. The muscular man reached out and took hold of her left bicep, and sudden fear wrapped around the inside of her throat, threatening to cut off her breath.

"I'm coming," she said mildly, but the man didn't acknowledge that she'd spoken. Lina turned to Frau Hoffman and saw a flash of excitement there, shining under the supervisor's censorious gaze. Somewhere, deep in her gut, Hoffman knew Lina was in trouble, and she liked it.

Nobody said anything else. After that brief eye contact, Hoffman turned and began to march back down the aisle between the desks. The two men followed, Lina trapped between them by the iron hand on her bicep. She held her head up, eyes straight ahead, and forced herself to breathe slowly. If she couldn't be calm and collected, she could at least appear calm and collected. An innocent person would have nothing to fear, right?

I'm surprised you can think that, Paul said. *You can't be that naive.*

What do you mean? I'm innocent!

No you aren't, you're working with me. And anyway, you of all people should know innocence is no guarantee of safety. I bet you sent plenty of innocents into the Reich's prison camps. Paul's words came flat and emotionless, and were somehow the worse for it.

Every person I condemned was a criminal enemy of the legal state! she shot back, fear-fueled anger bursting hot and ready into her mind. It stiffened her spine and burned away the choking dread that made it hard to breathe. *They were working against their government in a time of war! They were traitors, and deserved to be punished so.*

Were they? You spent time in Poland, didn't you? Ferreting out those who resisted the foreign occupation of Nazi Germany? That seems less like treason and more like irregular warfare to me.

They'd lost! They were a conquered people! If they'd just ceased to resist—

Now you sound like the Soviets.

Shock hit her like a smacking wave of frigid water. Total, icy fury flashed through her, instantly calming the whirling firestorm of fear and distress. Her thoughts sharpened, crystallized, and her steps steadied between the two men.

Good, Paul said. *That worked. You've got to keep your head, Lina. Remember you have advantages they don't know about.*

I am not like them.

You are, and that's what might just save your neck. You know how they're going to play this. You've been on the other side of the game before. Just keep your head, steel your nerve, and stay with me. We'll see where they take you. Maybe, if we're lucky, this will help us find Thanhouser. That's our mission, remember. Focus on the mission.

Lina forced herself to take a deep breath as they emerged from the front door of the building and headed for a black sedan parked nearby. *The mission,* she said. *Yes.*

A strange pause from Paul, and then, *Are you all right?*

Fine, she said, ducking her head and letting the muscular man pull her into the back seat of the sedan. *I'm fine, enemy of my enemy. We're moving. I'll keep the link as strong as possible, but you'd better be prepared to move, too.*

Lina...

The engine roared to life.

We're going, she thought to him, and said nothing more for the remainder of the ride.

* * * * *

Chapter Four – Captive

The black sedan didn't take them far. It wasn't a terribly comfortable ride, with Lina squished between the two men in the cramped back seat. Frau Hoffman didn't accompany them. Lina got a last glimpse of her brutish face as the car pulled away from the curb and sped off down the street, only to arrive a few minutes later at another grey government building. The hulking edifice squatted next to the street, its façade half-obscured by scaffolding as work crews labored on the far end. The car drew to a stop next to a set of double doors, and Lina found herself being pulled from the backseat and marched in through them.

The two men took her down a twisting stairwell and a long, dimly lit hallway, then stopped before a metal door. One of the guards opened it and pushed her into the small, windowless room beyond. No one said a word, not even when the door clanged shut behind her, and the heavy *thunk* of a lock slammed home.

Where am I? she asked, reaching out to Paul. Something that might have been nerves fluttered in her stomach, but she simply focused on the icy calm she'd found and made it stop. *We didn't travel very far. Can you see where they've brought me?*

I think so, Paul said. His mind touch felt stretched and distant, but not unbearably so. *I'm moving toward your location now. What do you see?*

Nothing, she said. *They've locked me in a cell. They'll leave me here for a time, long enough for me to get hungry or need to relieve myself. Then they'll pull me out when I'm uncomfortable and use that in my interrogation.*

All right, Paul said. *See what else you can learn. I'll get as close as I can.*

Lina sent a pulse of acknowledgment and looked around her small cell. Bare concrete walls stared back at her, featureless but for the shadows she herself cast in the harsh light from the bare bulb set into the ceiling. A circular stain on the floor suggested one of the corners had held a toilet can at one point, but it had been removed. Likely to assist in creating her discomfort, though a stinking can would've created discomfort enough, as far as Lina was concerned. She let out a sigh and walked to the opposite corner, then slid down to sit with her back against the wall, her knees drawn up in front of her. She tucked her arms in close to her body and shivered. It was chilly in the cell, despite the warm summer sun she knew shone outside.

Without much else to do, Lina closed her eyes and started working through some of the control exercises she'd learned at the *Reichschule.* She started by just breathing in and out, focusing on the sound and the feeling of the air filling her lungs, stretching her chest before letting it all out in a long, whispering exhale. After a few iterations, she expanded her attention to the rest of her body, noticing how her muscles and joints felt. The cement floor was cold under her derriere and behind her back, and her neck and shoulders felt corded and tight with tension. She took several more breaths, willing her body to relax and loosen up, willing the chill to seep into the core of her being, to insulate the center of herself from whatever was going on outside.

What are you doing? Paul asked. *If you disconnect, our deal is off.*

I'm not going to disconnect, Lina said, and even to herself, her mind tone felt dreamy and slightly distant. *I'm simply weaving in another layer of protection. It's likely this interrogation will get…unpleasant.*

Paul apparently didn't have anything to say to that, as his mind got very quiet. Lina let him be and turned her attention back to the task at hand. Once she finished wrapping herself in cold, she decided to take a chance and see what she could sense with her power. She opened her eyes and let them rest, unfocused, on the seam between the metal door and the concrete floor. Another deep breath in...and on the exhale, she reached out.

Torment bordering on madness swirled around her as the minds of her fellow captives writhed in agonizing fear or pain, or both. The sickly-sweet stench of sweat and excrement rose up, threatening to choke her. Her ears began to ring from the echo of screams that someone, somewhere uttered. The taste of blood filled her mouth.

Deep inside herself, she flinched, but she hadn't spent time piling up layers of icy insulation for nothing. She forced her mind to steady, to *be* ice. She took the agony and used it as fuel to push herself onward, to keep skimming across the surface of those wretched minds and reaching out beyond them.

A pair of thoughts, both male, stood out from the rest. Their level of fear was significantly lower than that of the captives. Their surface minds moved briskly through the tangles of agony all around, getting stronger, drawing nearer.

Guards. Approaching her cell? Was it time already?

The heavy *ker-thunk* of the locking mechanism turning said it was. Lina blinked her awareness back to herself and realized her muscles were stiff and cold, her fingers nearly numb. She must have spent longer reaching out than she'd realized.

The door squealed on its hinges as it swung open, and a male face looked in. It wasn't one of the men who'd brought her from the typing pool. This one had a shock of blond hair and wire-rimmed glasses.

"Stand up," he ordered in guttural, Russian-accented German. Lina pushed against the wall and levered herself slowly to her feet. Glasses motioned for her to come forward. She complied, moving slowly so as not to present a threat. Outside, the other man waited, the light from her cell doorway shining on the moist bald pate of his head. A tiny corner of her mind wondered how he could be sweating in this chill, but then she remembered outside this subterranean hallway, it was still the middle of summer.

"Come," Glasses said, beckoning again, then he turned and continued down the hallway, away from the stairwell Lina had come down before, past more of the heavy metal doors that hid the screaming, tortured minds of her fellow captives.

At the far end of the long hallway, they entered another stairwell. Glasses led her up two flights, while Sweaty followed close enough she could feel the heat of his labored breath on the back of her neck. He didn't appear to be in peak physical condition, for he wheezed as they climbed. They exited the stairwell into another long corridor, though the doors on either side were wood, not metal. When they came to the fifth one, Glasses opened it and gestured for her to precede them inside.

"Have a seat," he said. The tone of his harshly-accented words made it clear that it was an order, not an invitation or a request. Lina licked her lips and walked over to the lone chair sitting in the middle of the floor. She sat down, placing her hands in her lap.

Sweaty stomped over, still breathing heavily, and grabbed her right wrist, wrenching it up and slamming it onto the armrest of the chair. Only the ice she'd wrapped herself in saved her, for her instincts screamed at her to lash out with power and fight back against this violent man with the punishing grip. She could feel the power coiling in her mind as if it had a mind of its own, and it thirsted, eagerly, for the blood of one who had harmed her.

But that was fanciful, not helpful. Whatever was about to happen had to happen. So while Sweaty locked the heavy iron manacle that had been built into the chair around her right wrist, she obediently laid her left wrist in the corresponding manacle on the other side.

"You have committed a crime," Glasses said once she'd been securely bound to the chair. "Do you admit this is true?"

"I-I offered Frau H-Hoffmann some money," she said, making her voice small and trembly, "b-because I missed work for a day."

"And you knew this was wrong?"

"Y-yes," she said, letting her head drop down as if she were ashamed. She sniffled, wishing she could summon up some tears.

"Then why did you do this?"

"I was afraid," she said, hunching her shoulders forward. "I didn't want to lose my job."

"Why were you not at your job for a day?"

Tell them you met me, Paul said in her mind. *Remember our cover story.*

Not yet, Lina said. *They won't believe it if it's too easy.*

This short exchange took long enough that Glasses apparently believed she was hesitant to answer. He nodded at Sweaty, who stepped forward and cracked the back of his hand across Lina's cheek. Her vision exploded in stars, and her head snapped hard to her right, sending a wrenching pain shooting through her neck. Once again she tasted blood, but this time it was her own, from where her teeth had cut the inside of her cheek. She let out a cry and tried to hunch down into the chair, curving her spine and trying to draw her shoulders up to protect her face.

"I was sick," she whimpered. "I didn't feel good—"

Sweaty reached out and grabbed a fistful of hair at the top of her skull. He pulled, slowly, making the nerves in her scalp scream in tearing agony. She let out another cry, and tears began to fill her eyes from the pain.

"I was si—" she started to say again, but Sweaty slapped her again, open-handed this time, but with no less force. She felt a hunk of her hair wrenched free from her scalp, and she began to sob in response.

"Lies will not help you," Glasses said, his voice silky under the raucous sound of her crying. "Only the truth will help you. Do you understand that?"

Lina whimpered and affected a nod.

"So I'll ask you again, where were you when you weren't at work?"

Lina sucked in a breath and tried to control her sobbing, feeling her chest heave as she did. She swallowed hard and inhaled again, feeling the buzz of hyperventilation in the skin of her face. She pressed her lips together and tried to breathe through her nose while Glasses stared at her, his expression darkening. Sweaty raised his hand again, but Glasses waved him off with a sharp, cutting gesture.

"I-I was on the west side of the city," Lina said, allowing herself to gasp a little as she did, "in the American zone. I visited a friend there."

"This is not prohibited," Glasses said. "Why would you lie about this?"

"M-my friend is a-a m-man…"

"So you're a typical German *Hure*," he said with a sneer. "Why should that surprise anyone? But then, you must be a hypocrite, too, if you are pretending otherwise."

He walked around behind her chair, leaving her facing only Sweaty with his fleshy, impassive face and heavy hands. She felt Glasses reach out and take hold of a lock of her hair that had slipped loose from its usual bun. He twisted it between his fingers until it pulled tight just above her ear, and elicited a little gasping sound. Then he tucked it behind the curve of her ear and bent to whisper to her.

"You German girls are all alike," he said, his lips brushing against her skin. The moist heat of his breath filled her ear. "I saw it when we conquered your city. The way you all moan for the taste of the Russian cock. Old, young, it doesn't matter. In the end, every single one of you begs for it…"

She felt his fingertips trace the line of her spine up under her hair, then his fingers curled into a fist and he yanked her head back until her skull banged painfully against the back of the metal chair. His mouth crushed down over hers, forcing her jaws wide as his tongue drove deep enough into her throat to make her gag. Her body bucked against him, but the chair's restraints held her fast, and in the end, she had to accept the crushing, bruising mockery of a kiss.

But she wasn't powerless.

Quick as a thought, Lina focused her power down to a pinpoint and connected with Glasses' mind through his punishing touch. Faster than any bullet, she sent that needle-like, surgical pulse of power into his brain, into the part that lit up with desire and pleasure at her fear and pain. She pulled on the fear and revulsion coursing through her and drove it deep into that shining target. She shredded wherever she touched, carving out a hollow until nothing but blankness inhabited that part of the man's psyche.

Then she withdrew to find him backing off, releasing her hair. He looked at her, his eyes narrowing behind his wire-rimmed glasses.

Lina dragged in a breath, and then another. Her stomach heaved as bile rose in her throat.

Glasses spat three words in Russian. Though vitriol dripped from his words, Lina could see his eyes as he walked around her chair, and his expression held a kind of suspicious wonder. As if he knew she'd done something, but he couldn't quite put his finger on what. He slapped her again, making stars sparkle in her vision. She turned her head to the side and let herself whimper.

I can come, Paul said quietly in her mind. Violence roiled beneath his words. *I'll find a way to break you out.*

Not necessary, Lina said, closing her eyes and letting tears slip from beneath her lashes. *This is actually fortunate.*

Lina…

Think about it, she said, *this is the security headquarters for the whole city. Chances are, Rolland was brought here. He may still be here, as a matter of fact. And even if not, someone here is likely to know something about him. This is the best place to pick up his trail.*

Sweaty grabbed her by the hair and forced her head back again, baring her throat. Glasses stood in front of her, staring.

Lina they're hurting you.

Do you think I didn't notice?

I'm coming to get you. You don't need to go through this. There has to be another way.

I can handle myself, enemy of my enemy, she said. *This is the only way. Be quiet now, I must concentrate.*

Lina didn't sever the connection, since that would violate their agreement, but she did sort of turn away from Paul's white-knuckled, impotent fury, shunting it to the back of her mind. His sense of helplessness saturated their link, dragging at her attention until she had to lock it away so she could focus on the here and now.

Sweaty drove his fist into her stomach. The breath exploded from her lungs. She gasped, clawing for air. He slapped her, open-handed, skewing her body to the left as the iron manacle cut into the skin of her wrists. She pulled herself straight just in time for his meaty hand to crack against the side of her face again. The iron taste of blood filled her mouth. Lina spit, trying to clear her mouth, then something huge and heavy clubbed her in the back of the head.

A high-pitched ringing exploded in her ears. Her chin bounced off her chest. Bright sparkles of light coalesced to blot out her vision, and the world spiraled slowly away into oblivion.

* * *

Lina gasped and sat up so suddenly, the pounding in her head made her eyeballs feel like they were about to burst. She let out a grunt of pain and covered her head with her hands as she curled into herself. An incessant, high-pitched ringing in her ears knifed through her, making the pounding worse, and she felt as if she might start vomiting at any second.

Where am I? What happened?

Lina?

She hadn't realized the connection was still there until he spoke. Paul's voice came through stretched and thready, and Lina instinctively reached out to shore up the link.

Pain kicked her between the eyes, and she pitched forward, dry-heaving from the strain. Agony wreathed her middle as she moved. She could breathe, though, so her ribs must only be bruised, not broken.

Lina! You're all right! Paul's palpable relief rolled down the link.

Not really, she thought back. That was all she could manage while fighting to master her body and bring it back under control.

You're conscious, he pointed out. *I knew you weren't dead, because I could still feel you… barely. How badly are you hurt?*

That was an excellent question. Lina put her trembling hands flat on the concrete floor and pushed herself up on shaking arms until she could maneuver to sit, once more leaning against the cold hardness of the wall. Slowly, experimentally, she opened one eye, and then the other.

The same concrete cell as before…or possibly another one. She couldn't imagine they looked terribly different from one another. This one, though, held a pair of stinking toilet cans in the corner.

No, wait. She squinted as the light from the ceiling stabbed into her brain. A single toilet can, doubled in her vision. She cursed softly and held up a hand with ten fingers.

Concussion, Paul said, his tone grim. *Double vision, ringing in the ears, headache…we have to get you out of there.*

Not yet, Lina said. *I think I can find him.*

A concussion could kill you; Lina, don't be an idiot.

I'll be fine. Where are you? she asked, mostly to change the subject. She leaned her head back against the wall and closed her eyes again. It helped with the nausea and the piercing pain from the light as well.

In an office building next door, he said. *I can get to the roof and find a way over to you—*

Too risky, she said, cutting him off. *They'll kill us both if you're caught, and I still haven't found out anything about Rolland.*

You can't stay in there, he protested. *It's not worth it. We can find out what happened to him without letting them beat you to death. You're more valuable alive!*

I'll stay alive, she said. *I don't really have any information they want, and I'm only accused of a petty crime. I suspect they'll leave me here for a few days, maybe a week or so, and let me think they've forgotten me. Then they'll either release me or move me somewhere else.*

What makes you so sure? Paul's suspicion wasn't pointed at her, but it prickled uncomfortably at her mind just the same.

It's what we would have done, she said. She tried to remain matter-of-fact, but the throbbing pain in her head and ribs made her thoughts sound shaky, even to herself.

Lina—

Don't, she said, though she wasn't sure exactly what he intended to say. *I'll be fine. I just need to rest for a while.*

Paul didn't answer for a long moment. Lina shifted, trying to avoid jarring her middle or her head. She slowly lowered herself to the cool floor, sighing with relief when she finally laid herself flat. She couldn't stop herself from whimpering as she straightened her body out. But then, there was no one to hear, so what did it matter?

Fine, Paul said, his mind touch dark and just this side of sullen, *but if they beat you like that again, I'm coming to get you, no questions asked.*

How do you propose to do that without compromising us both?

I'll think of something.

Lina thought about saying something else, but the waves of exhaustion washing over her made the effort overwhelming. She let it go.

How long was I out?

Not long. A few minutes. Ten at most, Paul said, still brooding.

Just long enough for them to move me, then. Lina said, letting out her breath slowly. The pounding in her head eased a fraction with her release of tension.

I don't think you should sleep, Paul said.

I won't, Lina said, though exhaustion dragged at her mind, and she just wanted to let her battered body sink into the floor. *You can help. Stay with me. Since I've got some time, I'm going to reach out and see what I can find.*

I'm right here, Paul said, and he was. Lina felt the strength of his mind like a promise on the other side of the gulf she'd built between them.

He was not her friend.

His mind felt so good.

She gave up the fight and let all that fortitude pour through the link, bolstering her, muting the scream of bruised ribs and concussed head. He was cool, healing water on her wounds, soothing her abraded psyche, bringing her back to life. Or something like it, anyway. She took a deep breath without wincing and felt her mind relax.

Thank you, she said.

For what?

For...never mind. Lina turned her attention away from the seductive healing his mind offered and focused on the cool hardness of the concrete floor. To forestall any more questions, she pushed her awareness out.

As before, the agony and terror of her fellow prisoners pulled at her, but she focused on skimming over the surfaces of their minds. She wasn't looking for more pain; she had enough of that on her own. What she wanted was information. This was a government institution. Surely someone was in charge of organizing, documenting, and keeping records, right?

Somewhere, vaguely "up," she found calmer, more orderly minds. Some had razor-edged violence in their surface thoughts. Muscle, she decided, like Sweaty and Glasses earlier. Bully-boys trained in low-level interrogations and torture. Lina had never had much use for their skills when she was on the other side of the manacles, but she knew others valued what they could do.

Wait...what was that?

Lina halted her skim and used her lightest touch to examine one particular outer mind she'd found. It was a woman, so the mental landscape felt slippery and hostile, but her skills were coming back with practice, and she had years of experience getting in and out undetected. Just as she'd done with Glasses, she sent a needle-sharp thread of awareness into the woman's thoughts.

...scientist. Express to Moscow. Seven eighteen PM.

* * *

That's him! It's got to be!

Paul's words snapped Lina back into her own head and aching body.

We don't know that, she said. *It could be anyone being transferred or sent back to Russia.*

She thought the word 'scientist!' If it's not Thanhouser, it's likely the same route he took! You found a solid lead, Lina. I'm coming to get you.

How do you plan to do that? If you're caught, you'll be tortured, and we'll both be executed!

Have a little faith in me, Lina. I know what I'm doing, Paul said, his irritation leaking down the link. *You did your part, just try to relax and trust me. I'm not your enemy.*

You're not my friend.

Lina wasn't sure whether she actually transmitted the thought or not. Paul didn't answer, so she let it drop and focused on ignoring her increasingly insistent hunger.

Once again she took refuge in her training. She ran through the full gamut of focusing techniques, then doubled back and ran through them again. By the end of the exercise, three things had changed.

Her thoughts had cleared, and she was calm.

She'd built some distance between her conscious mind and her body's pain.

And someone had opened a slit in the bottom of the heavy door and shoved a small tray of food inside.

Well, "food" was a bit optimistic. The dark brown lump resembled bread, inasmuch as there was a crust, and it had a spongy look to it. It felt like a rock, and Lina grimaced as she plucked it off the metal tray and held it up.

You should eat. You need your strength.

I need my teeth intact, she shot back to Paul, knocking the lump against the tray with a satisfying *whack*. A corner of the lump broke off from the force of her blow.

So break it up like that and eat it. Don't be stupid, Lina.

As much as she longed to defy him, Paul was right. She did need to eat. Her stomach gurgled with need from her psychic exertions and general deprivation, so she picked up the smaller chunk and put it in her mouth. It tasted as dry and awful as she'd expected, but the hunger eased as she choked it down. She used the tray to break off another chunk and kept at it until she'd eaten it all.

Afterward, the "bread" sat like a lump of coal in her gut, but at least she didn't feel like an animal was gnawing at her insides anymore. She lay back down on the floor and tried not to bump her head or ribs.

I think I'll try to sleep now, she said. *Call out and wake me if it feels like our link is slipping away. I don't think I'm in danger from the concussion, but it's better to be prepared. I'd like to conserve as much energy as possible in case they decide to interrogate me again.*

Good idea. I'll be awake anyway, Paul replied. He sounded distracted, like he was working on something. Lina was tired enough not to care, so she didn't bother looking through his eyes or delving into his thoughts to find out what. She laid her head down on the cold concrete and let her eyelids drift closed.

Seconds later (it might have been hours, but it felt like seconds) Lina started awake to the heavy *ker-thunk* of the lock on her door. She pushed herself up to sit against the wall, hissing through her teeth as she jarred her bruised ribs.

Lina—

Something's happening, she said, panic flooding her sleep-addled brain. *Someone's here.*

Go with it, Paul said. *This is my doing.*

The door swung into the cell, and Glasses stared down at her, the light from the hallway glinting through his lenses. Fear swelled within her, threatening to wrap around her throat and choke the life out of her. The Russian didn't say anything, just stepped into the tiny concrete cell. His partner, Sweaty, followed him in without a word.

Lina scrabbled toward the corner, but to no avail. Sweaty reached down and grabbed the front of her torn, soiled blouse with his meaty fist and hauled her up onto her tiptoes. Her bruised side exploded in pain, and a whimper slipped past her lips.

Lina, Lina, it's all right. This is my doing. You have to trust me!

But the shock of seeing her tormentors again so suddenly was too much. Lina exploded into panic and fury. She kicked and clawed, her feet connecting just below Sweaty's knee, her nails raking red lines in his thick skin.

The big man grunted and slapped her, wrenching her head to the side and bringing tears to her eyes. She hung limply in his fist and barely heard Glasses' voice over the renewed ringing in her ears. He snapped something in Russian, and Sweaty replied with another grunt.

But he didn't hit her again.

He put her down, holding her up by her blouse as her knees threatened to buckle. Glasses said something else, then turned and walked out of the cell. Sweaty reached into his pocket and pulled out a short piece of rope that he tied around her wrists. Then he clamped his hand around her bicep and forced her out into the hallway after Glasses.

Dimly, she felt Paul's presence in her mind as she walked.

Lina!

What?

Good gods, woman, what in the hell were you thinking? I said this was my doing!

What?

I'm getting you out of there! I told you to trust me! Why did you fight him?

I can't...he hurt me...

Confusion swirled with pain and terror inside her mind. She stumbled on leaden legs as Sweaty dragged her up the stairs, each step echoing in the concrete dimness.

It's okay, Paul said eventually. *He won't hurt you again. Just don't fight anymore. You've got to trust me, Lina. Can you do that?*

She didn't answer.

She didn't know the answer.

* * * * *

Chapter Five – Retrieval

They took her out into the night and put her in a car.

Sweaty hauled open the rear door and shoved her inside. Unable to catch herself with her bound hands, Lina fell hard onto her left side. She gasped as she landed on her bruised ribs. Spots of light danced before her eyes, and the ringing in her ears got loud enough she barely heard the car door slam.

She felt the acceleration, though, as the driver stomped on the gas, and they lurched forward, away from the security headquarters building. She grunted in pain and pushed upright, letting the force of their acceleration press her against the seat back.

"Lina," Paul said out loud, glancing over his shoulder at her. He kept both hands on the steering wheel, but she got a quick pulse of impatience through their link. He wanted to reach back and untie her, make sure she was all right. The feeling was so strong, it cut right through her surprise at seeing him.

The impression disappeared as he retreated behind his barriers. Once again, Lina realized the sister who had taught him must have been incredibly skilled.

"How badly are you hurt?" he asked out loud. "Besides the concussion? I couldn't tell through the link."

"My ribs are bruised, but not broken," she said. Her voice sounded rusty and hoarse. "At least, I don't think so. They don't hurt enough to be broken, I think."

"Good," he said, steering around a corner that sent her sliding across the backseat again. Lina reached out and braced her hands on the door. She managed to keep from hitting it with her body, but only just. Another soft grunt of pain escaped her control.

"I'm sorry," he said. "I'm just trying to put as much distance between us and that place as possible. I don't know how long it'll be before they realize the prisoner transfer order I cooked up was a forgery. It could be minutes, it could be forever."

"Why do you say that?" she asked, more to distract herself from the way the movement of the car was roiling her stomach than for any other reason.

"The administration of the Soviet zone is in flux," he said, glancing back at her again. Belatedly, she realized he wore a dark suit. In fact, he looked quite similar to the two men who'd arrested her…had it been only yesterday? Paul started speaking again, and Lina pulled her scattered thoughts together to focus on his words.

"They're working toward transitioning from Soviet occupation to re-establishing local infrastructures and processes, albeit ones very much in the Soviet mold. But nothing is complete, so it's easy for things to be missed, or out of the ordinary. I think that'll give us an advantage, but I want to get clear, just in case."

"Where will you go?" she asked. "Back to the west side?"

"No," he said, regret in his voice. "It would draw too much attention to cross, and then cross again. I've got a safehouse outside the city, to the east. We'll go there."

"And then what?"

"And then we'll see," Paul said. He didn't elaborate, and Lina fell silent as the meager lights of the city streaked by her window and faded away into the darkness that wrapped around them.

She must have dozed off. Eventually, their tires left the relative smoothness of pitted asphalt streets and bumped and jolted down a gravel road. When the car slowed in a rattling shower of rocks against the undercarriage, Lina opened her eyes to find the eastern horizon pink with dawn.

"We're here," Paul said, and for the first time in their association, she heard fatigue in his tone. He cut the engine and slewed around to look at her over the back of his seat. She blinked and looked back at him, unsure what to say. Despite their ever-present link, he kept his barriers tight, so if he expected something from her, she had no idea what.

"I can't get out by myself," she said softly, lifting her bound hands. Paul blinked and nodded, then got out of the car and opened the rear passenger door. He extended a hand to help her, and she put her fingers in his. The warmth of his skin surprised her. She wasn't sure why.

"Let's get inside," he said. "I'll find a knife, and we'll get that rope off you."

Lina nodded and pressed her lips together in pain as he pulled her out of the backseat. As soon as she stood on her own two feet, she dropped her hands from his and turned away. When he didn't move, she looked back up at him.

"Which way do I go?" she asked softly. "It's too dark to see anything in the trees."

They'd followed the gravel road to its rounded end. In the slowly growing dawn light, Lina could see at least two trailheads, and maybe another one a little further down.

"Over here," Paul said. He reached out his hand as if he'd take hold of hers again, but when she didn't reach back, he let it go and turned for the nearest break in the trees. Lina followed him, stepping gingerly over the rocks and sticks that littered the forest floor.

The trail wasn't long, but it sloped gradually upward, and Lina had started the journey exhausted. Her legs dragged as if they were made of lead, and her ribs ached more with every step. By the time they turned the last corner, the sun had cleared the horizon and morning light streamed through the boughs to illuminate the stone cottage set well back amid the trees.

"Who lives here?" Lina asked, her eyes tracing over the sharply slanted roofline. The place looked ancient, as if it had once been the domain of some child-eating witch out of a Grimm Brothers' tale.

"No one, now," he said. "It's part of an estate that belonged to one of our contacts during the war. He signed it over to our people when he and his family decided to emigrate after the Soviets came through. It's a remote spot; I don't think this cottage appears on any government records, so it should suit us nicely."

Paul gestured for her to follow him and walked up the path toward the house. He pulled a key from his pocket and used it to unlock the modern dead bolt that marred the smoky beauty of the heavy oaken front door. He stepped to the side and waved her through, ducking his head to keep from hitting it on the lintel above.

The interior of the cottage looked just as fey and brooding as the exterior. A huge, hulking fireplace stood opposite the door, with a wooden mantel crammed full of old books, rocks, unidentifiable pieces of machinery, and other detritus. Two large shapes squatted on either side of the hearth, both covered in furniture shrouds. To the left, a narrow, arched opening led to a miniscule kitchen. To the right, a set of heavy wooden stairs marched up along the stone wall.

Underneath the stairs, some enterprising individual had built shelves that lay crammed with more books and junk.

Paul bustled in behind her and headed straight for the fireplace.

"The floor above is a bedroom loft," he said. "There's a bathing tub up there. We'll have to heat and haul water, but you can at least get the smell of that place off you."

"Is it so bad?" Lina asked, trying for lighthearted banter, but simply sounding passive-aggressive instead.

"No," Paul said as he snapped a smaller stick into kindling. He laid the pieces atop the wood already stacked in the grate and reached for more. "I could feel your disgust through the link. I'd want to get clean as soon as possible, too. I'll draw you a bath, then you can sleep until tonight."

"What about you?" she asked. "You've been awake longer than I. You need sleep, too."

"I'll take the sofa," he said, pointing behind her. She turned and saw another low shape covered in a furniture shroud. "One of my colleagues is gathering some information for us and will meet us here shortly after sunset. We'll have a plan by then, Lina."

He pulled a long match from a cup mounted on the wall beside the hearth and struck it, then lit the tinder and kindling he'd laid. Lina watched, entranced, as the fragile flames licked along the wood until they finally caught hold of the logs below, and the spicy-sweet aroma of wood smoke trickled out into the room.

"Are you hungry?" Paul asked, pulling Lina from her reverie. "It'll take me a moment to get your water heated. There should be some food in the kitchen. Go and eat. I'll call you when it's ready."

Lina nodded and walked through the low-ceilinged room to the tiny kitchen beyond. It held an ancient icebox, which she found mostly empty, save for a few slabs of cured bacon. Though she rarely cooked, she rummaged around in the cupboard until she found a frying pan and some knives, along with a dented tea kettle that looked like it predated the Kaiser. She lit her own fire in the wood stove in the corner and soon had thick slices of bacon sizzling in the pan while her stomach growled its impatience at her.

"I've got the fire going," Paul said, walking in just as the scent of frying bacon started to permeate the air. He sniffed in appreciation and looked at the stove.

"I found some bacon," she said, pointing, "and I've started some water heating in the kettle. I thought it might be faster than the fireplace."

"Good thinking," he said. He pulled a giant stock pot off an upper shelf and carried it to the large sink basin. "I'll heat this out there as well." He lifted the pump handle and began to work the mechanism. A moment later, a spurt of water clattered into the bottom of the pot, and Lina couldn't help but shiver as she thought about the likely temperature of the water.

To distract herself from that thought, she turned back to the stove and used a long-tined fork to flip the bacon, then went back to the cupboard to find plates. She wasn't sure exactly how long to cook the bacon, and the uneven heat was tricky, but the slices of meat were only slightly on the dark and crispy side when she pulled them out of the pan and onto the chipped plates she'd found.

"I wish we had some bread," she said, turning with plates in hand. "Or cheese. I'm not much of a cook, I'm afraid."

"It's great," Paul said, grunting as he lifted the now-full stockpot and muscled it toward the other room. "Be right back."

Lina huffed out her breath as he left. She'd slept during the drive from Berlin, and she'd been in so much pain during the hike to the cabin, she hadn't been able to notice much else. But being in these close confines, doing mundane household tasks together…it lent the situation a surreal sort of domesticity.

She pushed the thought away, hoping Paul hadn't caught the edge of it as he walked back into the kitchen. She placed the plates on the table and seated herself, while he took a moment to wash his hands at the pump before joining her.

"Thank you," he said. "It smells delicious."

"We have to eat," she said, and winced inwardly at how ungracious she sounded.

"You're right," Paul replied, and said nothing else. Instead, he applied himself to the pile of bacon, eating with neat economy. Regret trickled through her thoughts as she watched him. Too late, she realized he'd been trying to be personable and kind, rather than the ice-faced operative she'd met a few days ago.

But he's not my friend, she reminded herself behind her mental barriers. *No matter how kind he is, he's merely using me. Between the Americans and the Soviets, the world will be torn asunder, and they care not for their tools. I can't forget that. Anything else is a lie.*

Even as she framed the words in her mind, her power pushed at her in denial. His delicious mindscape called to her with the promise of comfort and companionship. She'd been alone for so long…

No, I haven't! I've had Isa, and Rolland, and the girls! I made them a promise. I'll find Rolland Thanhouser. I'll keep the girls safe. And I won't be seduced by the kindness of my enemy's enemy. I won't.

She bit into another piece of bacon, refusing to acknowledge the tiny voice in the back of her head that suggested perhaps the lady did, indeed, protest too much.

* * *

Once they'd eaten, fatigue hit Lina like a motorbus. True to his word, Paul hauled the stock pot of now-lukewarm water up the stairs and poured it into the bath tub. Lina added the boiling water from the kettle, and while it wasn't enough water to soak in, she gladly climbed in to wash her hair and body clean. The small lump of soap next to the tub looked homemade and smelled harsh, but it was infinitely better than the stench of excrement, fear, and pain that had clung to her since that first interrogation.

After rinsing her hair several times, Lina stepped out of the bath and wrapped one of the large and surprisingly soft towels around her body. Since Paul had mentioned something about using the kitchen sink to wash up, she pulled the plug and watched as the water—grey with soap, dirt, and the dried blood she'd scrubbed from her face and neck—swirled away down the drain.

Amazingly enough, Paul had clothes in the small wardrobe for her. Well, not for *her* exactly, as they were clearly cut for a taller woman than she. But with two pairs of wool socks, the boots fit well enough, and Lina actually appreciated the extra-long sleeves, as they kept her soap-roughened hands warm in the morning chill. The trouser legs weren't so easily handled, but she eventually folded them over and rolled the hems up, and they served well enough. She tried everything on, then removed only the boots and crawled into the long, low bed fully clothed.

She laid her head on the pillow and closed her eyes, willing her mind to think about nothing at all. For a few moments, she heard the sounds of Paul moving around downstairs. It wasn't hard to imagine him down there, pulling the dust cloths off the furniture and getting settled on the low couch she hadn't yet seen uncovered. Eventually, though, he quieted, and the only sounds she heard were the birds chittering in the morning sunlight as she fell inexorably into dreamless sleep.

By the time she woke, the birds had gone, but the sun poured brightly through the tiny window to spill a puddle of light over the floor next to the bed. She heard the muted rumble of male voices downstairs and stretched her arms over her head, feeling her spine pop and her ribs ache as she did so.

They don't hurt as badly as they did, she thought. *I suppose I'll take that as a good sign.*

A very good one, Paul thought back to her, though she hadn't been addressing him. She hadn't been thinking behind a shield, either, so it wasn't odd for him to answer, she just wasn't expecting it. *I was worried they'd cracked them.*

I told you I didn't think that was the case, Lina said, rather mildly.

Yes, but unless you have a secret medical degree you're not telling me about, you're not an expert, are you?

It's my body, she shot back, smiling despite herself at the banter. *That makes me more of an expert than you.*

I suppose you're right. Are you coming downstairs? Doc is here with some very good intel. We have plans to make. He brought more food, too.

I'll be down shortly, she said and reinforced her privacy barrier. She felt Paul turn his mind to other things, as he'd done when she'd bathed last night. She'd been almost too tired to notice it then, but she noticed it now and was grateful.

Since she hadn't saved any water to wash her face, she contented herself with relieving her bladder, combing out her hair and re-braiding it close to her scalp and out of the way, and pulling on the sturdy hiking boots she'd found. Then she walked down the stairs with only a very small hitch in her stride, and managed to keep from cradling her ribs with one hand.

Sometimes in life, it's the little victories that count.

"Adalina Sucherin, may I present Doktor Philip Wholrab, formerly of the University of Frankfurt. Doc, this is Lina, the psychic I told you about."

"Doc" was shorter than Paul, but taller than Lina, with a medium build. He had light brown hair, and an engaging smile that reached all the way to his spectacled eyes. He reached out a hand to take hers, and raised her knuckles to his lips in the old way of greeting.

"*Enchanté*," he said.

"Likewise, I'm sure," she replied to his French in tart German. She pulled her hand back out of his grasp, causing him to take a step back and laugh, looking over at Paul.

"You weren't kidding," he said, speaking American-accented English. "She really is a spitfire! I apologize if I've offended you, Fräulein. I meant no harm."

"Doc is an orthopedic surgeon," Paul said. "I thought perhaps he might take a look at your ribs."

"I told you, I'm fine," Lina said, impatience in her tone.

"I think you're right," Doc said, finally speaking proper German. "Shall we take a look and prove Paul wrong? He really hates that."

In spite of herself, Lina laughed, which made her wince as it jostled her ribs. Compassion flowed over Doc's open features.

"Ah, not totally fine at all, hmm? Come have a seat over here, next to the fire."

Lina sat on one of the squishy armchairs that had been under the dust cloths while Doc knelt on the floor in front of her. She unbuttoned the sturdy flannel shirt and raised her cotton undershirt so he could see the red and purple bruising that bloomed all across her side.

"Hmmm," Doc said. "I think you're right, they're probably not broken, but I'm afraid I must palpitate slightly to check. I apologize, Fräulein. This will hurt."

And it did. Lina pressed her lips together and willed herself not to scream as Doc's fingers gently prodded her bruised flesh. Once again, spots of sparkling grayness began to dance in front of her eyes, and she had to force her breath through her nose.

"There," Doc said, his voice soft. "I'm so very sorry, but I had to check. Bruised, but not broken. You're made of stern stuff, it seems."

"Doktor," Lina murmured, without really meaning to do so, "you have no idea."

"Dear lady, I believe you," Doc said, causing Lina to look up and meet his frank gaze. "We all do what we must."

"Yes."

Doc smiled and patted her shoulder. "I have some bandages in my bag. We'll wrap your ribs to give you some more support and protection against bumps, yes?"

Lina nodded, and Doc pushed up to his feet.

"Don't go anywhere," he said. "I'll be right back."

He turned to walk into the tiny kitchen, pushing past Paul. Lina hadn't even realized that the American had absented himself, but as with the psychic barriers, she appreciated his courtesy.

"Everything all right?" Paul asked.

"No," Lina said, "but it's like we thought. Bruised, not broken."

"I can't imagine you broken," Paul said, and Lina blinked rapidly as she realized he wasn't talking about her bones.

"Everybody can be broken," she said, thinking of a blood-soaked tent in a snowy forest in Belgium.

"Is that your professional opinion, Oberhelfer?"

"It's the truth. Anyone can be broken, eventually. The world itself is broken. The question is whether or not it can be put back together again."

"Or put ourselves together again."

Lina shrugged; it was all one and the same. Paul looked as if he'd liked to say more, but Doc bustled back into the main room with a black physician's bag in his hands.

"Here we are," Doc said, pulling out a length of bandage. "This ought to do nicely, and it's better than cutting up Paul's sheets here, eh?"

Lina pulled her eyes from Paul's intensity and smiled at Doc. He'd been so kind, even while hurting her, and he was much easier to deal with than the prickly American. Though Paul still held his mental shields in place, Lina felt a stab of discontent echo down the lines of the link.

Jealousy? That she'd smiled at Doc? It didn't make sense, but in a tiny, petty, mean corner of Lina's mind, she was glad.

* * *

While Doc bandaged Lina up, Paul disappeared back into the kitchen. He emerged several minutes later, carrying a plate of sandwiches that immediately made Lina's mouth water and stomach growl.

"Doc brought more supplies," Paul said, offering the plate to Lina. She reached for the top sandwich, trying not to wince or move her torso more than necessary as Doc continued to wrap the bandage. "Let's eat, and we'll hear what else he brought with him."

"All done," Doc announced, tying the bandage off. He sat back on his heels and looked at his handiwork with a critical eye. "That should hold unless you're doing really vigorous activity, which I strongly advise against. Rest will heal those ribs better than anything else."

"Thank you, Doktor," Lina said and smiled at him again. He grinned back at her and winked, then snatched a sandwich from the pile Paul still held and practically fell into the other chair. "Paul, I brought some beer, too. Why didn't you bring that as well?"

"Because we have work to do," Paul said in the tone of someone repeating an old argument.

"Beer is good for work," Doc said and pulled himself back up out of the chair. "Besides, Lina needs it for her healing. I'm a doctor. You have to believe me."

Paul rolled his eyes, but obligingly waited as Doc went back into the kitchen and returned with three glasses and a large, unmarked bottle.

"It's my own brew," Doc said. He set the glasses on the mantel and unhinged the bottle's top before pouring a beautiful, honey-colored liquid into the glasses. It gleamed like amber in the light of the fire, and Lina found herself smiling again. Despite the pain in her

ribs and the danger of her situation, something like happiness bubbled up inside her. It was such a foreign feeling, she almost didn't
recognize it. Prickly tears threatened to fill her eyes, and she blinked
rapidly and took a deep, appreciative sip of the beer. Flavors of honey and wheat flowed over her tongue, and she focused on identifying
the specific notes, rather than on the pleasure the taste brought her.

You're allowed to be happy, you know, Paul thought to her from the
seat he'd taken on the couch opposite. She looked up to find him
watching her, an uneaten sandwich in his hand, and a glass of beer
on the small table at his elbow. He sat with his back to the room's
front window, and the fading light of the afternoon sun cast him in
silhouette, but the flickering light from the blaze in the fireplace let
her see his dark eyes fixed on her face.

I thought you were giving me privacy, she shot back.

*That was when you were changing. You're fighting so hard not to feel any-
thing good, I couldn't help but notice.*

How can I be happy when Isa and the girls are at risk? she asked, turning back to the fire, desperate to turn the subject as easily.

*Pffft. They're fine. They're likely on a plane to New York right now. We
don't welsh on a deal. We're honorable.*

We?

The United States of America.

Lina turned to look at him, raising her beer glass again, but letting
him see the skepticism in her eyes over the rim.

People are honorable, she said. *Nations are pragmatic.*

Yes, but we're not your enemy anymore, Lina.

No, she said. *You're my enemy's enemy. But you're not my friend.*

Paul's dark eyes narrowed, and she felt the quick heat of his anger through the link.

So you keep telling me, he said and turned away.

"All right, Doc," Paul said out loud. "You've eaten a sandwich and a half of the food you brought for us. Time to pony up the intel you promised. What's going on?"

Doc took a swig of his excellent beer to wash down his latest bite and grinned at Paul. Then he set his beer down on the floor beside his chair and reached into his pocket, pulling out a folded paper. He held this out to Paul and sat back before taking another bite.

"What's this?" Paul asked.

"It's a hospital transfer order for a patient going by train to Moscow. The patient is a former commander of a Nazi prisoner of war camp. He's to be transported with the utmost security. His train, too, leaves at seven eighteen tonight, but it isn't taking the usual route to Moscow. It's an express, and it's routing around the cities along the way."

"It's got to be the same train," Paul said. "How good is your intel on this, Doc?"

"I had it from the mouth of the prisoner's security detail himself. He likes his vodka, and I have a nice little recipe I cooked up in my still...anyway. I trust it."

"Good enough," Paul said, "but then the question is, if it's not following the normal routing, where's this train going?"

"Ah, but that's on the transfer order as well, my friend," Doc said, looking pleased with himself. "You see the string of shorthand on the bottom? Those are the distances and directions to the nearest hospital for every fuel stop along the way. The patient isn't in the best of health, you see. And the Soviets are *very* eager to get him alive, so they can use his execution to best fuel their propaganda."

For the first time since meeting him, Lina heard something other than open kindness in Doc's tone. He spoke of the Soviets with an edge of savage venom, revealing a bone-deep hatred that rivaled Lina's own. It wasn't polite to pry, but Lina would've bet everything she owned the Red Army had destroyed someone or something Doktor Philip Wholrab loved, and he was determined to get his revenge.

"Perfect," Paul said, looking up at Doc with a small, savage smile. "This will do very nicely. Let me just grab my map, and we can figure out where and when this train will be traveling."

"Finish eating first," Doc suggested, lifting his beer and sliding seamlessly back into the persona of the harmless, fun-loving doctor, "and let me get out of here before I hear any of your nefarious plans."

"Good idea," Paul said. "As always, you're invaluable, Doc. Thank you."

"Yes," Lina said, lifting her glass toward the doctor. "Thank you for everything."

"My dear, you are very welcome," Doc replied. "You both are."

* * *

After they finished a rather convivial meal, Doc wished them, "Good Hunting," and hiked back out into the trees toward his vehicle. Lina remained in her seat while Paul rummaged through the books and detritus on the various shelves for a few moments.

"Ah!" he finally said in satisfaction. "Here it is! I knew I had an atlas in here."

He blew the dust off a long, thin book and carried it over to the small end table he'd used earlier. Then he lifted this and brought it over to set in front of Lina so they could look together at the pages within.

"How old is this book?" Lina asked as he flipped through.

"It predates the war," he said, shrugging slightly, "but the topography should be the same, as will the rail lines, if they survived. We should be able to still plot the route closely enough."

"I hope you're right," she said.

"Me, too. Here, you take the paper and read what it says at the bottom." He handed her the transfer order Doc had given them, and he set about marking the ranges and distances she read. After a few minutes' worth of work, they had an approximation of the express route drawn in pencil on the pages showing the territory between Berlin and Warsaw.

"Here, I think," Paul said, pointing. "This town…Treplin? I think this will do. The atlas says it has less than five hundred people. It's remote, and the track goes through a perfect choke point here, between these two lakes."

He looked up at Lina.

"Can you swim?" he asked.

She blinked, startled. "Yes, why?"

"Because I have an idea, but if we're going to make it work, we have to go now. The train departs Berlin in an hour, and from there it's just over two to Treplin, I'd guess. We need to be in place before the train arrives."

He pushed up to his feet and took the atlas from the table in front of her, ripping out the relevant page and throwing it into the fire.

"What are we going to do?" she asked.

"I'll tell you in the car," he said. "Gather your things. Let's go."

Lina didn't have any "things" to gather, so she simply busied herself with tidying up their glasses and wrapping up the remaining sandwiches for later. Paul, on the other hand, had quite a lot to gather.

Without saying a word to her, he went to the bookshelf under the stairs and pulled three separate books halfway out of the shelf. Lina's eyebrows went up when she heard the resulting *click* and the bookshelf swung out, away from the staircase. Underneath lay a shallow cabinet lined with rifles, shotguns, pistols, and what looked like hand grenades.

"Clever," she said, fighting not to peer over his shoulder.

"I like to be prepared," he said, glancing back at her. "Can you use any of these?"

"I've fired a pistol," she said, "and I used to hunt waterfowl with my father as a child."

"Shotgun, then," he said, lifting one out and handing it to her, "and here's a Luger. You ought to be familiar enough with that."

She took the weapons and the holster belt he handed her, as well as the extra ammunition for both. She put the belt on under her flannel shirt, which was long enough to cover the pistol if left untucked like a jacket. The shotgun had a sling attached to it, and she slung it over her shoulder. Ammo went in the pouches on the belt, in her trouser pockets, and the breast pocket of the shirt.

"What exactly are we going to be doing?" she asked as he handed her yet another packet of shells for the shotgun.

"I'll tell you on the way," he said. "We don't have a lot of time."

She'd been concerned with her own weapons, so hadn't watched to see how many he'd stashed about his person, but the cabinet was significantly emptier when he stood up. He took one last thing from the hidden trove—a knife as long as her forearm—and closed it back up with a *clunk*.

"Ready?" he asked.

"I suppose so," she said, hefting the small packet of sandwiches.

"Good. Let's go."

* * *

The drive to Treplin took a little over an hour and a half because some of the roads hadn't been fully repaired from the war. Paul drove as he had before—aggressively, taking turns at speed that made Lina cling to the door handle and fight not to slide across the seat.

"So here's what I'm thinking," Paul said once they left the gravel of the trailhead road and were back on solid—albeit pitted and torn up—asphalt once again. "You saw the map near Treplin. The train tracks go right between those two lakes, Greater and Lesser Treplin-er lakes, right?"

"Yes," Lina said, grunting as he wheeled the car around a tight corner, and she bumped the door on her side. "Why?"

"Well, that's a perfect choke point! If we can stop the train there between those two lakes, they can hardly get away from us."

"But how will we get away from them?" she asked. "If they'll be trapped, so will we."

"We'll swim," Paul said, giving her another of his grim smiles. "You said you could swim, right?"

"Yes," Lina said, shaking her head, "but I've never done it while people are shooting at me! And you don't know if Rolland can!"

"I'm a strong swimmer. If I have to, I'll knock him out and drag him along. Look, I know this sounds like a crazy plan, but fortune favors the bold, Lina. This is the best shot we've got before they cross the border into Poland, and we've got a whole other set of problems."

Lina took a deep breath and watched as they passed a slower-moving vehicle.

"All right," she said. "So we stop the train...and then what?"

"Then we go get Thanhouser."

"And how will you find him?"

Paul glanced over his shoulder at her.

"You'll find him," he said, "using your gifts. Is that something you can do? My sister could always find us, even in the middle of a crowd."

"Do you have other siblings?" Lina asked, distracted.

"What? No...us. Me and my friends. But answer the question, please. Can you find Thanhouser?"

"Your sister could likely find you because she was used to linking with you," Lina said. "That's the bond at work. Once a psychic has linked with a man, her power gets a taste for him, and actively seeks to reestablish and maintain the link. That's part of the reason you felt so strongly about getting me out of the security prison."

"I was trying to protect you," he said.

"Yes, exactly. We've been linked for several days now. The bond is growing between us even now, and it makes you protective of me. After this experience, I could certainly pick *your* mind out of a crowded train. It would call to me like a beacon shining on a hill. But the problem is, I never linked with Rolland Thanhouser. I didn't use my power again until after he was taken."

"So you can't find him?"

"I don't know," she said. "I'll try, but I can't make any promises."

Paul blew out his breath in a sigh. Frustration leaked down their psychic link and made Lina shift uncomfortably in her seat. Was he disappointed in her?

Did it matter?

"It doesn't matter," Paul said. "It's still the best shot we've got. If you can't pick his mind out, we'll just have to search the train visually. I hope it doesn't come to that, but we have to try."

"I'll do my best," Lina said softly, unable to help herself.

"I'm counting on it," Paul replied, his voice hard.

They drove in silence for a while after that. Lina contented herself with staring out the window as isolated farmsteads and villages lit up one by one. Behind them the sun sank below the horizon, and the night rose up all around.

"Why did you shut your power down?" Paul asked suddenly, his voice startling over the hypnotic *whir* of the tires on the road beneath them.

Lina pursed her lips and looked down at her hands.

"When Berlin fell to the Red Army," she said, keeping her voice neutral, "it was a very bad time, especially for the women and girls. I'd hidden with Isa's daughters—Johanna was only a baby then—and she'd charged me with keeping them safe. Some soldiers found us, and I could feel what they wanted to do. Not just to me, but to the little ones as well."

"Did you shoot them?" Paul asked, his voice even and devoid of judgment.

"I didn't have a gun," she said, "but I killed one of them anyway."

"With your power."

"Yes."

The confession hung in the air between them. Lina had never told anyone other than Isa what she'd done. Isa had told Rolland that Lina had saved the girls, but she hadn't said how. To let a man know the full extent of her power was to court death. Lina had learned that as a child, even before she'd ever gone to the *Reichschule*.

"My sister had to do that once," Paul said, still speaking in that casual tone, as if discussing the weather. "She and one of her girlfriends were in the city, and they were attacked by a pair of drunks intent on rape. She lashed out and stripped the attackers' minds of their external shielding, leaving their psyches wide open to every stimulus. She said they'd be mad in minutes, and dead in hours. Is that what you did?"

"Not exactly," Lina said, "but similar. I pumped my power into the part of the brain that regulates circulatory functions and caused all his cerebral capillaries to burst at once. He died instantly."

"Ah. Efficient," Paul said, and this time his voice held a note of...approval? "But messy, I imagine."

"Yes."

"So you shut down after that in horror at what you'd done?"

"Partially," Lina said. "Partially because it was just easier that way. There was so much pain everywhere in the city, I could feel it bleeding past every shield. It was just easier to hunker down and hide."

"I can understand that, too. We heard some stories in the American zone...well. I'm glad you survived. And I'm glad you kept those girls safe. They seemed like nice girls."

Lina felt the ghost of a smile turn up the corners of her lips. "They are," she said.

It was full dark by the time they found the town of Treplin. As advertised, it was small enough to fit inside Lina's old neighborhood in Berlin, and looked completely deserted.

"They must roll the sidewalks up at dusk out here," Paul said as he wheeled the car around and headed back the way they'd come. They'd left the highway a little while back, and the road was little more than a glorified cart trail at this point. Lina gritted her teeth and hung on while they bumped and jostled back to the woods, where they'd caught glimpses of moonlit water through the trees.

Fortunately, it wasn't too far.

"I think this is our best bet," Paul said, pulling up to a railroad crossing Lina hadn't even noticed their first time through. But sure enough, the winding cart track crossed right over the metal tracks at a spot hemmed in by trees. Paul cut the engine and the lights, then looked at his wristwatch. "It's actually kind of perfect. Get your stuff. We've got about an hour by my watch. Let's find an observation spot."

Realization dawned on Lina.

"You're leaving the car?" she asked, incredulous.

"Yes. It's big enough it should derail the train. It happens all the time back home. Some drunk leaves his car on the tracks, and *boom*. Massive delays, etc. No one's usually hurt, though. Except maybe the drunk, if he didn't get out of the car in time. So let's go, all right?"

Lina blinked at the sheer audacity of it, then shook her head, obligingly opened the car door, and stepped out. The gravel of the road crunched beneath her boots, and she tried very hard not to think about what else might be making crunching noises soon.

Paul retrieved their weapons from the trunk of the car, then disappeared into the trees. Lina gaped. Had she not been mentally linked with him, she'd have thought herself completely alone. He moved so silently and smoothly, she instantly lost him in the shadows.

Paul?

I'm here, he said, *walk toward me.*

Unshield a little, she said. *How did you do that? You were just...gone!* She felt him drop his shields and light up like a bonfire in her mind. She took a tentative step toward him, then another, and she could feel his dark amusement at her fumbling.

Right here, he said, and she suddenly saw him again, standing next to the trunk of a large, ancient tree. He reached out a hand for hers, and without thinking, she took it.

Lina's power surged between them like lightning arcing from cloud to cloud. She felt her eyes go wide as the fatigue and constant ache of her ribs faded into the background, and the barriers she'd erected for privacy dissolved. His mental landscape lay wide open before her, inviting her to slide all along that deliciously strong masculinity.

What was that? Paul's words echoed inside her brain. *What just happened?*

I don't know, she admitted. *I've never had that happen before. The bond...it just...*

My shields are gone, and I don't want to put them back up.

Invisible hands closed around Lina's throat, cutting off her breath as agony, betrayal, and old loss made new again stabbed through her. She doubled over, reaching out to catch herself on a nearby tree. The roughness of the bark under her fingers registered as something solid, and she clung, figuratively and literally, as she tried to put herself back together.

Shields are necessary, she said as she spun hers out of nothing and slammed them back into place, despite her deep desire not to do so. *The bond is too seductive, otherwise.*

Lina, Paul thought, reaching out to touch her hand on the tree. *I'm not trying to hurt you…I'm not…*

Stop! Her mental scream reverberated down the link, and his fingers fell away as he backed up a step. *You're not my friend! You've insisted I stay linked with you, and I've complied, but I will protect myself from you!*

His mind stayed silent, but his fingers dropped away from hers on the tree. With her shields locked down tight, she couldn't feel his emotions, but that was all to the good. Only once before in her life had she allowed a man to have such deep, intimate contact with her psyche, and it had ended in a blood-soaked tent in the snow.

Deep in the recesses of her mind, that damned little voice whispered that this was a different situation. There was no enemy here to turn that deep connection against them…but Lina shut the voice down. Paul was not Josef. He didn't care for her. She was a tool to be used for the advantage of the United States of America.

The country that had been her enemy. That had killed her family.

The country whose psychic had killed her love, killed her adopted brothers, and left her for dead.

The country that was holding her new family hostage to her behavior.

The enemy of my enemy is not my friend, she thought, not caring if he picked it up or not. *Simply a means to an end.*

The train's coming, Paul said, his tone flat and lacking emotion. *We need to get undercover.*

He took her hand again, but she was prepared and fought down the resultant power surge. Paul pulled her forward into the darkness between the trees, and she focused on keeping her footing. He led her up a bluff overlooking the railroad crossing and pulled her down to crouch beneath the lowest branches. The ground was cold and damp from recent rains, and Lina couldn't help but grimace. Though she hadn't said a word out loud, Paul put a finger over his lips and pulled his slung rifle around to the front.

When they hit the car, it'll be noisy and chaotic for a few moments, Paul said into her mind, *I'll head down this bluff as soon as we hear the initial impact. I need you to pinpoint Thanhouser's location as quickly as possible, and vector me in.*

I'll try, Lina said.

Stay quiet and hidden, Paul said. *The lakeshore should be just on the other side of this hill. As soon as you find Thanhouser, head that direction. I'll grab him and meet up with you at the lake. Work clockwise around the lake until we meet up. We'll stay linked, which should help us find each other.*

That's a very loose plan, Lina said, peering into the darkness to the west. A far-off light started to paint its way across the trees in the distance.

The train.

That's why it's going to work, Paul thought with a grim, dark humor that slid down the link to Lina's mind. She snorted softly in response, but said nothing else.

Before long, they heard the steady rhythm of the train's wheels rocking its way down the tracks. From her vantage point up on the bluff, Lina could see it approach the final curve before passing between the two lakes. Excitement threaded through her, speeding her pulse as she watched multiple tons of metal speed, all unknowing, toward the obstacle in its path.

The light from the front of the locomotive swept across the base of their hill, then lit up the tracks in front of them. The abandoned car's metal bumper gleamed a warning.

Here we go, Paul thought and stepped forward to skid down the bluff toward the tracks as the train's engineer let out three quick, ear-splitting blasts with the train's whistle. While the echoes of the whistle faded in the trees, a horrendous screeching followed as the engineer applied the emergency breaks in a vain attempt to avoid the inevitable.

Lina clapped her hands over her ears and ducked her head as the locomotive struck the abandoned sedan. The crunch and scream of tortured metal rose up as the train left the track, gouging a great furrow in the narrow strip of dirt before the trees. The first row of trees exploded into splinters as tons of machinery plowed into the woods, pushed forward by the inexorable momentum of an express train running at top speed.

Lina! Where is he?! Paul yelled into her mind.

Lina looked up, heart racing, and reached out with her power to the mechanical carnage below. There was Paul running down the hill, his mind shining its siren call to hers. She followed his path for a few moments, trying to get her bearings amid the chaos of terror below.

As she'd done in the prison, she skipped her attention from mind to mind, never staying long enough to be detected. She sampled the surface thoughts of each individual, and when she didn't find what she wanted, jumped on as quickly as possible.

Every mind felt shaken, literally and figuratively, by the crash. Some wondered if they still lived, others defiantly screamed they did, and fought to calm themselves and decipher this new situation. Still others felt regret that the crash was over and they still breathed. One of these pictured his wife and three daughters' faces...

Oh!

I found him! Third car from the end!

She felt rather than saw Paul change direction, running west over the uneven ground. Cries of pain, shouts of fear and command rose up through the darkness toward Lina as people began to emerge from the damaged train. She forced herself to focus, despite the sickening smell of heated metal and gasoline—

Boom.

The explosion showered Lina with sticks and leaves from the trees around her. The ground pitched under her feet, causing her to clutch at the nearest tree to try to keep her feet. Down below, Paul was not so lucky, as the force of the blast picked him up and flung him forward on his face in the chewed-up dirt.

Paul!

I'm all right, he thought back, dazed. He pushed up on arms and legs that trembled, and started to stumble forward, shaking his head to clear it from the internal fog. *Where is he?*

Ahead and to the right—look out!

A figure loomed up out of the smoke and darkness in front of Paul. A huge man wearing a Red Army uniform stumbled forward, speaking in Russian. Paul didn't hesitate. Though Lina could feel his head throbbing in pain, he launched himself at this stranger before dropping to one knee and sliding in the mud and loose dirt just to the Russian's side. Paul pulled his long knife from its sheath and drove it deep into the back of the stranger's unprotected knee. Though the Russian wore leather boots, they only came up to mid-calf, and the big soldier bellowed in pain as Paul wrenched the blade free before springing back up to his feet.

The Russian stumbled, tried to turn, then fell heavily onto his wounded side. Through Paul's senses, Lina could smell the iron-rich tang of blood as the Russian's severed artery pumped his life out onto the muddy ground.

Where now? Paul demanded, his mind as cool and collected as ever. Lina, startled by the sudden extreme violence and nauseated by the echoed scent of blood, swallowed hard and fought to focus.

Fifty meters, she said, guessing. *I don't…there are more people with him. Probably other guards…*

I'll handle it, Paul said, starting forward again. *Can you reach Than-houser? Tell him what's happening?*

I-I can try.

Do it.

Lina shoved another shield in place to keep the sickening smell of blood away and reached out with her power once again. She skipped from mind to mind, trying to find the man who held Isa and her daughters close in his thoughts.

Fear. She mostly found fear and confusion. Desperate frustration welled up within her. Had Rolland put those thoughts away from himself? Or worse, had something happened to him? From the pain ricocheting through the wreck after the explosion, Lina could tell dozens had been injured. Was Rolland one of them?

Please, Rolland, she thought. *Please be there! Please be all right, for Isa's sake, and for your girls!*

Isa?

The thought was faint, too confused and weak to be either hers or Paul's. But it was there, a flicker of recognition in the swarm of chaos ahead. Lina locked onto that thought and wove a quick and dirty connection to bring Rolland into a rudimentary network with her and Paul. It wasn't a solid connection, by any stretch of the imagination, but it was there.

Rolland, it's Lina! Isa's safe. Your girls are safe, but they need you! Rolland, say something so I know you understand me.

Lina? Weak, still, but slightly clearer. Lina felt Paul change direction slightly.

Keep him thinking. I'm almost to his car. There are people all around. This could get tricky.

Who's there? Rolland demanded, his mind shading toward panic. Lina reached out again and did her best to soothe his fear.

Rolland, it's I, Lina. The other voice you hear is Paul. He's helping me. We're going to rescue you and take you to Isa and the girls. You just have to stay with me, all right? Just stay with me, and trust me. Let me help you.

Slowly, slowly, Lina persuaded Rolland's natural mental barriers to open just enough to let her in more fully. She slipped in with the lightest of touches and immediately regretted her decision. Unlike Paul's deliciously seductive mind, Rolland's psyche felt like a warzone. Pain and fear tangled together like concertina wire crisscrossing his mental landscape. Jagged blades of agony lanced through his channels at random, and it was all Lina could do to remain in control and not flee, screaming, back to the safety of her mind and Paul's.

What is it? Paul asked her as she withdrew just slightly.

His mind! I think—they've tortured him. He's more than half mad!

Will he be able to work? If we get him back to safety?

Sharp, incandescent anger bloomed through her, rocketing down the lines of the link toward Paul. Even Rolland felt it, because he flinched away from her, whimpering. Lina tamped down hard on her sudden emotion, and spent the next several breaths reestablishing the tenuous link with Rolland. It took everything she had to send him soothing, calming thoughts, when all she wanted was to unleash her fury on Paul's thoughtlessness.

Don't worry, she spat on a private channel to the American, once Rolland had stopped retreating. *He'll be able to decode that damn book! You'll get your money's worth out of him, never fear!*

I know I will, Paul said, still in that frighteningly calm tone. *Calm down, I'm at the train car. Who's inside?*

Lina swallowed hard and reached out once again.

Rolland, she said, *I think he's sitting, or crouched? Close to the back of the car, against the wall. Besides him, there are five—no, six others? Mostly prisoners, I think. Two, maybe three are guards.*

How do you know?

The prisoners have more pain in their thoughts, Lina said, fighting down nausea once again.

Ah. See if you can get Rolland to move toward the hatch in the back of the car. Paul held his rifle low and ready, and crouched as he rounded the rear corner of the train car.

Rolland, Lina thought, *Paul's coming to rescue you. We're coming to take you to Isa. Can you help us? Can you move toward the door in the back of the car? Just scoot toward the door. Trust me, Rolland. We're going to get you out of there and take you to Isa and your girls, but you have to trust me and do what I say.*

Isa, Rolland's mind whispered. He may have actually said the word out loud, but more importantly, the confusion and fear in his mind stopped its chaotic swirl. With agonizing slowness, and a whole lot of stabbing pain, Rolland used his legs to push his body across the floor of the car.

Meanwhile, Lina felt Paul easing the back door open just a crack and peering inside through the sights of his rifle. Inside the car, someone was holding a lit match for light, which was either a very brave or very foolhardy act. Especially considering that there had already been one explosion that night.

Lina watched through Paul's eyes as he visually identified another Russian soldier at the far end, leaning out and shouting to someone in the next car. The match-holder, too, wore a Red Army uniform as he held his tiny light source high.

Rolland is just to your right, Lina said, *leaning against the wall next to your barrel.*

Got it, Paul said and fired. Twice.

Time slowed down for Lina, and she watched through Paul's eyes and Rolland's as first the match holder, then the soldier on the far end crumpled and fell. Paul reached out with his free hand and grabbed Rolland's collar, then hauled him backward out of the car. Pain exploded in Rolland's mind as Paul dragged his battered body out onto the ground.

Can you stand? Paul shouted through the link. Roland responded with a wordless affirmative, and used the external frame of the train car to push up to his feet.

Inside the car the match had fallen onto the straw that littered the floor. Smoke started to billow upward, and for the first time, Lina realized that men still inside the car had begun to scream.

Paul grabbed Rolland's bicep with one hand, slung his rifle with the other, and took off running. At first he kept to the shadow of the shattered train, but once away from the crowd gathering to evacuate the burning car, he angled out across the short open area and sprinted for the trees, dragging an exhausted, pain-wracked Rolland Thanhouser with him.

When they reached the safety of the first line of trees, relief and exultation surged through all three of them, each one amplifying the other's joy.

Almost here! Lina sent. *Not far now, just up the slope—*

Something cold and round poked into the back of Lina's neck.

"Stand up," a voice said in harsh, Russian-accented German. "Slowly, Fräulein."

* * *

*L**ina?* Paul's anxious query echoed in her head as Lina slowly pushed up to her feet, keeping her hands visible on the trunk of the tree.

"Turn around," the Russian grunted, and Lina complied. At first glance, her captor wasn't much to look at. He was young and scrawny, with a uniform that hung on his too-thin frame, and dirt around the edges of his fingernails. His hands, though, were steady on the rifle he held pointed directly at her face.

Lina? What's happening?

I got careless, she admitted, feeling an eerie calm settle over her, filling the spaces within her psyche. *I didn't go to the lake like you said. I stayed close to help direct you, and one of them found me. I'm sorry, Paul, but I need to break our connection. You have Rolland now, so I've fulfilled the terms of our deal.*

Lina! Wait—

With a wrench she severed the link, her awareness of him going suddenly dead as her mind and power found itself confined to her own senses once again. She blinked, forced herself to breathe, and pushed down the bond that wanted nothing more than to reach out, reach for him…

No, she told herself. *I can't. I can't let him feel this. He's not my friend.*

"Don't move," the Russian said as he stepped closer. He kept his rifle pointed at her with one hand, while he reached out with the other and yanked on her shotgun sling, pulling it off her shoulder. The sling twisted, causing the stock of the weapon to crack painfully across her shins. She winced and flinched, and found the Russian's metal barrel pressed hard against her forehead.

"Don't. Move," he repeated, his voice hard and savage.

"I-I'm sorry," she said, trying to sound small and helpless. "It hurt me—"

"Quiet." He tapped his belt buckle with his free hand and pointed at the belt she wore. "Drop this."

Lina's mouth went dry. She needed him to get closer. Close enough to touch. She slowly lowered her hands to her waist and began to fumble at the buckle. She let out a tiny cry of frustration as her clumsy, shaking fingers couldn't loosen the stiff tightness of the belt.

The Russian muttered something that may have been a curse, or may just have been innocuous words, but he lowered his rifle and stepped closer. He reached out to help her, yanking on the front of the belt so she stumbled toward him. She reached out, her hand brushing the back of his…

And she struck.

With cold, calculating fury, she forged her power into a point and drove it deep into the young man's brain. Then as she'd done once before in a Berlin cellar, she made her power explode, shredding every blood vessel in the boy's brain. He stumbled, his eyes looking up to her before they pinkened and began to flow with blood. His body fell heavily toward hers, blood trickling from ears and nose, and from the sides of his mouth. She staggered under his weight and felt her heel catch on a root from the nearby tree.

She went down hard, elbow and head cracking against the wood, her bruised ribs screaming in protest as the dead man pinned her to the forest floor. She lay against the tree's massive trunk as stars exploded in her vision. For just a moment, she wondered if there had been another explosion from the train.

Through the high-pitched ringing in her ears, she could hear the sound of men's voices calling out in Russian. Fear skittered under her skin. She gritted her teeth against the pain in her body and head and pushed against the soldier's dead weight. The smell of blood mingled with the burnt gasoline and smoke stench from below, and she closed her eyes and fought the rising tide of nausea.

The voices called out again. She couldn't stop to be sick. She couldn't let them find her helpless like this.

Eventually, by swiveling her upper body in excruciating pain away from the trunk of the tree, she was able to slowly worm her way out from under the body. Blood from his face covered her hands, streaked across the front of her shirt. Her holstered pistol caught on the dead man's kit, and she reached down, whimpering, to unfasten it and wriggle free.

At last! She reached out, used the same tree to steady her as she pushed up to her knees, then feet. She scrubbed her bloody hands on the tree's rough bark, not caring how it scratched her skin. She'd rather feel gritty and scraped than covered in the Russian's tacky, cooling blood. A man's voice called out again, seeking, and her fear bloomed into full panic.

Lina fled on unsteady legs, stumbling up the rise toward the summit. Branches snagged at her skin and clothing, but she pushed on, needing to distance herself from the wreck, the body, and the men searching in the woods. When she topped the rise, she could see more trees spread out below, and the distant gleam of moonlight on water. She lurched forward. Her foot tangled on something, a branch? A root? Pain shot through her leg from ankle to knee. She fell hard, leaves and sticks skittering around her as she slid down the steepest part of the slope before coming to rest next to a natural deadfall.

Get up, go. Her fear pushed at her, drove her onward. She pressed up onto her hands and knees just in time for the agony in her head, ribs, and legs to come spilling out. She spewed her stomach's contents onto the forest floor. For several long, terrifying minutes, all she could do was hold herself there and shake as her body convulsed with violent heaves. But the fear wouldn't let go, so she reached out with trembling hands and used the deadfall to pull herself up to her feet.

On this side of the hill, away from the lights of the road and the wrecked train, the night wrapped her in inky darkness. A sudden image of Paul gliding through the shadows surfaced, and the bond kicked and screamed within her psyche like an angry child.

No, she told herself. *He has Rolland. That's what he wanted. He has no further use for me. It would be foolish to return to him now. I would be a liability that must be removed. The girls are safe, I've done my part. Now I can disappear.*

Lina stepped forward into the blackness, walking tentatively at first, but with more confidence as she went on. She didn't hear any more shouts for the moment, so she made herself move slowly, cautiously. Her head still throbbed, and her ribs felt as if they'd been bruised all over again, but she was up and moving, and she wanted to keep it that way.

The forest continued to slope downward, the trees growing thinner and sparser until she finally emerged onto a thin ribbon of moonlit sand. Ahead, the lake gleamed like a jewel, reflecting the light from the mostly full moon overhead. After feeling her way through the darkness of the forest, so much light felt like a luxury, and Lina took a moment to look around and appreciate the view.

Crack.

Lina flinched, ducking as the sound of a rifle shot echoed across the water. Panic rose up within her again and she looked wildly around to see if she could pinpoint the shooter's direction.

Crack.

Were they shooting at her? She suddenly realized how visible she must be, standing on the beach in the moonlight. She glanced at the trees behind her, but if the shooter was one of the men she'd heard, they'd be coming from that direction.

Crack!

This time the shot startled a flock of waterfowl roosting in front of her on the surface of the lake. They took off en masse, squawking and honking their displeasure at the disturbance. Opportunity crystallized in front of Lina, and without hesitation, she took it.

She ran forward into the small, choppy waves the birds had left behind. The frigid water numbed her skin and took her breath, but she pressed on, wading forward until it lapped at her waist. Then she dragged in a deep breath and dove in.

Icy cold wrapped around her entire body. She kicked against it, driving herself down toward the murky, muddy clay bottom. Overhead, she heard the muffled echo of another gunshot. Only her considerable will kept her breath contained and saved her from surfacing in a panic.

Out, she thought. *I must get away from this beach!* Her fingers brushed the slimy muck at the bottom of the lake, and she changed the angle of her body. Instead of pulling down, she pulled out, away from where she had been. She opened her eyes, but the darkness under the water was absolute, so she closed them again and focused on feeling her way forward with her body's swimming strokes.

Inside her chest, the pressure to breathe began to build. She resisted, but it grew with every second until she couldn't help but let a bubble slip past her lips. She opened her eyes again and looked up and around. It might have been illusion or hallucination, but she *thought* it looked slightly darker over to the left. The shoreline? Would she be shielded if she surfaced there to breathe?

Shielded or not, sparkles danced in her vision, and her chest and throat felt like they might explode at any moment. She let out another slow bubble and noted the way it rose along her face. Then she angled her body once again to follow and kicked upward.

When Lina broke the surface, she wasn't totally hidden, but she wasn't far from the shore. She turned her head, listening, searching, but she couldn't hear anything else, so she moved slowly to propel herself toward the edge of the water.

Unlike the small strip of beach where she'd entered, the shore at this point consisted of a sheer clay cliff overhung with tree branches. Several roots protruded from the dirt face, and eddies in the water promised hidden obstacles beneath the surface. Lina felt her way through the water, her heavy, booted feet searching for the bottom. Despite the way the boots dragged at her, she was glad she had them, for once she kicked a submerged log with enough force to ripple the surface water. Plus, eventually she'd have to get out of the lake and walk again, and she'd want the boots at that point.

She stepped onto the log she'd found and stood up slowly. The cool night air wrapped around her numb skin and soaked clothes, making her movements heavy and sluggish as she reached for the protruding tree roots. Eventually she got a grip on one and used it to pull herself up to where she could step to a foothold on the cliff. So far, so good.

The cliff was maybe two meters tall; not a daunting obstacle, under normal circumstances. But with everything she'd just been through, plus the sodden weight of her clothing, it seemed completely impossible.

Still, she had to try. Lina pushed up on legs that trembled harder than ever and reached up to grab another protruding root. She reached up with her left foot, found another foothold, and started to pull herself up when her hand slipped down the length of the root. She hissed through her teeth as fire erupted in her palm and fingers. By blind instinct alone, she reached up and grabbed at the crumbling clay of the cliff. Her raw hand found the rounded point of a rock, and she used this to haul herself high enough to belly flop over the lip of the bank. Fear pushed at her, and she wriggled forward like a grub, desperate to get her legs under the dubious shelter of the overhanging limbs.

That done, she rolled to her side and curled into a ball, desperate to stop the convulsive shivers that wracked her body and made her teeth clatter together. Grinding fatigue seeped in on the heels of her fear, blurring the edges of her mind. She let her eyes drift closed and willed herself to be still, to be warm, to be safe.

Crack.

Another shot, closer this time. Lina's eyes flew open as panic reared up in her mind once again. She tensed, trying to push herself up to continue running…

But why? She couldn't have found a better hiding place if she'd tried. She lay in a small depression next to another deadfall between two thick, heavy tree trunks. The trees' interlocking branches spread low on all sides, obscuring her spot from everywhere except directly below the cliff, where she'd surfaced. Furthermore, no one had fired when she'd been climbing out of the water. She'd have been totally exposed then, with the moon highlighting the contrast between her body and the dark clay of the bank. If someone wanted to kill her, that would have been the perfect opportunity.

Maybe they didn't want to kill her. Maybe they weren't shooting at her.

Then who—?

Paul! Her panic flared anew, igniting her bond-driven urge to reach for him, to connect with him. He had to be all right. He had to be—

Lina's power flooded outward, reaching kilometers in every direction until it found what it sought.

There! Like iron to a lodestone, her power locked onto the contours of his mind and flooded her psyche with the sudden, delicious, overwhelming awareness of *him.*

Lina? Lina! You're alive! Where are you? I'm—we're coming for you. Are you all right?

I'm safe, I'm hidden. Where are you? I heard the shots—

You're by the lake then. Yeah, the Russians sent out a few scouts, but I handled it.

Handled...oh. Lina drew in a deep breath as realization dawned. Paul had been armed, too. And unlike herself, *he* was unlikely to have been so careless as to lose both of his weapons. *Was that you shooting, then?*

No, he said. *Shooting them would have made too much noise. Tell me where you are. I can feel that you're close.*

Indecision rippled through Lina. The small, emotionless voice in the back of her mind urged her to sever the link. She'd already been linked with him for too long, and there was no need to expose herself to more danger by continuing their association.

But on the other hand...

On the other hand, her body continued to be wracked with cold, and the touch of his mind in hers held the promise of warmth and comfort...and despite everything, of safety. His initial touch had been so frantic, so relieved, she knew the bond had acted upon him as well. She *mattered* to him. He would protect her, and after what she'd just gone through, what she'd just done, Lina found herself badly in need of protection.

I'm on the lakeshore, she thought. *Not far from a tiny beach, just off to the right if you're standing on the sand and looking at the water. I'm under some trees at the top of a cliff, and I'm very, very cold. I think you'll have to swim to get to me. I had to swim to get here...*

She trailed off as her mind, overcome by the cold and fatigue and the exertion of it all, wandered into oblivion.

* * *

L ina woke, gasping. The world rocked around her, bringing her nausea back to the fore. She opened her eyes to darkness and the heat of her own breath. Something lay over her face. She tried to move it, but her arms felt leaden and trapped against something warm and solid. She whipped her head from side to side, panic surging within.

Shhh, I've got you. Paul's thought came down a link she hadn't known still existed. *I'm getting you out of here. Getting you both out of here, if it kills me.*

The world suddenly made a whole lot more sense. Her arms were trapped because Paul was carrying her cradled close to his chest, like a child. He'd covered her with a blanket or something. The world lurched with his steps.

He was moving fast.

I can't breathe, she thought, her tone small and half apologetic. She would've liked to protest that he should put her down, that she could walk or run very well by herself, but she knew that to be a lie. All the injuries done to her mind and body had come home to roost, and she was as helpless as a half-drowned newborn kitten.

Sorry, he thought. The suffocating fabric peeled away from her face, and the cold night air rushed in again. She blinked and could make out the rough shape of his shoulders and head against the midnight sky. *You're hypothermic, so I was trying to keep you warm.*

Thank you, she said, though it seemed the most ridiculous thing in the world. *Where's Rolland?*

I stashed him in your hiding spot, Paul said. *He was too badly hurt to keep up, and I've got to get you warm. I can't lose you.*

I'm not going to die, she protested, *and even so, you have what you came for—*

Shut up. I'm too busy to argue with you right now.

We're not arguing—

Shut. Up.

Lina gave up, at least for the moment, and focused on trying to see. Despite her weight, Paul moved in a kind of half-run loping motion. He seemed to be on some kind of trail or footpath through the trees. She wondered idly how he'd found it and where it led.

The latter, at least, she found out before too long. The tree branches above them cleared out, and Lina could see a larger, unbroken stretch of star-studded sky. She fought to lift her head, to look up from Paul's chest and see where he was taking her.

She didn't see it at first, but eventually she made out the outline of a long, low building that might have been either house or barn, or something entirely different. Paul didn't hesitate, but carried her up to the building and walked along it until they reached a door. He shifted her in his arms so he might use his fist to pound on the wood, and then stepped backwards, turning his body slightly and holding her closer than ever.

"Hello the house!" Paul called out in German. "Please, I need help! My wife fell into the lake and nearly drowned!"

A light flickered at the edge of Lina's vision. She tried to raise her head again, but Paul prevented her from doing so, stroking her wet hair away from her face as he guided her back down to rest against his shoulder. She heard the heavy *ker-thunk* of a latch, and the squeal of hinges.

"Grandfather," Paul said again, his tone managing to be both respectful and desperate. In the back of her mind, Lina found herself impressed with his acting skill. "Thank God. Please, can you help us? My wife and I, we were going to take our boat out...it's such a beautiful night...but then it overturned, and I couldn't find her, and..."

"Come in." The male voice was rusty, as if the speaker hadn't interacted with another human being in a while. "You damned fool, come in."

Lina felt Paul move forward out of the night and into a warmer darkness.

"Put her there, next to the fire," the householder said, and Lina felt Paul turn, then felt herself being lowered into an upholstered armchair. She shivered and curled her body up on the seat, trying to conserve as much heat as possible. Paul settled her in place, then grabbed a blanket from a nearby sofa and began tucking that in around her clammy arms and legs.

She saw an unfamiliar figure move behind Paul toward the massive stone fireplace. The man stirred the banked coals into a blaze, then turned and pointed an ancient pistol at the back of Paul's head. Lina's eyes widened and she let out a tiny squeak of surprise.

"Now," the man said, his eyes hard, "suppose you tell me how you managed to rescue 'your wife' from the lake without being wet through yourself? Who are you? Criminal trash, trying to take advantage of an old man?"

Paul raised his hands slowly out to either side. Through the link, Lina felt his mind go calm and empty as he prepared to act.

Wait! she cried down the link. *Please don't...just give me a minute!*

"Grandfather, please," she said, forcing the words through her chattering teeth. "We mean you no harm!"

"He's lying," the old man said, his voice like iron.

"About the boat, yes," Lina said, "but not about needing your help. We're not criminals!"

"Then what are you doing out on the lake in the middle of the night, Fräulein?"

For no reason she could name, Lina's eyes fell upon a framed object mounted above the mantle. She blinked, and the lines and whorls of the object became clear, though it was hard to see the telltale blue color in the flickering firelight.

"The Blue Max," she whispered, then cut her eyes to the old man's face. "You're...a flying ace?"

"What about it?" the old man snarled. She felt Paul's readiness rise inside his mind.

"You're a patriot!" Lina said, grasping onto this one fact. "You flew and fought for Germany! You're just like us!"

The old man's eyes narrowed, but he didn't fire. Nor did he lower the gun.

"We both fought for our country in the recent war, too," Lina said, hoping that he wouldn't ask too many questions. "We're out in the night because we were rescuing a fellow patriot who'd been taken by the Soviets. He's a scientist, and they wanted to take him back to Moscow and make him use his research to help the Red Army grind us down!"

The old man stared at her for a long moment, then finally decocked his pistol and pointed it at the floor.

"They run the Moscow trains near here," he said. "Your friend, he's to be on one of them?"

"He was on one," Lina said, "but it crashed, and in the confusion, we got him out and away. He's hidden nearby, but he's very badly hurt."

"And you? Why are you wet?"

"Soldiers from the Red Army saw me," she said, shrinking into the blankets a little. It felt good, and it helped sell her story. "I ran and dove into the lake to escape them. They were...not kind to us when Berlin fell."

"Nor when they marched through here," the old man said, sorrow and long-held rage crossing his face. "I'll help you, if nothing else, because it causes those pigs harm. Where's your friend?"

How do you know we can trust him? Paul asked, his eyes staring daggers at Lina. *You gave him too much information! What if he betrays us?*

He didn't shoot you, she said. *We don't have much choice at the moment. He hates the Russians like I do, like we both do. The enemy of my enemy, right?*

So you'll trust him, but not me? Paul said, then slammed his barriers home, indicating he didn't expect an answer.

"I'll get him," he said, "if you'll keep my wife safe here. I can find my way back."

The old man nodded. "Yes, good. Let me heat up some stew for you all. Don't dally." He turned, his pistol still in his hand, and went out through a narrow doorway into what Lina presumed was the kitchen. Paul, too, turned without a word and walked back to the front door.

But before he crossed the threshold, he paused and looked back at her.

Kill him if he looks to harm you. I'll be back soon. Believe it or not, I am your friend, Lina.

Lina didn't respond. She huddled in her blankets and watched as Paul opened the door and went back out into the night.

* * *

The old man's name was Aldaric Tollenbach. He told Lina to call him "Erik" and gave her his daughter's warm clothes to change into. Afterward, he smiled brightly at her as he brought out a steaming bowl of stew, along with fresh bread.

"This is delicious," Lina said once she'd devoured about half the serving. "Did your wife make it?"

"I did," Erik said, leaning forward to stir the fire with his iron poker. He sat in another armchair facing hers, and looked pensively at the pile of wood near the door. "My wife died three years ago."

"Three...oh."

"Yes," Erik said, stabbing at the fire once more and standing up with a soft grunt. Lina heard his knees clicking as he walked to the woodpile and took two split logs off the top. He carried them back and placed them carefully on the dwindling blaze. "When the Red Army came through. Our daughter was home then. Her husband was in the Luftwaffe, and she was staying with us in town. When Maria heard that the Soviets were coming, she sent Elisabeth and the children away, and stayed to buy her time."

"I'm so sorry," Lina said, unsure what else to do. "She must have been a very brave woman."

"Yes," Erik said. He lowered himself back to his seat and looked over at her with dry, frank eyes. "She was. Like you, I expect. You said you fought in the war as well. What did you do?"

"I worked in the intelligence service," Lina said. "I was trained as an interrogator, and I was good at it."

"Where were you posted?"

"Warsaw first," Lina said. "Then Paris. Then…back home, until the end."

"They wouldn't let me back into the Luftwaffe," he said. "My eyes had gotten too bad. I spent most of my time at one of the flying schools, teaching. I was there when the word came. By the time I made my way back home, my daughter had buried my wife."

"Where's your daughter now?" Lina asked, her voice gentle.

"Bavaria," Erik said, "with her husband and children. He's an engineer."

"Well," Lina said, mopping up the last of the stew with a hunk of bread, "you're a very good cook, sir."

"Thank you," Erik replied, giving her a small smile. "My Maria always thought so. She was a wonderful woman, but she could burn water."

A knock on the door heralded Paul's return, and Erik went to let him in. Lina noticed the old man retrieved his pistol first, and filed that away. The man might have been old, with poor eyesight, and past his prime, but he maintained a warrior's caution.

Lina couldn't say she blamed him.

When Erik opened the door, Paul staggered in, supporting Rolland's weight. The American had the scientist's arm thrown over his shoulder, and Rolland looked semi-conscious at best.

"Bring him here, by the fire," Erik said, stepping forward to help Paul. Rolland let out a groan. As they carried him closer to the light of the fire, Lina gasped as she got a look at his face and hands.

The side of his face puffed out with swelling that nearly blocked his right eye. Purple bruises stained his face and neck. His hands hung in twisted claws from his wrists, with fingers sticking out at odd, unnatural angles that made bile rise in Lina's throat. Rolland moaned again, his head lolling as Paul and Erik lowered him into the chair.

"He's very bad," Erik said. "This man needs a doctor."

"I can get him one," Paul said, breathing heavily from the exertion, "but it'll take a day or two."

"You can all stay here tonight," Erik said, "then you go get your doctor in the morning. Lina will stay to help me care for him."

"'Lina,' is it?" Paul asked, looking over at her with raised eyebrows. She stared back, and Erik chuckled.

"You're a besotted young husband. Your wife and I talked while you were gone. She's a lovely girl, but too young for this old hawk. Besides, I lost my heart years ago to my Maria. You have no reason to be jealous, pup."

Paul opened his mouth, probably to protest being called "pup," but Rolland groaned again and lifted his head. Without thinking about it, Lina stood up out of the chair and walked forward to place her hand on Rolland's forehead, reaching out with her power as she did so.

The link didn't snap into place as quickly or eagerly as it had with Paul, but it created a strong connection, and Lina had to fight not to let her knees buckle as Rolland's pain bled down the lines to her brain.

Paul's eyes snapped to her as he wordlessly demanded the load. She could feel his exhaustion, but he was healthier and stronger than either she or Rolland, so Lina gratefully let the tearing agony flow to him. She felt him take a sharp breath in, and felt a lessening of the strain on her own system.

"You're all right, Rolland," she said, both mentally and out loud, for Erik's benefit. "It's Lina and Paul. You're in a safe place. We're going to get you a doctor. You need to rest."

"He would do better to pass back out," Erik said. "With these injuries, the pain alone could kill him."

"Grandfather," Lina said, "that's not helpful."

Erik shrugged, and Lina realized he wasn't entirely wrong. She reached out to Rolland again and laid down a soothing blanket of ease, then carefully, very carefully, nudged him toward the comfort of sweet oblivion. The battered scientist pulled in a shaky breath, then another, as his body sagged into unconsciousness.

"See," Erik said, giving her a wink, "perhaps I was helpful after all."

Lina snorted. The sudden cessation of Rolland's pain left her feeling giddy, and a full-blown chortle bubbled up from inside her. Paul, too, chuckled, and before long, all three of them laughed long and hard at just how helpful the old man was proving to be.

"Well," Erik said, wiping tears of mirth from his eyes, "it's getting late. Let's move him to my daughter's room. I'll make a pallet for him, and you two can have her bed. That way, if he wakes, you can help him."

"Right," Paul said and rolled his head on his neck as he prepared to lift Rolland's dead weight once more.

While the men carried Rolland up the stairs Lina hadn't noticed earlier, she busied herself by taking her dishes into the kitchen and wiping them clean with the dishrag that hung by the pump-style sink. Then she dried her bowl and spoon, and dished up another portion of the stew. The remainder of the loaf of bread sat on the counter next to a whole loaf. Figuring that was for breakfast, she took the remainder and balanced it on the edge of the bowl. Paul hadn't said anything, but she could feel his hunger through the link, and knew he'd need to eat before he slept.

She could feel his proximity, she realized suddenly. Without actively reaching out through the link, she could *feel* him coming closer. Deep within the secret parts of her psyche, something warmed and glowed brighter with every step he took.

The bond, she told herself, huddling behind her privacy barriers. *We've been linked too long. I need to disconnect.*

Don't, his mind whispered in response as the illusion of her barriers crumbled away. *Don't disconnect again. It isn't safe.*

It's never safe, she replied.

"It can be," Paul said out loud, his words pitched low. She turned to see him leaning against the kitchen doorway. Exhaustion lined his face, and his shoulders slumped in weariness. She held out the bowl without a word.

"It can be safe," he said again, taking the bowl. His fingers brushed hers, setting off jolts of lightning under her skin. "I can keep you safe, Lina, I promise. You just have to trust me."

"I do trust you," she replied, her voice sounding far steadier than she felt. "I don't have much choice."

"You did. You broke the link. You could have stayed gone. I never would have found you if you hadn't reached out to me."

Lina pulled her hand back as if he'd burned her. The bowl of stew wobbled, but Paul caught it. The light from the small kitchen lamp cast his eyes in shadow, but she could feel the weight of his gaze as she stepped backward until she felt the cool hardness of the sink basin at her back.

Why did you reach out for me?

I was scared, she admitted, unable to lie in her own mind.

Of what? Hypothermia? You were well hidden. No one could have found you.

I'm not afraid of dying, she said. *I suppose I'd welcome it, if I knew Isa and the girls were safe.*

I have Rolland. They're safe. You know my mind well enough by now to know I mean that. So what then? What scared you so much that you linked with me when you didn't have to?

Lina didn't answer. She just pushed off the sink and strode past him. Some hybrid of fear and fury burned coldly in her as she fled up the stairs into the tiny room where Rolland lay on a pallet that occupied most of the floor. She stepped carefully over the wounded man and climbed into the narrow bed. Exhaustion frayed the edges of her mind, making her movements clumsy and sluggish. Paul's presence hung heavy in her mind.

Lina...

No, she said, feeling the tears gathering behind her eyes. *No, I can't. Not tonight. Please. Just eat and come to bed. I...I can't right now.*

His silent acquiescence flowed down the link. Lina sent a pulse of grateful acknowledgment and laid herself down, spreading her hair out on the single, thin pillow. She closed her eyes and willed sleep to come.

And felt him.

Despite her exhaustion, his psyche pulled at her, inducing a rest-lessness, an unsatisfied need that skittered along her channels. She shifted, rolling from one side to the other. She pulled the blankets up, then flung them off. Fatigue hammered at her, and only her will kept the gathering storm of tears from breaking.

I'm here.

She opened her eyes to darkness. The sun wouldn't rise for hours yet, and Paul must have put the lamp out before coming upstairs. But it didn't matter, she felt him there, his lean frame slumped against the doorway. The same fatigue that ground through her rolled off of him as well. Before she could think better of it, she pushed herself up onto one elbow and reached out in the darkness.

Come, she said.

He stepped carefully over Rolland's sleeping form and took her hand. Once again, the touch sent a jolt ringing through their joined minds. Lina interlaced her fingers with his and pulled, urging him forward. Something ancient and feral reared up within her and awoke a need long-buried.

The mattress dipped beneath his weight and he was suddenly *there.* His free hand came up and touched the healing bruise on her cheek, then threaded through her hair. He hesitated, and she felt the words starting to coalesce in his mind, but she wanted none of that. The sudden, savage need inside her had no time for words, no time for thoughts. She pushed herself higher until her lips met his, and sudden fire flashed between them, searing down the lines of their connection.

Their connection that wove itself tighter, as skin slid over skin, and lips and hands tangled together. Power surged in her mind, spill-ing through the warp and weft of their bond, flowing over the delicious hard angles of his mental landscape. They moved together in the darkness, matching need for need, abandoning thought and filling the night with sensations that ricocheted through their joined minds, pulling them ever closer to one another.

Exquisite agony built inside them, pulsing higher with each breath, each slide, each touch until it ignited. Lina's body flung itself backward, bowing as her mind spiraled out in all directions while Paul clung to her, using all his strength to keep her from flying into a million pieces as the storm broke over them both in a second that lasted for an eternity.

Lina?

His thought came, breathy and ragged, but there nonetheless, and it brought with it a wave of aching tenderness. She rode this wave, putting herself back together again enough to form coherent thoughts.

I was scared, she said, her thoughts halting at first, but becoming more solid with each of their joined heartbeats, *because I heard them shooting again. I knew they couldn't see me. That meant they were probably shooting at you. I reached out because in that moment I was terrified of losing you.*

Paul didn't say anything. He just pulled her gently back down to earth, down to him, until her head came to rest in the hollow of his shoulder. She let him cradle her close and reveled in the feel of his strength and the coiled power of his body.

The fog of ecstasy dissolved slowly away, leaving nothing but honest fatigue and the sound of their entwined breath in the darkness.

* * * * *

Chapter Six – Travel

Lina woke, warm.

Sunlight streamed through the tiny window in the wall above her head. She rolled onto her stomach and buried her face in the pillow, breathing deeply. It still carried the scent of Paul's skin, and she took a moment to indulge in thinking about nothing but the sensations of the night before.

You're awake. Paul's thought carried with it a caress of joy, and the knowledge he'd missed her. Lina blinked rapidly and sat up, pulling the small blanket up to cover herself. *Get dressed and come down. Rolland's awake, and there's breakfast.*

All right, Lina thought back. She probably should have said something to address what they'd done, but the genuine feeling of happiness emanating from Paul's mind was so pervasive, and so unexpected, she just didn't know what to say. So she shrugged and looked around for the clothing she'd worn the night before.

A few moments later she walked down the stairs, dressed once again in Erik's daughter's work trousers and a sturdy blouse. The scent of frying meat drifted up to meet her, and her stomach rumbled.

"Good morning, Lina," Erik said, looking up from the fireplace with a smile as she walked into the room. "I'm sorry about the mess. I wanted to clean out the fireplace, since we used it last night. Your husband and your friend are in the kitchen. There's bacon and toast."

"Thank you, Erik," Lina said with an answering smile. "My other clothes were still wet, so I put these back on. I hope that's all right?"

"Of course!" His smile flashed larger for just a moment before he turned back to his work. "Elisabeth isn't using them, and I don't imagine she'll be back here anytime soon. She's safer with her husband in the American zone." He shook his head briefly, shrugging one shoulder as if to say that it seemed strange to him, but there it was. Though he couldn't see her, Lina nodded in sympathy. War made strange bedfellows, perhaps, but that was nothing compared to peace.

"Lina?" Paul's voice came from the kitchen, and he stepped through the narrow doorway a moment later. "Good morning."

He looked much the same as he always had—forbiddingly handsome, with an air of contained violence in the lines of his lean frame. But this morning, his dark eyes burned with something else as they found her face. Something that ignited answering fires deep within her center.

"Good morning," she said, her voice rougher than she would've liked.

Erik chuckled next to her and stood up, wiping his hands on a rag that hung from his belt.

"The two of you must not have been married long," he said. "You could scorch the air itself with the looks you give one another. Come, man! Kiss your bride good morning and feed her breakfast. Then we'll decide what to do next."

Paul didn't smile, per se, but the corner of his mouth deepened, and he moved like a hunting cat as he closed the distance to Lina. He reached out a hand, and she took it, allowing him to draw her close. As soon as his fingers touched hers, the bond surged between them with an echo of the savage joy from the night before. Lina blinked and fought not to gasp out loud at the strength of the surge.

"Good morning," Paul said again, his voice pitched lower, more intimately.

"Good morning," she replied.

I didn't want to leave you, he said into her mind as he bent to brush his lips against hers. *It almost hurt, but Rolland was awake and...*

It's all right, she said, returning his kiss. *I came to no harm. Thank you for tending to him.*

Paul lifted his head so he could meet her eyes again. *Why do I feel like this? You're like oxygen to me. It wasn't this bad yesterday.*

It's the bond, she said. *When we...sex makes it stronger. And we were already so tightly connected. I—I am sorry.*

I'm not. His words were immediate. Vehement. *Not at all. I just want to understand what happened. But I don't regret it. You were already important to me, Lina. Now you're essential. And I don't mind at all.*

I'm glad, she said, feeling his sincerity. She didn't feel regret, either, but two very different impulses warred in her mind. On the one hand, she wanted to pull him close to her and never let go. She wanted to cement their connection with more lovemaking, to entwine with him physically, mentally, emotionally until she couldn't tell where he left off and she began. On the other hand, icy fear stabbed through her, bringing with it the memory of a blood-soaked tent in the snow. For just a moment, she was back there, choking on the pain in her throat, the scent of death cloying in her nostrils.

Lina? Where did you go?

Everyone I've ever loved has died, she thought, without meaning to do so. *Only Isa and the girls are left. I have to keep them safe.*

You've done that. I have Rolland. They're safe, Lina. You have to trust me.

I do, she said. And she did, she realized. After all that had happened between them, how could she do otherwise? *But I don't trust your government. Not entirely. Isa and the girls won't be totally safe until Rolland is back with them, and they're all in America. We have to make that happen.*

I intend to, Paul said and kissed her again, lightly, on the lips.

"Come on," he said, "before we disgust Erik any further. You need to eat, and Rolland is asking for you."

Erik had apparently decided to be discreet, because he was no longer in the front room. They found him in the kitchen, cutting up more bread and chatting amiably with Rolland.

"Ah, here you are," Erik said, grinning at them as they walked in. "Newlyweds, I would swear it. I thought I'd give you a moment. I've been talking to your friend Rolland, here."

"Rolland," Lina said, letting go of Paul's hand to take a seat next to the battered scientist at the table. "How are you? You look much better!"

Much like her own face, Rolland's bloomed with a few colorful bruises—hallmarks of the beatings he'd received. But his eyes were clear and bright, and he managed a lopsided smile through cracked and broken lips.

"Lina," he said, his voice ragged but understandable, "I'm better now. How did you find me? And the girls...the girls are safe?"

"They are," she said, then looked up as Paul put a plate down in front of her.

"Eat first," Paul said, shooting a warning look at Rolland. "Then we'll talk about everything."

The sudden cramp in her stomach reminded Lina that she was, in fact, hungry, and she set to with enthusiasm. The homemade bacon was thick and crispy, just as she liked it, and the bread was just as delicious as it had been the night before. Perhaps hunger was the best sauce, but she decided then and there that Erik was one of the best cooks she'd ever met.

"I'm sorry there's no coffee, or tea," Erik said, sounding rueful. "There's been none at the market recently, and I don't like to reuse the grounds too much. It becomes weak and tasteless…for me it's better to have nothing at all."

"I agree," Lina said with a smile for the older man. "It's all wonderful. Thank you."

"Yes," Paul said, while Rolland nodded as he chewed. "Thank you very much, my friend. We are quite in your debt."

"No debt," Erik said. "It's my pleasure to help fellow patriots like yourselves. Confusion and death to the enemies of Germany, eh?"

"Indeed." Paul's voice was smooth and gave no hint of hesitation, but Rolland looked sharply at him. Lina held her breath and started to reach out, but the scientist said nothing and turned his attention back to eating his breakfast. His mangled hands meant that he struggled, but he was making it work for the moment.

"First, we must get Rolland to my doctor friend in Berlin," Paul said, and Lina could feel that he'd followed her line of thought. She glanced up to see him looking intently at Erik. "And for that I need a telephone. Is there one nearby?"

Erik frowned and tilted his head from side to side.

"Not in the town, no," he said. "Maybe in Fürstenwalde. You can walk there…well, you two could."

Rolland looked up. "I can walk," he said quickly.

"Yes, but Erik's right. You're injured and would slow us down," Paul said, shaking his head. Pain creased Rolland's features, and he looked down at his plate. Lina felt a stab of pity for him, but Paul spoke the truth.

"I have a cart I use sometimes," Erik said, "for hauling wood and the like. I can borrow a mule from one of my neighbors and take you down there. You might attract less notice in a cart than walking with an injured man."

Paul pursed his lips, then nodded. "That's what we'll do, then. Thank you, Erik. We're even further in your debt."

"Not at all, my friend," Erik said, smiling so his eyes nearly disappeared in his wrinkled, weathered face. "I'll go now and see Rald about the mule." He wiped his bread-cutting knife on a towel and placed it carefully in a drawer before walking out with a decided spring in his step.

Paul watched him leave, and the corner of his mouth deepened slightly. "I swear, that man looks ten years younger than he did when we arrived."

Lina looked up sharply as a tiny warning bell went off in her head. She reached out, focusing her power down to the finest infinitesimal needle, and followed Erik as he exited the front door of his cabin. She held her breath as she sent that power arrowing into his mind, not enough for him to notice, just enough to get his most surface thoughts.

Sky and smoke, the thrill of adrenaline, the boneshaking, teeth-jarring rattle of a machine gun as the world spun over and over again…and underneath it all, fierce joy and a pride so strong it threatened to close Lina's throat.

She withdrew as quickly as she could, before Erik could notice her eavesdropping presence, and looked down at her plate again as she let out her breath.

"We're safe," she said. "Erik is just who he says he is. It gives him joy to help us, to resist the Soviets. He will not betray us."

Paul met her eyes with a look of inquiry. She picked up her toast and bit into it, opening the channel to let him feel what she'd discovered in Erik's surface mind. Paul sent back a pulse of gratitude like a caress. She shivered from the force of it and looked back down at her plate, where it was safe.

"How do you know?" Rolland asked, panic threading through his voice, bringing Lina's attention back to him. "He could be going to find them right now!" He put his injured hands on the table as if he'd push up to his feet, and then flinched, curling them in to his chest.

"Rolland, be careful," Lina pleaded, reaching out to put a hand on his shoulder. "It's all right. I—"

"Lina talked with him extensively while I was fetching you," Paul said. He, too, reached out to pat Rolland's shoulder. "Erik is a German patriot and a hero of the Great War. He hates the Soviets as much as either of us, if not more. If she says we can trust him, we can trust him."

He doesn't remember much of his rescue, Paul thought to Lina. *Let's keep your power a secret for now. If it becomes necessary to use it, then do, but his ignorance may protect us all.*

How?

I don't know. But experience tells me if something's hidden, it's better to keep it hidden.

Amusement bubbled up inside her mind, and she let the silent laughter flow down their link toward him.

You're such a spy, she said.

Always. It's what's kept me alive.

The fountain of laughter vanished, like someone had severed the plumbing. Cold dread began to creep in at the edges of her mind, but Lina took a shaky breath and held it at bay. He *was* a spy. She'd always known that. And it had kept her alive so far, as well. He was the enemy of her enemy, but he was also her friend…wasn't he?

Paul looked at her. He wanted her to turn and look at him. She felt it through their link. She licked her lips and slowly complied.

You are important, he said, articulating the thoughts slowly, as if for emphasis. *You can trust me, Lina. I swear it. You've become like oxygen to me, and whether it's from the bond or not doesn't matter. It's real, and I won't let anything happen to you.*

Doubt tore at her, but his iron hard sincerity lay there at the other end of their link. Her memories of loss and pain, all her internal warnings against trusting this stranger—never mind that he was an admitted American spy, this enemy of her enemy—shrieked in her mind to disengage, to find a way out. Trust was too risky, she had too much to lose…

But he was still there, on the other side of her mind, as strong and inflexible as steel. The power of his will bolstered her own, and he gave it up freely at her touch. His need to protect her, to be near her radiated like the heat from red-hot metal, and that heat wrapped around her, filled her mind with pleasure and safety and peace.

Peace. What an odd feeling. It had been so long, she almost didn't recognize it. It made her nervous.

Trust me? he asked again, insistent.

I do, she said. *I told you that.*

I know. But I need you to believe it. I need you to know that I'm more than just your enemy's enemy.

Lina looked away, and then pushed up to her feet. "Are you finished, Rolland?" she asked. "Let me have your plate. I'll clean up the kitchen while we wait for Erik to return with the cart."

Paul didn't say anything as she collected the plates and took them over to wash in the sink. She felt him heavy in her mind. He'd let the matter drop for the moment, but he wasn't about to let it go entirely. That, too, could be the bond at work, she realized. It bound them ever tighter, pushing them toward deeper and deeper intimacy with every interaction. Paul's insistence on trust was probably just another manifestation of its power.

As was the way her body ached for him even now.

She pushed *that* supremely unhelpful thought away and forced her mind to focus on the mundane tasks of washing the dishes, wiping the table and the counters clean, and sweeping the kitchen floor. By the time she was finished tidying up, Erik had returned with the cart and a mule, and Paul and Rolland had gone out to him. She followed, wiping her hands on a clean towel as she stepped out into the balmy summer morning.

"It'll be most of the day to get to Fürstenwalde," Erik was saying as Lina joined the men. "The roads are still bad in some spots, so that will slow us down. But there are many carts, and you shouldn't arouse suspicion."

"Is there room for Rolland on the seat up front with you?" Paul asked, eyeing the cart with a skeptical frown.

"No, he'll ride in the back. I have some things I've been meaning to take to the orphanage there, mostly old clothes and such, so we can cushion him somewhat. You and Lina will walk beside."

"Good enough," Paul said. "Let's get loaded up. Where are your old clothes?"

"Inside. Follow me."

Besides the clothes, Erik added several blankets to the cart, including the ones that had served as Rolland's bed the night before. When Lina asked about it, the old man just shrugged.

"I'm not using them," he said. "You three are the first visitors I've had since the end of the war. What does an old man like me need with extra blankets? The clothes belonged to Elisabeth and Maria, but they don't need them anymore. There are German children in Fürstenwalde who have nothing. The war took their parents, took their safety and their livelihood. Maybe they can use these old things. You and your husband and your friend have reminded me that I'm not alone in the world anymore. Germany still exists, and our people will survive, if we can care for one another."

Lina had never been a very demonstrative person. Her mother and father had taught her and her sisters to be decorous with their emotions. But in that moment, Lina couldn't resist. She carefully placed the folded blankets she'd been holding down on the bedframe and threw her arms around Erik in a sudden embrace. She felt his body tense with surprise, and then his arms rose to wrap around her shoulders as he returned her hug.

"You're a good girl," he said quietly. "You remind me of my Maria. She would have liked you very much." He cleared his throat then, and blinked rapidly as he let Lina go.

"I wish I could have met her," Lina said. "She must have been a remarkable woman, to have the love of such a good man."

"Careful," Erik said, chuckling thickly. He swiped quickly at his eyes, and Lina politely looked away. "Don't let your young husband hear you. I don't want him thinking there's anything going on between us."

Lina laughed and picked up the blankets once again. Erik gave her another wide smile, and then turned to head down the stairs and out to the cart.

* * *

Thanks to Erik's efficiency and Paul's decisiveness, they set off a few hours before noon. Lina and Paul did their best to create a cushioned seat for Rolland in the cart, but as the cart started off down the gravel road, Lina pressed her lips together in sympathy and felt a surge of gladness that she was able to walk. Her bruised ribs still ached, but the previous night's rest had taken the edge off the pain, and despite everything that had happened, her body was healing with its usual resilience.

A few minutes into the trip, Paul dropped back to walk beside her as she followed the cart. She glanced up at him with a tiny smile as the bond leapt with joy in her mind at his increased nearness. He continued looking straight ahead and occasionally scanning the fields and trees on either side of the small road, but his left hand drifted down and caught her fingers with his. Lina swallowed hard against the now-familiar surge of power as they touched.

"Is this wise, do you think?" she said out loud, even as her awareness rolled ecstatically through the delicious landscape of Paul's mind.

"Erik would expect it, I think," he said. "He thinks we're married, after all."

"Rolland doesn't."

"He does now. We spoke about it before you woke up this morning."

"You talked about me?" Lina blinked rapidly, trying to force her mind to focus on Paul's words. Her attention felt like a recalcitrant puppy, determined to run away and lose itself in play and pleasure. She had to fight to bring it to heel so she could understand the import of what he was saying.

"Yes. He's very protective of you. Sees you as his family's guardian angel, of sorts. He saw us lying together when he woke up and asked me some pointed questions."

"And what did you tell him?"

Paul turned from his survey of the side of the road and looked at her with those dark, intense eyes. His fingers tightened around hers and he pulled her to a stop beside him.

"I told him we had begun as partners to find and rescue him, but circumstances had wedded us together, and now I couldn't survive without you."

Lina rocked backward as the world tilted around her. She inhaled sharply, shakily. The scent of his skin teased at her, tightened things low in her body.

"You could," she whispered.

"Maybe," Paul said, his voice dropping to a murmur, "but I don't want to." And right there, in broad daylight, he bent and brushed her lips in a kiss.

Desire exploded in her brain, spinning her head better than the finest champagne. She deepened the kiss, reaching up to his face as he pulled her closer for one long, exquisite moment before backing off. When he did, his ragged breathing matched her own.

"You love me," she said, and it wasn't quite a question.

"That's what I told Rolland."

"Is it the truth?"

"What do you think?"

She licked her lips, savoring the taste of his mouth.

"So, what? We're wed? Just like that?"

"It seemed the most expedient answer. I didn't think you were much for a church and the whole bit."

"I'm not religious," she said, "and with the occupation, the government is…"

"We'll get an American marriage certificate when we can," Paul said. "I meant it, Lina. The only way I'm ever going to be apart from you is if you want it that way."

"I don't," she said before she thought about it.

"I know. You love me, too." Paul reached up and stroked a strand of hair back from her face while the corner of his mouth deepened in one of his little smiles. He bent to kiss her again, lightly this time, and then tugged her forward.

"Come on," he said. "We don't want to fall too far behind."

It was like being a little bit drunk, Lina realized, as they hustled to catch up with the cart. She certainly felt half-intoxicated by Paul's nearness, the feeling of his hand in hers, the open feedback loop of his emotions as they tangled with hers and reinforced the ever-growing bond between them. They fell into step with one another; even the rhythm of their breath synched up, and Lina had to wonder if their hearts weren't literally beating in unison.

Up ahead, Rolland lay on the piles of clothing and bedding with his eyes closed, and Erik looked forward as he drove, so it appeared no one had noticed the earth-shattering change that had just happened. No one but Lina, herself, and Paul.

Her husband.

Because he was right. For better or for worse, they'd become so inseparable, so entwined, so *wedded* together, that no religious pageantry or officious bureaucracy could ever hope to unite them further. She didn't know how this story would end, but Lina knew one fact like she knew her own name. Paul was hers, and she was his. Nothing save death itself would ever rip their bond asunder.

Paul squeezed her fingers one more time, then let her hand go. He sent a pulse of desire and regret down the lines of their link, then followed it up with his steely resolve to complete their mission and keep them all—but particularly her—safe. She watched him as he stepped further toward the side of the road, his eyes always moving, scanning for threats. She felt his attention turn away, toward the task at hand…but not really.

Because she was there with him, in his mind. She looked through his eyes, listened to the birds through his ears. She felt the way his body tightened in response to her proximity, and the naked truth of her answering desire for him. She felt his iron will as he forced his mind to focus on the job, even while she whispered wordless promises of closeness and connection during the night to come.

I'm sorry, she thought, though, in truth, she wasn't. Not really. *I don't mean to distract you.*

You don't, he replied. *You give me a reason to focus. I said I'd keep you safe, and I will.*

I know, she said. *I trust you.*

* * *

A bout three hours into the trip, Erik called a halt so they could stretch and relieve themselves.

After handling the most pressing needs behind a screen of saplings, Lina returned to the cart and reached her arms over her head, grateful for the opportunity to stop and rest. The summer air lay thick and hot around them, and the road had been worse than she'd expected. The gravel was thin to nonexistent, and old craters rutted and pocked the hard-baked mud surface. Rusting equipment lay abandoned here and there along the side of the road, showing that someone had most likely used this route as a means of retreat not too long ago.

As soon as Erik and Paul helped him return to his seat in the cart, Lina went to Rolland. She couldn't imagine how he must feel, after being bounced and jostled for the last three hours. His face looked pale and drawn, but he gave her a smile as she approached.

"I'm glad for the break," he said. "Your man was right, I couldn't have walked this long, but I fear my teeth have rattled loose in their sockets!"

"The road's been very bad," Lina said, grimacing in sympathy. "I think there must have been a lot of fighting near her."

"There was fighting everywhere," Erik said, drawing Lina's attention as he climbed back up to his driver's bench. "All the roads are scarred like this. But it doesn't matter. We'll heal, yes? Like your lovely face."

Lina smiled, surprising herself. The old man was right, she realized. Her facial expressions pulled less, and while her ribs were sore from the walking, they weren't half as painful as they'd been during that desperate scramble away from the train's wreckage. Her eyes softened as she nodded acknowledgment of Erik's words, and then inexorably turned to find Paul studying her face.

"How much longer?" Paul asked, pitching his voice to make it clear he spoke to Erik rather than Lina herself. He reached over into the cart and pulled out a jug of water, uncorked it, and held it out for her. Lina drank, grateful for the coolness to cut the dust, then handed the jug over to Rolland.

"Another few hours," Erik said. He removed the broad-brimmed hat he'd worn and swiped his hand across his brow. "We're nearly halfway there."

"Then we should get moving, if we can," Paul said, anxiety bubbling in his mind. He turned to look at Rolland in inquiry.

"I'm fine," the scientist said, handing the water jug to Erik. "Our host did a fine job packing this cart. I can certainly ride as long as you all can walk."

"You must let us know if something hurts worse," Erik said sternly. He took the jug, took his own drink, then capped it and stashed it back in the cart within Rolland's reach. "But you're right, we should move on."

He clucked to the mule, who made an ugly braying sound, but started forward again. Lina gave Rolland a reassuring smile and resumed her walk.

The second half of the journey was harder than the first. They'd left the forest around Treplin behind, but they'd become used to seeing the occasional stand of mature timber between the farm fields.

No more.

Lina could see where the woods *used to* be, but the only living things in those areas was the occasional brave, stubborn sapling that forced its way through the splinter-littered ground and reached out for the sky. Though she wasn't much for whimsical thoughts, Lina couldn't help but feel those saplings carried some of the same defiant optimism as Erik. Their worlds had been shattered to kindling, completely rent asunder…and yet they grew.

The sun had started its slant toward the beckoning west when Erik pulled the mule to a stop yet again.

"The bridge over this creek is out," he said by way of explanation as he persuaded the animal to step off the main road onto a rough side track. "Fortunately there's a spot to ford nearby. We cross this, and then we're half an hour from the town."

"What happened to the bridge?" Lina asked.

"Bombed during the war," Erik said, "by the witches."

Icy fear shot through Lina at the word. She tensed and looked over at Paul.

"'Witches?'" Paul asked, his voice extremely casual. "What do you mean?"

"The *nachthexen*," Erik repeated. "The damn Soviets sent their own women out to die, can you believe that? I know you served, Lina, but we would never be so reckless as to put you into combat or deliberate danger. But those degenerate communists put their women in biplanes…biplanes! I had better aircraft thirty-five years ago! They gave them fabric biplanes and hand-dropped bombs and sent them out to destroy our bridges and towns! It was barbaric! But what can you expect from the Red Army, eh?"

"Right," Paul said. "I think I've heard of these…what did you call them?"

"*Nachthexen.*"

"Night witches, right. They were called that because of the sound their fabric wings would make on a bombing run."

"Well, and because they were enemy women doing unnatural things, but yes," Erik said. "I suppose that could be another reason." Erik chuckled and shook his head, then clicked his tongue at the mule again to encourage the animal to keep moving down the narrow track.

He doesn't know, Paul thought to Lina, *unless you've said something to him while I was gone.*

No, Lina said, *I wouldn't.*

I know, Paul said. *You're too smart for that. I don't think he'd be bigoted, but you never know.*

He called them 'witches,' Lina said, horror coursing through her. She fought it, wrestled it down and forced herself to remain as calm and analytical as possible. *That's what men call women when they burn them.*

They were enemy combatants, Lina, and I've heard of these Soviet women before. Everyone calls them the Nachthexen. *It's like you calling us Amis during the war.*

During the war, I would have burned you, too, she said. *You were my enemy.*

I'm not now, Paul said, exasperation edging his thoughts. *You know that. You said it yourself.*

No, you're not now, she agreed, *but…it just makes me nervous.*

I'll keep you safe, Lina. I promise. Erik doesn't ever need to know about your power. He likes us. He's helping us.

For now.

Take what you can get, Lina. Trust me.

I do. She sighed, willing the unease to go away. *I do.*

Erik pulled the cart to a halt again, and Lina looked up to see that they'd reached the wide, flat bank of a little stream. It didn't look like a particularly formidable crossing, though she knew fords could be deceiving. The creek itself looked lazy and slow, but she couldn't help but wonder what obstacles lurked beneath that calm-seeming water.

"I'll drive through," Erik said. "The water comes just below the axles of this cart, usually. The ford's wide, so you can both swim alongside. Can you swim?"

"Yes," Lina said. Paul nodded.

"What am I saying?" Erik asked with a wide smile. "You're strong young Germans! Of course you can swim. Rolland, hang on. I'm sorry, my friend. This will be bumpy." He swiveled back around in his seat and urged the mule forward. Lina felt Paul's sardonic amusement flow down their link, but he stayed silent, and his face gave nothing away.

Go first, he urged Lina. *I'll be right behind you.*

All right, she said.

She walked down to the bank of the creek, then sat on a rock to remove her boots while Erik persuaded the mule to step forward into the water. She struggled a bit with one of the knots she'd tied, which meant that by the time she got her boots off, the cart had already splashed into the water and begun to work its way across.

Her surge of frustration must have echoed down to Paul, because he looked up from his own preparations and came to her side.

"Tie the laces together, like this," he said, lifting his own boots so she could see. "Then put them around your neck. That'll leave your hands free to catch yourself if you slip. But please don't slip. That could be dangerous."

"Thank you," Lina said, smiling. Warm goodness began to suffuse through her mind, and she sent a pulse of it down the link to him. "That's a clever idea."

He didn't say anything, just reached out and stroked her cheek. The touch magnified their already broad connection, and Lina suddenly felt herself far away, experiencing something from his memory.

Night. Cold. The dull roar of rapids. The bite of icy water and the thump of boots against his chest. And the fear. So much fear, and it was made worse by the way he had to lock it up and compartmentalize it into a tiny box lest it start to affect the others, especially—

Paul grabbed her hand and the memory cut off as suddenly as if someone had severed the film reel in half. Privacy barriers he hadn't used in days slammed closed, and Lina gasped at the vehemence of it and looked up at him, hurt.

"I don't want to remember that," he said lowly, his eyes intense. "You don't need to see it; it's not a good memory."

"I—all right," Lina said, pulling in a shaky breath. She squared her shoulders and pushed the sudden pounding in her head away. Hard for her to argue, when she certainly felt the same about some of her own memories from the war. "Let's just go."

Paul squeezed her hand and sent a pulse of gratitude her way, then let go and gestured for her to precede him into the water. She finished tying her boots together and hung them around her neck, then stepped carefully into the welcome coolness of the wide stream.

The gravel streambed didn't pose any problem at first, but when she got about a quarter of the way out into the current, the gravel ended, and flat, slick rocks took its place. Lina curled her toes and tried to grip with every step, but as the water rose up over her knees and thighs, the flow got faster. She took another step and felt her balance falter. With a curse, Lina kicked her feet up and began to pull herself forward with practiced swimmer's strokes. She reached for the far side, but the current caught her, pushing her downstream faster than she'd anticipated.

Lina! Paul's thought snapped out. *Don't fight the current! You'll just tire yourself out. Swim at an angle. Be careful of the rocks!*

I shall do my best, she thought back, allowing her frustration and dismay to color her mental tone. She did as he said, though, angling her body downstream as she continued to pull for the far bank. Her hands scraped against a large, submerged rock, and she scrabbled against it, trying to get a grip. But the current pushed her onward, tumbling her around and bumping her shoulder and knee. Pain shot through her, and she couldn't suppress a gasp. Her mouth filled with water, and she choked, tried to spit.

Lina!

I'm all right! she thought desperately. She reached out again, half-blind from the spray, and tried to catch the far edge of the boulder. Her hand splashed down into the water, and her fingertips brushed against the stone just out of her reach. Anger surged through her, and she kicked out and down. Her toes impacted, hard, on something rough and sodden, but solid. A submerged log? Not that it mattered. More pain lanced through her body from toes to crown, but she straddled the log, then locked her feet together underneath and fought to sit up straight.

The water pushed at her middle, but she snarled and forced her body upright against its power.

"Lina!" Paul shouted. She turned to look over her shoulder at him, midway across the ford. "Are you all right?"

"I'm fine!" she shouted back, "but I'm afraid I'll be swept away again if I leave this log."

"Just stay there! We'll get you. Just hang tight." Paul pushed forward, crossing the ford in a couple of minutes. Lina turned back to face downstream, mostly because she didn't want to lose her balance and tumble back into the water. Her ribs pulsed with renewed pain, and her shoulder and knee felt abraded and raw. Her toes throbbed in time with her ribs, and she was wet through.

It was not her finest moment. She risked raising one hand long enough to push her sodden, clinging hair back out of her eyes. The bank she'd been trying to reach lay tantalizingly close, but Lina couldn't see any way of getting there from her current predicament. She'd managed to find a log that had fallen into the river and wedged itself up against the old bridge pilings. If she left her current perch, the current would sweep her further downstream, past the treacherous remains of the bombed-out bridge...

Oh!

Paul, Erik had some rope on his cart, right?

I think so, Paul said. *I didn't think we'd need it. The ford didn't look that deep, or fast.*

Don't worry about that now, Lina thought. *If you get it and walk down the bank to the old bridge, I think you could drop the rope down to me and pull me in.*

Got it, Paul said. Lina felt his relief at having a plan. She followed along in his mind as he finished pushing across the ford and ran up to the cart.

"Where's Lina?" Rolland called.

"The current got her! I need some rope!" Paul said, his voice snapping out like a whip. He threw his boots to the ground, cut the joined laces near the knot, and shoved his wet feet into them. Meanwhile, Erik sprang into action, jumping off the driver's seat and opening up the compartment beneath. He pulled out a coiled length of old rope and tossed it at Paul.

"I'll come with you!" Erik said. "I hope the rope is long enough!"

"Me, too! We'll be right back, Rolland!"

"Just get Lina safe!" Rolland called back, bitter frustration soaking his tone. "Don't worry about me!"

Paul and Erik loped downstream, sticking as close to the bank as they could. Lina felt Paul as he wove around the shattered remains of trees and fought not to fall down the crumbling bank and back into the water.

"What are we going to do?" Erik asked. The old man was breathing heavily, but keeping up. Lina felt just as impressed by this feat as Paul did, and her admiration for the war ace ratcheted up another notch.

"She's on a log up against the bridge piling. We're going to go out on the bridge and throw the rope down to her, then pull her up."

"The bridge is treacherous, my friend. There isn't much left of it."

"I know," Paul said, "but it's the best I've got right now."

"Very well," Erik said. "Let's save your wife."

The two men climbed up the short slope to the road, then walked out to the bridge to assess the situation. The old structure had once been a sturdy one, with thick stone pilings sunk into the streambed. Lina's log had wedged up against what had once been a center piling before the span had succumbed to the Night Witches' bombs. What remained stretched high enough over Lina's head that she didn't think she could get up on top of it. Even so, it was only half as tall as it had once been, judging by the ruins on either bank.

"Lina!" Paul's shout echoed over the water, and she turned her head in time to see him and Erik cresting the rise and walking out to the foot of the bridge. "All right?"

"As I can be!" she shouted back.

"Just hang on. We've got some rope. I'm going to weight it and throw it out to you, then Erik and I will pull you up, all right?"

"Fine. Please hurry!" As hot as the day had been, with her hair, clothes, and skin soaked to the bone, Lina shivered in the afternoon breeze. Her thighs and hips screamed with the effort required to stay in place atop her precarious perch. To distract herself, Lina reached out down the link to follow Paul's hurried consultation with Erik.

"What have we got?" Paul asked, looking around. "Maybe if we find a big enough stick, we could use that—"

"How about this?" Erik asked, pulling a bent metal ring out of his pocket. "When you mentioned throwing the rope, I thought you might want to weight it. This harness ring is no good for real use, but it should be heavy enough. You'll just have to take care not to hit Lina with it."

"Perfect, Erik!" Paul said with a tight smile. He reached out his hand for the piece and tied it on the end of the rope. Then he hefted it a few times, swung it around over his head to make sure it was secure, and nodded in satisfaction.

"Okay, Lina!" Paul yelled, turning back to her. "I'm going to throw this *past* you, all right? Don't try to catch it. Let the water push it toward you, then just grab onto the rope! Tie it around yourself, and then we'll pull you in."

"I'm ready!" Lina called back, flexing her skinned, sore hands.

It sounded easy enough, but it took several tries before Paul was able to toss the weight far enough past Lina that the current would push the rope toward her. On the fourth attempt, she reached out and grabbed hold, feeling a quick spike of victory as the rope caught on her abraded palms. She pulled it through the water toward herself, wrapping it under her armpits and tying a quick knot in front of her chest. Then she took a deep breath and sent an affirmative pulse to Paul through the link.

I'm ready, she thought again.

Good, he said. She felt him brace his feet and prepare to haul her in. *Jump off your log.*

Lina did so, unhooking her feet from their locked position as her muscles wept with relief. The current pushed at her again, threatening to tumble her around and disorient her, but the steady tension on the rope gave her focus. The water closed over her head once, and she gasped and spit it out of her mouth as she surfaced. She worked to streamline her body as meter by meter, Paul and Erik hauled her in to the base of the bridgehead. They kept pulling, hand over palm-burnt hand, straining backward so the weight of their bodies assisted as she started to rise up out of the water.

She tried to help. She reached out for the piled stone, seeking finger- and toe-holds that might allow her to support some of her own weight and ease the strain on her two rescuers above. Sometimes she was able to find something. Others, she scrabbled futilely against the spray-slick, explosion-blackened surface.

Eventually, however, the top of the roadbed came into view. Lina stretched her hands up and got her fingers hooked over the edge. The men hauled backward on the rope again, causing her chest to lurch her body up higher, and she slapped her palms down on the surface, then threw her torso forward and collapsed, legs still dangling down toward the water.

"Lina!" Paul gasped and dropped the rope. He stumbled, chest heaving, toward her, and fell to his knees beside her head as she dragged her knees in and tried to push up on shaking, trembling arms.

Erik, too, joined them, breathing heavily, his face a florid red. He reached out and helped Lina to her knees, then let her go as she fell toward Paul's waiting embrace.

Paul's arms wrapped around her, squeezed her tightly enough to make her feel secure. She dragged in one breath, then another, and took a moment to let his strength be her shield. Just for a moment.

"Rolland," she whispered as soon as she couldn't ignore the anxiety and guilt pushing in at the edges of her mind. She inhaled, drawing in the warm, sun-kissed scent of Paul's skin "We must go."

"Yes," Paul said, his chest rumbling as he spoke. "You're right." But he didn't move.

"Thank you," Lina said, leaning back and breaking the embrace. She turned and smiled at Erik. "Thank you both. I'm sorry I was so stupid as to get swept away."

"It's not your fault, dear Lina," Erik said with a gentle smile and a rueful shake of his head. "The creek bottom is treacherous. I should have waited and let you hang on to the cart as we crossed." He stood up and held out a hand to help her, which she gratefully accepted.

"It was an accident," Paul said, pushing up to his feet as well. "It happens. It's no one's fault. We handled it. Now Lina's right. We need to get moving."

Erik pulled some of the clothes from his haul out so Lina could change into dry things. The skirt and blouse were heavier than she would have ordinarily chosen for summer wear, but after being soaked through, she was grateful for the extra warmth, and Erik assured her they weren't far from their destination. She changed beside the cart, shielded from the road by a blanket held by Paul, while Erik and Rolland looked the other way. Her hair, too, was completely wet and had come loose from her usual chignon. She finger-combed it as best she could and left it loose, in hopes the summer sun would dry it out.

"I'm ready," she said, feeling slightly self-conscious. Paul lowered the blanket, then did a double take. She blushed and looked down at her feet.

I've never seen you with your hair down, he thought, and she had the sense he hadn't fully intended to articulate the feelings in his mind. *You look so…young!*

That's why I usually wear my hair up, she replied, letting him feel the dryness in her words. *I've spent my entire life convincing people to take me seriously in spite of my youthful appearance.*

You're beautiful, he thought. She looked up to meet the dark intensity of his eyes. *That's part of your problem. People see a woman with your delicate beauty, and have no idea of the steel that lies beneath.*

Thank you, she said. Even she wasn't sure which part of his statement she felt most gratifying.

Don't thank me, I'm simply telling the truth. That hidden steel is part of what makes you so dangerous, Lina Sucher…Rutherford.

But not to you.

Paul smiled, and she could see the intensity bleed away. For just a moment, she caught a glimpse of the bone-deep fatigue she knew edged his thoughts before he narrowed their connection again.

I love you, he said. *That makes you more dangerous to me than anyone. Let's go.*

And with that, he turned away and began to fold up the blanket.

* * *

Thirty minutes later, the rutted dirt under the cart's wheels smoothed out and gave way to cobblestones.

"You know," Erik said, looking back over his shoulder at Paul as the group walked through the remains of bombed-out houses on the edge of the town, "Fürstenwalde has a good hospital. My friend is a doctor there. We could take Rolland and have his hands treated now, by my doctor friend. Well before your doctor friend could arrive, I'd imagine."

"I wouldn't want to put your doctor friend to any trouble, Erik," Paul said with an easy smile. "Rolland is...you're all right, are you not?"

"I can manage," Rolland said, but his voice was tight, his face pinched with pain. The long journey hadn't been easy on him. Lina, walking next to him, wanted to reach out and comfort him somehow, but she had no idea what to do.

"Nonsense! Why wait and extend his pain?"

"A hospital is too official," Paul said firmly. "My friend can be here in a matter of hours. I don't want to endanger you, or anyone else, any more than I've already done."

"Ach, so stubborn," Erik said with clear affection in his voice. "What, then?"

"This is a big town. Is there a hotel, or somewhere you usually stay when you come?"

"Yes, you wish to go there?"

"Do they have a telephone?"

"Of course."

"Then yes, let's go there, please. I'll get us all a room, and we can at least make Rolland more comfortable while we wait."

"Fine," Erik said, gathering up the reins and urging his mule forward again, "but you must pay for the room," he added with a grin. Lina felt Paul's answering pulse of amusement and let her own lips curve in response. She wondered if Erik had had this much fun since his own war, a generation ago.

The hotel, like most of the town of Fürstenwalde, had obviously sustained some damage during the war. Still, it seemed a respectable enough place. Someone had clearly done a lot of hard work to make the toughest repairs, and the receiving yard and stable area looked immaculate. Cheery firelight spilled out from shuttered windows, and a large, smiling young man came to greet them as they drove up.

"Herr Tollenbach! You're back so soon! Welcome!" the young man said, stripping off his gloves as he approached. "And you've brought friends?"

"Yes, Fritz," Erik said, pulling the mule to a stop. He climbed down out of the cart, and greeted the strapping Fritz with a hearty handshake. "These are neighbors from my village, come to help me at the market tomorrow. Only Rolland, here, twisted his ankle on the way out and had to ride in the cart."

"Oh, how unfortunate; will you need help getting to your room, sir?"

"Oh, I think we can handle him," Erik said smoothly, patting Fritz on the shoulder. "If you will put my mule and cart up? Are your mother and father inside?"

"Yes, sir! Go on in. I'll handle this handsome man," Fritz joked, taking hold of the mule's bridle. He reached into his pocket and produced a twisted orange carrot, which the animal gleefully snatched. "We're old friends, are we not?"

"You seem to be," Erik said with a laugh. "Thank you, Fritz. Paul, you come help me with Rolland, and watch his bad ankle! Then we'll just go through those double doors there. Don't worry, they're not as heavy as they look…"

The old war ace kept up a steady stream of chatter as they filed into the foyer of the hotel. Like the outside, the place was scrupulously clean, if a bit spartan for a hotel. Lina could see someone was doing their best, however, for fragrant flowers stood here and there in vases, and every shuttered window had its complement of bright, checked curtains.

"Ah! Herr Tollenbach!" a woman's cheerful voice greeted them, drawing Lina's attention back from the surroundings. The woman smiled at Erik, and then let her eyes go wide as she caught sight of Lina, Paul, and Rolland behind him. "How may I help you today?"

The woman was Marta, Fritz's mother and, with her husband, owner of the hotel. Erik and Paul spoke with her about a room and food, while Lina hung back beside Rolland. To her great relief, the men concluded the business quickly enough, and before long, the sturdy matron led them down a long hallway to a room at the end.

"This is our largest suite," Marta said as she unlocked the door and held it open. "With four of you, including a young couple, you'll be needing two bedrooms, so I put you in here."

"Thank you, Marta, that will do nicely," Erik said as he accepted the key she held out and stepped past her into the room. Paul and Rolland followed, leaving Lina to bring up the rear. She smiled at the woman and murmured a quiet word of thanks as she passed, but

Marta didn't seem to hear her. She simply stared right past Lina and seemed to focus only on Erik.

Strange, Lina thought. Perhaps she doesn't like my clothing?

She's just comfortable with Erik, Paul said as he inspected the suite, looking out each of the windows and figuring out the layout of the rooms. *Strangers probably make her nervous.*

Then she should choose another career, Lina thought tartly. But as a rude hostess was the least of their problems, she let the matter drop and walked further back to explore the accommodations.

The suite wasn't particularly large, but it was more than Lina had hoped for. There were, in fact, two small bedrooms, each with two narrow beds. Between lay a small sitting area, where a sofa and two armchairs bracketed a low table. Both bedrooms featured wide windows secured with tight shutters that could be locked from the inside. There was no glass, though if she looked closely, Lina could see the frames for it. If she had to guess, she'd say the windows had been blown out by a bombing during the war, and the family had yet to procure enough glass to reglaze the whole establishment. In keeping with the rest of the hotel's appearance, the slightly threadbare rugs on the floor looked scrupulously clean, and someone had attempted to cheer the place up with a vase of wilting wildflowers.

"It's perfect, Marta, thank you," Erik repeated after he'd looked around briefly. "We'll stay tonight, and then leave after we finish our business at the market in the morning."

"I'll have the girl bring a tray," she said. "You won't need anything else?"

"No. Thank you."

Marta glanced at Lina then, finally, and looked quickly away before exiting and closing the door behind herself. Something uneasy twisted in Lina's belly, but she told herself it was merely hunger. The woman was a friend of Erik's. She was trustworthy, surely?

"Where's this telephone?" Paul asked as soon as the door was firmly shut.

"At the marketplace," Erik said. "I can take you whenever you like."

"Let's go now," Paul said, looking over at Lina. "Rolland can rest here, and Lina can wait for the food. Once I reach Philip, it shouldn't take him long to arrive, as he has his own car."

"Will it be dangerous for him to come to us?" Lina asked as the uneasiness refused to die inside her.

"I shouldn't think so. He's a doctor; he is forever being called out to help with this person or that."

"Your husband's right," Erik said. "No time to waste. Lina, you'll wait here with Rolland?"

"Of course," she said, turning to her old friend. "Let's get you settled."

By the time she'd helped Rolland use the small washroom and stretch out on one of the beds with a sigh of relief, Erik and Paul were gone. She sent a tendril of thought after Paul, just enough to let him know she was there, and felt his answering pulse of...something. She didn't dare name the feeling. She didn't want to think too closely about it.

A knock on the door heralded the arrival of a tray full of food and a bottle of good local beer. She brought Rolland a plate of the sliced sausage and onions and put it beside the bed for when he awoke. Then she made herself comfortable on one of the sofas and had her own share of the plain but hearty food.

Erik and Paul returned just as she was finishing up. Lina had known they were coming, of course, but she couldn't suppress a surge of gladness when the door to the suite opened and Paul, dark and handsome, walked through.

"Hello," she said, her lips curving softly.

"Hi," he answered. He didn't smile, but his eyes lit with that intensity she'd come to realize belonged only to her. The look in his eyes sparked desire into a low, smoldering flame deep in her center, and she stood up quickly to distract herself.

"Let me make you both a plate," she said.

"Serve your man first, my dear," Erik said from behind Paul. He gave Lina an indulgent smile and a wink. "I've taken care of myself for many years now."

"You care for us, I can care for you as well," she retorted softly, but with just a little sass.

"Just like my Maria," the older man laughed, "keeping us men in our place. You're in for a wonderful life with this one, my friend." He clapped Paul on the shoulder then walked past, back toward the washroom.

"Doc will be here in two hours," Paul said, his even tone at odds with the heat in his gaze.

"Will you bring him here?"

"At first. If he has what he needs, he can treat Rolland here and stay the night with us. If not, he can take us by car back to Berlin or elsewhere."

Icy fear streaked down Lina's spine. She shivered

"I don't want to go back to Berlin," she said. "That seems too dangerous."

Paul nodded. "I know. It's not my first choice, either, but it depends on what Doc needs to treat Rolland. Berlin may be our best option." He reached out and touched her cheek. "Your bruises are fading."

"Finally," she said, snorting softly. She wanted to argue more about their future plans, but Paul was right. They didn't know what the doctor would need to help Rolland, and until they did, there was no value to be gained in wrangling.

"How's your side?"

"Also better."

"Good," he said, stroking his fingertips along her cheekbone and tucking a stray strand of hair behind her ear. His touch ignited trails of fire under her skin, and she shivered again. "Are you tired?"

"Yes," she said.

"We should lie down and rest, then." His voice dipped low and got rougher. She licked her lips, and his eyes followed the movement of her mouth.

"You should eat first," she whispered.

I don't want to eat. You're all I want, he said, and she felt his desire searing through her mind. *I just need to feel your skin.*

Food is strength, don't be foolish.

Is it foolish? he asked. *You want me too. This also makes us stronger, Lina.*

Thanks to the heat from his touch and the liquid need rising inside her, Lina's head started to spin. She blinked, swallowed hard, and then nodded.

"Yes," she said, "but please, at least bring a plate with you..."

The corners of his mouth deepened, and triumph leapt inside his mind. He touched her shoulder, then slid his hand down her arm to entwine their fingers. She lifted her chin, reached for him, and he was there. His lips felt warm with the promise of more to come, and Lina's sudden need threatened to drown her.

Paul broke the kiss first. He stepped back, but didn't let go.

"Yes?" he asked, eyebrows raising.

"Yes," Lina said and pulled him back toward their bedroom. "You can eat later."

* * *

They both ate later. Lina even managed a bath, though it was mostly accomplished standing up in front of the water basin. She'd managed to get hot water sent over from the kitchen, and Paul had helped her with her hair. By the time Doc knocked at the door of their suite, Lina felt cleaner than she had in days.

"Where's this patient?" Doc asked with no preamble when Paul opened the door.

"This way," Lina said, indicating the bedroom where Rolland and Erik both rested. She thought about offering some small talk, but decided against it. She had no problems with being all business, especially when there was work to be done. Doc hefted his small bag and walked past her without another word. She glanced at Paul, then turned to follow the doctor.

"Open the shutters, please," Doc said. "I need more light in here." While Lina moved to comply, Doc walked over to the bed and gently nudged Rolland's shoulder.

"Hmmph?" Rolland asked, rolling from his side to his back and blinking in the sudden brightness as the last light of the day streamed in. In the other bed, Erik sat up and rubbed his eyes, blinking owlishly at all of them.

"I'm Doktor Wholrab," Doc said to Rolland. "I'm here to help you."

Rolland struggled to sit up, and Paul stepped forward to help him.

"Easy, easy," Doc said, holding out a steadying hand. "Try not to strain yourself until we know what's going on. Where are you injured?"

"My hands," Rolland's voice was rusty with sleep. He lifted his hands and Lina felt a twist of nausea as she looked fully at the mangled claws where his delicate, skillful hands had once been.

"What did they use?" Doc asked, his tone even. He took hold of Rolland's wrist and eased the fingers apart. The scientist's face creased, and he squirmed in the bed.

"Hammer," Rolland said, pain tightening through every word. Lina pressed her lips together and tried not to imagine it.

"Your fingers have started to heal," Doc said. "I won't be able to put them back exactly as they were, but I may be able to help. A little." He looked up at Paul.

"You can't do it here?" Paul asked. Doc shook his head.

"The bones have to be re-broken and set. I need an operating room, or at least proper anesthesia. Anything I do here would only make it worse and increase the possibility of infection."

"Where?" Paul asked. "Berlin's too hot."

Doc looked up, meeting Paul's eyes with a sober expression. "Frankfurt," he said. "One of the doctors in Oberursel is a hand specialist, and there are modern surgical facilities there. That's our best chance."

Paul pressed his lips together, then nodded. "We were headed that way anyway," he said. Lina looked up at this cryptic statement, but Paul's expression and the lines of their connection stayed opaque. Clearly, he didn't wish to elaborate.

"Frankfurt is hundreds of kilometers away," Erik said, sitting forward on his own bed. "It will take more than a day of travel with my cart."

"I have a car," Doc said. "It'll still take several hours, but we can be there by morning if we leave now—"

A heavy, rapid knock on the shuttered window made Lina jump. She reached for the latch with shaking hands, then looked at Paul. He pulled a pistol from where he'd had it stashed in his clothing and gave her a single nod. She lifted the latch and stepped quickly to the side, out of the way.

"Erik, my friend!" Fritz's broad, open face was pale under his tan. He gasped a little as he spoke, as if he'd run at a dead sprint to come talk to them. "I'm glad I caught you! My mother…I'm so sorry. My mother recognized the lady." He tilted his head in Lina's direction. "There was a flyer circulated. I'm sorry, Frau, you're being called a traitor and a criminal. I told mother that a hero like Erik would never take up with one of these…"werewolves" is the word they're using, but she didn't listen. I'm still her little boy, you see, and she's just trying to protect me. But she's gone to the police station, and I think it would be best if you all left now. She'll return, likely with the police, any moment now."

Lina reached out, skimmed the surface of the boy's mind. He shivered and looked oddly at her, but she ignored it.

He speaks the truth, she whispered into Paul's mind.

"Shit," Paul said. "All right. Let's go."

"I'm parked out front," Doc said. He gently placed Rolland's mangled hand down on the bed and straightened it up. "We can leave this moment."

"My apologies," Fritz said, leaning back and looking around the building, "but they're coming toward the front of the building now."

"Out the window," Paul said. He holstered his pistol and bent to lift Rolland like a small child. "Doc, you go first and take Rolland. Erik—"

"I'll come with you," the old man said, "and perhaps I can speak with Marta. She's an old friend."

"Erik…" Fritz said, misery and worry in his tone. "Mother is…different lately. She's frightened of everything, but especially that some doubt or disfavor may be cast upon me. You should go with your friends. I don't think she can be reasoned with right now."

Understanding dawned in Lina's mind. She'd seen that phenomenon before. She'd *used* it, back in Warsaw. Paranoia was a powerful motivator, and when the general climate of a community was one of fear and suspicion, people would do anything to keep their families safe. Including turn in other members of their family who weren't as close.

"Paul…" she said softly.

"No." He didn't even look at her, just nodded for Doc to precede him out the window. "Don't even think about it, Lina. I'm not letting them take you again."

"But I can…"

"No," Paul said again. Doc put one foot out the window, then swiveled around on his rear and stepped out. He and Fritz reached out to take Rolland and maneuvered him carefully through the aperture.

"But…"

"No!" He turned and grabbed Lina by the upper arms. "Lina, no. It's not an option. You're being branded a criminal. It won't be like last time; they're just as likely to shoot you as take you prisoner." He dragged in a deep breath and put his forehead against hers. "Please."

Lina closed her eyes and leaned into Paul's touch. Wave after wave of wordless love ran down the lines of their link, surging back and forth between the two of them.

I can't let you go through that again, and I can't risk losing you.

"Listen to your husband, my dear," Erik said, putting a hand on Lina's shoulder.

"You must come with us," Lina said, reaching out to catch the old man's hand in her own.

"We're all going, now!" Paul said, his tone leaving no room for argument or further dithering. He put his hand between Lina's shoulder blades and pushed her gently toward the window. Outside, Doc held up a hand to help her step through and out. Erik followed close behind her, and Paul came last, pulling the shutters closed behind himself.

"My car is just there," Doc said in a low tone, pointing to a line of vehicles parked in front of the main entrance to the hotel.

"You brought an ambulance?" Paul asked, raising his eyebrows.

"I thought it might help. You said we were in a hurry. That thing is fast!"

"But not inconspicuous!"

"You didn't *say* inconspicuous," Doc said. "Don't worry, it's getting dark. Without the lights, it looks just like another truck. Let me take Rolland. I'll help him walk as if he's drunk, and we're stumbling home."

"Doc, I don't think—" Paul's caution fell on deaf ears, however, because Doc slung Rolland's arm carefully over his shoulder and they began staggering out across the yard toward the line of parked vehicles. After a few steps, Rolland began to sing a slightly bawdy old song in a truly unique key.

Come to think of it, "sing" might have been a generous term. Bellow, maybe? Bray like Erik's trusty mule?

Whatever the word, the diversion clearly worked. Paul peeked around the corner of the building, and Lina could see through his eyes that a small group of men—some wearing police uniforms, some not—turned from the front door with varying expressions of tolerance and exasperation. They watched the show as Rolland and Doc stumbled across the yard toward the truck.

Any minute now, their attention is going to swing away from where we are, Paul thought to Lina. *Be ready. When they turn away from this corner of the building, we'll start moving. Keep to the shadows, and if they look toward us, turn into me for a kiss. Maybe Doc's idea about faking being drunk isn't so terrible after all.*

Lina sent him a pulse of acknowledgement, then reached back to squeeze Erik's hand.

"Be ready," she whispered. He squeezed her hand twice in response and let it go.

Now! Paul said, giving her a mental push. He straightened slightly and stepped out from behind the building, angling first away from the cars, toward a low hedgerow that offered a hint of some concealment. Lina followed, hurrying after him, reaching out for his hand...

Whizz-CRACK!

Lina hunched, heart racing as she heard the sound of men shouting and more gunshots. A pair of iron-hard hands appeared at her waist, and Lina felt herself lifted half off her feet as Erik picked her up and bodily hauled her across the rest of the yard to the parking area. Paul reached out and grabbed her hand, hauling her down to the ground behind the dubious cover of the sedan on the end of the row. Erik followed, dropping heavily to his knees before fighting to get his feet back under himself

"Keep her safe," Erik said, his bright blue eyes intense as he stared at Paul. "Cherish her always, my friend."

"Always," Paul said, his own eyes narrowing in confusion.

"Erik! No, you can't—" Lina said, struggling against Paul's restraining grasp. She reached out and grabbed at his jacket.

Erik leaned forward and pressed a kiss to her forehead. He reached inside his jacket and pulled out a small object with a trailing chain. He gently removed her fingers from his lapel and closed them around what he held.

"Care for your husband, my dear. Give him strong children," he said. And before she could do anything else, he surged to his feet and ran toward the police, firing his trusty Luger as he went.

"Go!" Paul yelled. Lina felt herself lifted and hustled along, her feet barely touching the ground as she watched the hail of gunfire arc toward her friend.

She didn't see him fall. Paul heaved her up and into the back of Doc's ambulance. She fell hard on her shoulder and barely kept her head from banging on the metal floor. Paul hit the deck next to her, and Doc stomped on the accelerator. The ambulance leapt forward, sending them sliding back toward the doors, which flopped open.

Paul cursed and braced himself with his feet, then sat up and reached out to pull the double doors closed.

Lina pushed herself up to a seated position and drew her knees up to her chest. The ambulance took a sharp corner, and she swayed, but caught herself with her closed fist on the floor. When the vehicle righted itself, she slowly opened her fingers and looked at the object Erik had given her.

The blue-enameled cross's sharp corners had cut into her skin, and the gilt lettering had worn nearly away, but there was no mistaking the shape and sheen of the Pour le Mérite medal. Lina swallowed hard against the tightness in her throat.

"He sacrificed himself to save us," Paul said, his voice low over the rumble of the ambulance's engine and the road noise. Lina nodded, not quite ready to speak. In her mind, she screamed and raged…but there was no time for that now. So she locked it away.

Later. She would mourn Erik later. When they were safe.

"Lina?" Rolland's voice came weak and broken from the litter mounted above them. "Paul?"

"We're here, Rolland," Paul said. "Erik didn't make it."

"We may not, either," Doc said, his voice drifting back to them from the front of the vehicle. "One of them is following us. I'm going to cut through town and try to lose him. Hang on to something if you can."

Lina reached out with her free hand without looking away from the medal she still held. Paul caught her fingers in his and tugged hard enough to get her attention.

"Lina," he said. *Stay with me. I need you. You can fall apart later, but I need you now.*

Lina swallowed hard and gave him a nod. She closed her fist around the medal once more and felt one corner bite into her palm hard enough to draw blood. The sharp, quick spike of pain zinged through her, but it allowed her to focus and settled her nerves. She nodded again and put Erik's chain around her neck, dropping the Blue Max inside her shirt.

Doc drove like a demon, sliding around corners and barreling through narrow alleyways as he fought to shake the police car that followed them. The scent of diesel exhaust mingled with the aromas of cooked meat and livestock as they cut through the busy market area in the center of the town. Without warning, Doc spun the wheel and sent them careening across the compartment as he took a sharp right turn.

Darkness dropped around them like a curtain, followed by an uneasy silence as Doc cut the lights, then the engine.

"Doc?"

"I doubled back to a warehouse and pulled into a loading dock," Doc said. "I don't think they saw me go this way. If they don't show up in the next few minutes, I think we might be all right."

"Won't they see us when we leave?" Paul asked.

"That's another reason I brought the truck," Doc said. "This whole area was a field hospital during the war. The town is lousy with old Ami ambulances like this one. Believe it or not, my friend, we'll just blend in."

It seemed too good to be true, but sure enough, when thirty minutes passed by and no one came looking for—or shooting at!— them, Doc cautiously backed the ambulance out into the street and joined the sedate flow of traffic.

A tense few minutes followed as they wound their way through the darkened streets and out to the highway. Lina shifted and tried to find a more comfortable seat on the floor of the vehicle. Paul must have felt her movement, because the next thing she knew, he handed her a blanket from a stack next to the wall.

"You might as well sleep if you can," Doc said as they sped deeper into the night. "Paul, I'll wake you to spell me in a while."

"Stretch out," Paul urged Lina. "It's not the most comfortable thing, but it might allow you to get a little rest."

"Thank you," she said. She took the heavy, scratchy wool blanket and shook it out, then wrapped herself in it, and laid down next to the foot of Rolland's litter. After a few moments, she felt Paul's warmth curling around her. She reached inside her shirt and pulled Erik's medal out again. She ran her thumb over the points and ridges of the object, and closed her eyes to focus on the ache in her chest.

How many? she wondered, her mind drifting somewhere between discomfort and misery. *How many good people need to die before this broken world can heal?*

Paul held her close in the darkness, but didn't answer.

He didn't know either.

* * *

Despite her discomfort, fatigue eventually won out, and Lina slept. She woke with a start when the ambulance slowed to a stop. Paul's arm was a comforting weight across her middle, and her shoulder and left arm were numb from lying on the floor of the vehicle. She still held Erik's Blue Max, and she lifted her hand to slip the chain back over her head and tucked the medal inside her shirt.

"What's happening?" Paul asked, his voice holding no trace of the sleepiness Lina knew clouded the edges of this thoughts. He let go of Lina and sat up, stretching his neck to peer out the back window into the darkness beyond.

"Fuel stop," Doc said. "This seemed a good place for it. We're out of the way, so it should be safe to take a quick break while I fill the tank."

"Want some help?" Paul asked.

"Thank you, yes," Doc said. "I've got extra fuel cans in the cargo compartment. It should be enough to get us to the American zone."

Paul worked his way over to the rear door of the vehicle and stepped out. Once he was gone, Lina had room to get up onto her knees and check on Rolland.

"Were you able to sleep at all?" she asked.

"Some," the scientist said, giving her a wan smile. "Mostly I was thinking of Erik."

"Me, too," Lina admitted, touching the slight lump in the front of her shirt. She swallowed hard and shook her head, pushing the wave of emotions back away from her conscious mind.

"Come," she said. "They'll be a few minutes refilling the petrol. Let's get out for a moment and breathe, away from the gasoline smell."

"All right," Rolland said. "Help me sit up."

With a little bit of maneuvering, and several quickly suppressed grunts of pain from Rolland, Lina managed to help him climb out the back door and step out onto the uneven ground. Rolland's legs were still unsteady, so he kept one hand on the side of the truck and walked slowly around it.

The moon rode high in the cloudless sky, and the lights from a nearby village weren't enough to obscure the millions of stars overhead. Lina tilted her face up and tried not to think about anything at all.

"I think I know where we are," Rolland said then, surprise spiking through his tone. Lina turned to see him looking around, pursing his lips as he took in the local landscape.

"Really?" she asked.

"Yes! I think we must be near the factory where I worked at the beginning of the war. In fact, unless I'm mistaken, this is the road that led to the camp where we got the workers." He turned again and then nodded, pointing up a hill a few hundred meters to their left.

"Look up there. You can just see the corner of a building. That was where they were kept until they could be put on a train to our tunnels."

"Tunnels?"

"Oh, yes. We were building rockets, my dear, so the entire complex was underground, for fear of Brit and Ami bombers."

"That was smart."

"Yes," Rolland said. He turned to face her, the moon and starlight throwing the lines on his face into stark relief. "Smart, perhaps, but it made it all the more miserable for the wretches who worked there."

"What do you mean?" Lina asked. "Were your facilities substandard?"

Rolland let out a bitter laugh. "No, not at all! That's the great irony of it. My lab at the factory was the envy of every chemist in the Reich. There was nothing we could not get, and our procurement channels were second to none, so we got it all very quickly. We were even, as I said, hardened against bombardment, so there was little danger there. At one time, it was even suggested that we bring our families to the complex to live, for their own safety. But I refused. I couldn't expose Isa and my sweet girls to that place."

"Why?" Lina asked, shaking her head slightly. "Maybe not bring them near the lab and its toxins or whatever you had, but surely the complex itself was safe—"

"Not for their souls, my dear friend." Rolland looked at her, and for the first time, Lina saw an intensity deep in his eyes that made her skin shiver. "I couldn't let them see this place. I couldn't watch their sweet innocence fade as they realized what we'd done—were doing."

"What were you doing?"

"We worked them to death, then left them where they lay. We gave them almost no food, only a little water. When they protested, we hung them from the great equipment cranes in lots of ten for the rest of them to see. We stationed SS guards to stand over them with rifles and orders to shoot if they didn't produce satisfactorily. We gave them no medical care, no place to sleep, no respite. When they took the train from those buildings down into our tunnels, that was the last time they would ever see the sun."

"Your workers?" Lina whispered, swallowing hard against the nausea his words elicited.

"Workers? Ha, yes!" Rolland gave another bitter laugh. "That's one name for it. Workers, slaves, prisoners. Take your pick. This place became known as *Konzentrationslager Mittlebau*, but it was originally part of the Buchenwald system."

"Buchenwald," Lina said, feeling the word slip from her lips as her mind tumbled back in her memories. "Why do I know that name?"

"You were an interrogator, yes? For the intelligence system? Rooting out dissidents and such?"

"Y-yes."

"Then the people you found probably ended up there," Rolland said, lifting the corner of his mouth in a horrid parody of a smile. He turned his head and looked around them at the moon-dappled landscape once more. "And maybe even here, worked to death next door to my laboratory."

"Rolland…" Lina breathed out.

"That was why I dared not bring my family here. So they were in Berlin when the Red Army rampaged. Surely Berlin should have been safe, no? But I had to work, here, where yes, we were doing evil…but it was for a greater good! That's what I told myself—it was for the greater good. And as horrible as it was that these political prisoners and criminals and dissidents died here, maybe their death meant something if it helped Germany to be victorious, to protect her people and give us what we needed to succeed on the world stage, right?

"But then we failed, and not only did all these deaths here mean nothing, all of a sudden, my wife's life, my precious daughters' lives meant nothing, *nothing* to the ravening monsters who sacked our capital. And I couldn't protect them. I couldn't be there to help them, because I was here, neck deep in futile evil."

Moonlight glinted off the tear-streaks that ran down Rolland's face. He took a deep, shuddering breath and looked around again. Lina followed suit, taking in the hills around them, the buildings, and the lights in the valley below. Her thoughts roiled, tangling and twisting with the disgust and horror and dread that bubbled up from within at his story.

Lina? Are you all right?

She took a deep breath and shoved everything back, put it in a box, and slammed the lid, locking it away for later, when she could deal with it all.

I'm fine, she said. *Can we go soon?*

"We're just about done," Paul called out to them from the other side of the vehicle, where he and Doc were finishing up. "If you two want to get loaded back up, we should get back on the road."

"Come on," Lina said to Rolland. "All that is past. We must go."

* * *

The road wound on into the night.

Doc had given Rolland morphine for his pain, so he slept for the remainder of the trip. Lina, curled once more on the metal floor of the ambulance, envied him. Her thoughts continued to race, careening from topic to topic, and veering uncomfortably close to the box where she'd shoved the whole of the conversation during the fuel stop. Every time her mind's eye pictured Rolland's tear-streaked face, or the corner of a building on a moonlit hill, she flinched away and forced her mind to think of something, anything else.

Well. Not *anything.* Not the blood-soaked tent in the snow. But anything else.

You should sleep some more, Paul said into her mind. His mental tone was soft, almost tentative. He rode up front in the ambulance's passenger seat, next to Doc. Lina could feel his protective drive rumbling in the background, but how was he supposed to protect her from her own thoughts?

I'm trying, she sent back.

I know, he replied, almost apologetically. *It shouldn't be too long now. A few hours to Frankfurt, if a constabulary patrol doesn't pick us up first. Doc's been avoiding the towns because of curfews, but the sun should be up soon, and that'll let us make better time.*

What will we do in Frankfurt? Lina asked, as much to distract herself as for any other purpose.

A few things, Paul said. *First, we have to take Rolland to the hand specialist, just outside Frankfurt proper. Then, once he and Doc are settled there, I thought…*

What? she asked, when he trailed off.

You want me, don't you? I mean, as your husband? You want to be married to me?

I am married to you, she said, not as surprised as she should be to find it true. Oh, perhaps the words hadn't been said, and they still lacked legal documentation, but in all the ways that mattered, Paul was hers. His steely devotion buoyed her, stiffened her resolve to make it through this, to get Rolland to safety, and to see Isa and the girls again. His volcanic passion lit her up from the inside and made her ache for just the smallest touch of his fingertips. She focused his considerable will and gave him more of a purpose than he'd had in…well, she didn't know how long, but she could tell it had been longer than he liked. Their psyches fit together like lock and key, and Lina wasn't entirely convinced either of them would survive a severing. Perhaps it was the fault of the psychic bond, but at this point, what did that matter? All that mattered was that they were together, intertwined, inseparable. No god could have joined them more completely. No man could ever put them asunder.

I know, he thought to her on a caress that made her skin tingle with need, *but do you want to make it official? Legal? You want to come home with me and everything?*

I won't be parted from you, she said. *I don't care about the rest. If we must do paperwork, I'll do paperwork. If I must pray, I'll pray. You don't need me to say this, you can feel the naked truth of my thoughts. I'll do whatever it takes to remain by your side, Paul. As you'll do—have done—to remain by mine.*

There's so much you don't know about me, he thought. Lina saw herself in his imagination, her skin bare to flickering firelight. She tasted the heat of her own lips in his memory. *I'm not a good man.*

None of our hands are clean, she said. *The war tore the world asunder and took us with it. We're just trying to put everything back together. You and I...well. I'm not going to pretend it isn't because of the bond. Maintaining a psychic link for so long has side effects, we know that.*

It isn't because of that, Paul protested, *or at least not only because of that. I've been linked up for an extended period before.*

Yes, but with your sisters. It's different when there's no blood relation. But it doesn't matter. In the end, it doesn't really matter why we're bound together, the fact remains that we are. And so I need you, and you need me.

Just like when we met, he said, and Lina couldn't miss the hard edge of irony in his tone.

Yes, and no. Then I needed you to keep people I cared about alive. Now I need you to keep me alive. Because without you...

Don't think it.

I won't. Because we're together.

You won't leave me, Lina?

Never, while I breathe.

The ambulance hit a bump, and Lina grimaced as the resulting jolt spiked pain through her still-healing ribs. Paul dropped his barriers and let her pain flow into him, lessening the ache and filling her psyche with the hot deliciousness of his presence. They stopped communicating in words after that, their minds silent but full of the back-and-forth ebb and flow of need and fulfillment. Lina focused her attention on him and reveled in the silky feel of his landscape, until the rocking motion of the ambulance pulled her back into an uneasy sleep.

Lina, wake up. We made it.

Paul's gentle prodding penetrated the uneasy formlessness of Lina's sleep, and she opened her eyes to see that the inside of the ambulance had begun to lighten. Was the sun rising?

Only just. But more importantly, we've made it to the American zone. Doc's turning into a US Constabulary station right now. Things may happen fast, so wake Rolland up and follow my lead.

She sent him a silent acknowledgment and pushed up onto her knees to shake Rolland's shoulder. In the dawn light, the scientist's face looked even more grey and wan than it had the day before, and fear prickled at the edge of her mind. Was something wrong with him beyond his hands? He'd obviously been beaten all over…had he sustained internal injuries beyond what they knew?

Doc will figure it out, Paul said. *Just leave him be if you can't wake him. Here come the Circle C Cowboys.*

* * *

Paul notwithstanding, Lina found she still didn't really like Americans.

The "Circle C Cowboys," as Paul referred to the United States Constabulary troops, were a brusque lot. Normally, Lina didn't mind such things from government officials. It usually spoke to a higher level of efficiency, which she appreciated. But these men, wearing the uniform of U. S. Army soldiers, but with insignia that declared them something like police officers, seemed content to waste everyone's time with a million and one questions.

Meanwhile, Rolland still didn't wake. Doc stayed with him, under guard, while Lina and Paul were each taken to separate rooms to be interviewed.

"Frau Rutherford," one of the constables said, locking his gaze on her face, "tell me again how you met your husband."

"I was visiting mutual friends in the American zone in Berlin, and we had lunch together."

"And this was how many days ago?"

Lina thought back, trying to count them up. The days and nights had run together, and she really had no idea how long she'd been held in the security facility before Paul got her out.

"A week, perhaps? Maybe a little more," she said.

"That's a quick courtship." The constable's tone dripped disbelief and suspicion. "And when were you married?"

"Two nights ago, in Brandenburg."

"And do you have a marriage certificate or any sort of documentation from a priest? How do we know you are really married?"

"I don't have any papers," Lina said. "My husband said we can get them here in this zone, since he's American."

The constable leaned back in his chair; it creaked under his muscular weight, but didn't collapse. Lina felt a tiny, mean stab of disappointment.

"You have to understand how this looks, Frau Rutherford," he said, emphasizing her name.

"How does it look?"

"It looks a lot like you might be a commie plant, trying to worm your way into the US Army's intelligence secrets as a honeypot. That man of yours, he does pretty much whatever you want? He looks right smitten to me."

Lina pressed her lips together, but the laughter bubbled up inside her and spilled out anyway. It wasn't humor, it was something between derision and hysteria at the idea of her being a communist spy.

Lina? Paul's attention turned from his own interrogation as he sensed her suddenly volatile state.

He thinks I'm a spy. I'm tempted to scramble his mind.

Don't do that, he's just doing his job! Paul's words rushed into her mind, nearly tumbling over themselves in their eagerness. Lina ignored him, pulling in her power. She felt it like a glowing heat along every nerve. With a thought, she gathered that delicious searing together, twisted it into a point, and held it poised to strike.

Lina! Don't! Paul shouted in her head. *Just...just wait a moment, will you! Damn it! Just wait!*

In the back of her mind, a tiny corner of her consciousness flowed through the link to look through his eyes and hear with his ears. She saw him look at his own interviewer; the senior constable at the station.

"Lieutenant," Paul said, "I haven't been perfectly honest with you up to this point." He reached into his shirt and pulled out a small folding wallet. He flipped it open to reveal a printed card, which he handed to the constabulary officer. The young man took it and read it, his eyes widening as they scanned the text.

"S-sir," the lieutenant stammered. "I-I had no idea…"

"I know," Paul said. "I wanted to keep it that way for your protection. You did just as you should have. However, I have to cut this short because your trooper is in terrible danger. The one interrogating my wife? She…well…she's one of my assets for Operation Confiscate. She has a colorful history, and I didn't do a good enough job preparing a cover story for her. I need you to stop her interrogation immediately."

"But, sir…"

"I know, I know, it's irregular. But you see that card, and the signature on it. Please, lieutenant, help me save your man before she damages him permanently."

"How could she—"

"We both know I'm not going to answer that. So just get off your ass and protect your trooper, Lieutenant." Paul's voice cracked like a whip, and the young lieutenant visibly jumped.

"Fine," he said, his voice cooling significantly, "but I'll have to report this—"

"No you won't, you read the card. I'm telling you, kid. This is your only way out. Go stop the interrogation, and we'll wait here while you phone Bamberg."

The lieutenant stood up and tugged on his uniform jacket.

"Fine," he said again. "Please wait here, sir."

Paul gave the young man a nod and watched as he exited the small interview room. Then he reached back across the lines.

Lina?

I haven't killed the man yet, she reassured her husband. *He's staring at me. I think he expects me to crack under the pressure. You Americans do your interrogations much differently than we did.*

Sometimes, Paul said, *not always. Look, I'm sorry. I screwed up. I should have prepped a better cover story for us all. Instead, I had to tell the lieutenant who I am and that you and Rolland are assets I'm looking to acquire.*

I saw, Lina said. *I didn't realize that I was intended to be more than a key to Rolland.*

The truth is, the Army's as interested in what you can do as what he can do, but now...

Now what?

Now I don't want them to have you.

Lina wanted to ask what he meant, why the thought of the US Army Intelligence service using her as an asset made a deep unease roil through his mind, but she didn't get the chance. The door to the interview room flew open, making both her and the constable jump. He tried to cover his surprise by popping up to his feet as his senior officer walked into the room.

"Lieutenant," the constable said.

"Trooper, you've done very well here, and I'm proud of you, but you need to stand down this interview. Mrs. Rutherford and her husband and party are cleared into the Zone."

"But, sir—"

"I know what it looks like," the lieutenant said, holding up a hand, "but I checked with Headquarters in Bamberg. Rutherford's one of ours, and they said to help him bring whoever he's got across." He clapped the constable on his big, beefy shoulder. "You did well, trooper, but this is above our pay grade."

The trooper squinted suspiciously at Lina one more time, then shrugged and nodded to his commanding officer.

"Yes, sir," he said.

"Good man," the lieutenant said. "Mrs. Rutherford, if you'd like to follow me, I'll escort you to your husband and party, and we'll see what we can do to get you all to Frankfurt."

* * * * *

Chapter Seven – Integration

The constables gave them some petrol and food and sent them on their way. Paul offered to let her sit in the front of the ambulance, but she demurred. She reasoned that it might be useful to have him up front with his US Army identification and such. Besides, she wanted to keep an eye on Rolland.

He had woken, briefly, as they were loading him back into the ambulance. He was delirious, and his skin burned hot with fever, but even that little bit of consciousness gave Lina hope.

"We're almost there, my dear friend," she whispered to him, stroking his face with a damp cloth as the ambulance wound its way out of the constabulary station and back onto the highway. "Not much longer now. We're taking you to Frankfurt. They have wonderful doctors there. You'll be well in no time at all!"

Rolland's head rocked from side to side with the motion of the vehicle, but he gave her a wan smile before closing his eyes once more. She sighed and turned to look out the front window.

Before too long, she started to see houses and buildings cropping up alongside the road. Plenty of them were still in ruins, but there was much evidence of new construction, and the whole place looked almost cheery in the midmorning light. When they pulled to a halt,

239

Lina looked out the back window to see a group of children playing ball not far away in a field dotted with summer wildflowers. A sudden ache of longing to see Johanna, Aleda, and Ginette slammed into her, and she swallowed hard and forced herself to smile at the sight.

She turned back around to see that they'd arrived at a security checkpoint. Paul handed his little folding wallet to the guard outside, who studied it and returned it without any of the astonishment the lieutenant at the border had shown. The guard raised his hand in a salute, and once Paul had returned it, he stepped back and waved them onward. Doc put the ambulance in gear, and as it rolled forward, Paul turned around in his seat to look at her.

"Welcome to one of the most secret locations on Earth," he said.

"Frankfurt?"

"Oberursel," he said, his lips curving just a little at her flippancy. "Home of Operation Confiscate."

"What's that?" she asked. "You mentioned it before, in Berlin when we met."

"You remember when I said there are mechanisms to allow German scientists like Rolland to work for the United States? Operation Confiscate is one of them, but it's the most secret one, because we work to retrieve assets who may be trapped in the Soviet sectors."

"Retrieve?"

"Liberate."

"Blackmail?" she asked, an edge to her voice. She might need Paul like she needed to breathe, but that didn't mean she'd forgotten that he'd held the safety of the Thanhouser girls as surety for her cooperation.

He swiveled around to look more fully at her as Doc stifled a laugh next to him.

"If necessary," Paul said, his tone calm and even. "Blackmail, kidnap, coerce. We'll do whatever it takes to keep the assets out of Soviet hands."

Including marriage?

Now you're just trying to trap me.

No, I'm trying to understand you. I know you love me, but I'm not sure what else to believe.

You don't have to believe anything else, he thought to her. *You feel what I feel, you know what's on my mind. I told you, you're more than an asset to me now, and I'll do whatever it takes to keep you safe, too. But that may mean allowing them to treat you as an asset. Do you understand that?*

Better than you, I imagine, she replied tartly, *but you need to understand this: I won't be parted from you. I've lost everyone I've ever loved, and it was your government that took them from me. They* will not *take you as well.*

Her steely conviction caused a shiver of unease to run up the length of his spine; the sensation ricocheted down their connection to her.

Don't do anything crazy, Lina, Paul warned her.

Don't let them make me, she shot back.

Doc pulled into a building that bore a large red cross on a white field and parked the vehicle. He stepped out and yelled something in English, and four large men came running. They opened the back door, pulled Rolland's litter out, and carried it inside, Doc hot on their heels. Paul stepped out, too, and came around to the back of the vehicle, then held out a hand to her.

Lina looked at him for a long moment, then put her fingers in his and allowed him to pull her from the vehicle. He pulled her close, wrapped his arms around her, and held on like a drowning man. She felt his biceps flexing iron-hard against her frame and his chest shudder as he dragged in a deep breath.

We did it, he thought to her. *We made it. We're safe.*

She opened her shields and let his relief and pent up fear flow through her mind and out, content to give him the catharsis he needed. In the back of her mind, however, so quietly Paul couldn't have noticed if he'd tried, a tiny doubt raised its voice:

Are we, though?

* * *

Oberursel was an interesting place.

It had the feel of a military installation, something that made Lina vaguely uneasy. Still, she told herself as Paul offered her his arm, she *was* now married to an American military officer. She supposed she'd have to get used to it.

"Where are we going?" she asked a few minutes later as they headed down a sidewalk away from the hospital building where Rolland had been taken. The day had started to reach its summer heat, but a cool breeze skittered across her skin as they walked, bringing with it the fresh scent of cut grass. Somewhere in the distance, a lawn mower droned through the melodic chirping of birds in the trees overhead. Much like that morning in Berlin a week and a lifetime ago, the day felt surreally pleasant.

"Doc said he thought they'd take Rolland to surgery right away, and there may be other injuries to contend with, so I think they'll be busy for a long while. There's a small chapel down this road a ways; I thought we might speak with the chaplain and make things official."

She felt his bicep flex under her fingers as he spoke, and despite his best attempt at shielding, a bit of sudden anxiety leaked through to her. She stroked his arm and sent a pulse of love and need and desire his way.

"If you like," she said, and felt a stab of pleasure at the way his pupils dilated in response to her emotions. He swallowed, his Adam's apple bobbing up and down, and nodded.

They continued down the sidewalk and turned down a pretty cross street with neat, identical houses all in a row. They looked newly constructed, with saplings rather than trees in the yards, and flowerbeds with that same uniform look to them.

"Who lives here?" she asked.

"Hmm? Oh, this is family housing for our assets. There's a school a little further down, too, past the chapel."

"For the assets? Are Isa and the girls here?" Lina asked with a surge of sudden, irrational hope.

"No, they went with her sister to Virginia, as we promised." *Because of the girls' talent,* he went on silently. *They're assets as well, and more valuable than even the scientists here.*

They'll be safe, won't they? Lina asked, once again disturbed at the idea of the US Army turning the sweet little Thanhousers into "assets."

I gave you my word, Paul said. *Remember, Connor is their uncle, too. No one wants to see three little girls exploited.*

Pretty to think so.

None of us do, anyway, he amended. *Look, here's the chapel.*

Lina looked up to see a small building with an unassuming white spire nestled in next to the trim houses. A message board declared it to be a US Army chapel, and it had times for various denominations of services—including a Jewish one on Friday, she noted. Lina herself had never really had a problem with Jewish people, so long as they weren't enemies of the state. She'd heard the anti-Jewish rhetoric during the war and had figured most of it was simple rabble-rousing. In her mind, it didn't matter what one believed, or what family one was born into. What mattered was whether or not one did one's duty. During the war, she'd done her best to do hers, for her country, and her dead family, and her lost love. Now...

Well, now she was doing her duty by her neighbors, who'd become her new family, and by Paul, who'd become her new love. And maybe, maybe she had a duty to herself as well. In this broken world, didn't she have a duty to try to make herself whole?

These thoughts tumbled around in her head as Paul led her up the brick walkway and short wooden steps to the front doors of the chapel. He opened the door without knocking and ushered her into the cool darkness beyond.

"Can I help you?" The voice that spoke the English words was soothing and warm, and Lina blinked rapidly to try to help her eyes adjust to the dim interior after the bright summer day outside. Her English was spotty at best, but Paul understood the words, so she pulled the meaning and import from his mind.

A smiling man wearing the uniform of a US Army captain stepped forward. On his chest, where Paul wore his aviator wings, this captain wore a simple device in the shape of the Christian cross.

"Chaplain, yes, yes you can," Paul said, stepping inside and reaching around Lina to offer his hand for a shake.

"Major Rutherford!" the chaplain exclaimed. His smile grew, and pure delight flowed across his features. "I'm glad to see you! I'd ask where you've been, but I don't believe you'd tell me."

"Probably best I don't," Paul said with a small smile. "This is Lina."

"Hello, Lina," the chaplain said. "I'm Chaplain Bryce Saunders. What can I do for you today?"

"We'd like to be married," Paul said, and the chaplain blinked rapidly.

"Major?"

"That's right," Paul said. "We'd like to be married as soon as possible. Now, in fact."

"But…Major, that's a big decision; why the rush?"

"Look, Chaplain," Paul said, his voice patient, his internal mind decidedly not. "I can appreciate your position here, but you know me, I'm not some young reckless soldier who found the first fräulein that wasn't going to charge. Lina and I are already wedded together, but we need to make it official in the eyes of the Army. Because we will not be separated."

The chaplain looked at Paul for a long moment, his penetrating gaze odd for someone of such apparent youth. Paul stared right back, and Lina could feel him willing the chaplain to feel his sincerity as the seconds ticked by.

"And this is what you want, Fräulein?" the chaplain asked.

"Yes," Lina said, twisting her tongue to pronounce the English words as clearly and firmly as possible. "I stay with Paul. I am his wife."

The chaplain let out a sigh, then smiled at them both.

"Well," he said, "you both seem quite determined, and I'm here to serve your spiritual needs. If this is what you need, then I shall serve. Meet me there in front of the altar; I must go get my vestments and the ceremony from my office."

As the chaplain left, Paul led her further into the chapel itself. It wasn't a large building, and it was barely adorned, especially compared to the great ancient cathedrals she'd visited in her youth. But the summer sun shone through the high, arched windows and gave the polished wooden pews and floor a warm, lit-from-within kind of glow. The altar itself lay under a snowy cloth with a beautiful, multicolored embroidery around the edge. As they walked closer, Lina could see the embroidery contained an intricate vine and dove motif, and she felt a stab of awe for the seamstress who'd created such beautiful work.

Despite her lack of religious sentiment, Lina couldn't deny that the chapel held a peace that sank into her being, soothing frayed and worried nerves as it went. She slid her hand down Paul's arm and laced their fingers together, prompting a smile from him.

"Are you ready?" Paul asked as the chaplain returned through an unobtrusive door behind the altar, this time with an ecclesiastical robe over his uniform.

"Yes," Lina said and let her husband lead her up the two steps toward the altar.

The ceremony itself was short and to the point. Essentially, the two of them swore to love, honor, and cherish one another, to forsake all others, and to be loyal unto death. These were easy promises for Lina to make, especially since she'd already made them back in Erik's cabin. Chaplain Saunders then prayed over them, invoking the blessings of his god upon them, their marriage, and their future children.

Children.

That was something she hadn't considered.

Nor did she have time to consider it then, for the chaplain was congratulating them both and shaking Paul's hand. He offered Lina a hug, but she demurred with a smile, and he accepted that with good grace.

"Thank you, Chaplain," Paul said. "You don't know how much this means to us."

"I think I might have an idea," the chaplain said with a bit of a mischievous twinkle in his eyes. "Now we're all finished, except for signing the marriage contract. So let's do that now, and then you're all official."

"Excellent," Paul said. A signature from each of them later, and it was done. They were officially married in the eyes of the United States Army.

Not that it mattered much to Lina. But it made Paul happy, and that was enough.

They walked back out into the summer sunshine, and the dark, enigmatic American she'd once feared as her enemy's enemy wore a smile that reached all the way to his eyes. That alone was enough to let Lina carry a bit of the chapel's peace away with her in her heart. Deep contentment saturated their link from both directions, nearly intoxicating in its comprehensiveness.

"You must be tired," Paul said after a few silent, joy-filled steps.

"A little," Lina admitted, stifling a yawn as the breeze fluttered through the saplings along the street.

"I have a small billet here," he said, "in Oberursel. It's not much, but it will be quiet. Let's go there, and we can get some rest."

"When will we hear about Rolland?"

"Probably not for a while; though I think there's a dinner tonight. We should see Doc there, and we can ask him for an update then."

"A dinner? Formal?"

"Yes, why?"

Lina looked up at him and shrugged. "I don't have anything to wear. Is that important here?"

Paul blinked, then pursed his lips. "You know, it might be. That's a good thought. I'll see what I can do about finding you something while you rest, all right?"

"What about you? You were up all night, too; don't you need to sleep?"

"I slept in the ambulance some."

"So did I," she pointed out, "but I mean real sleep, in a real bed."

He shot her a lightning-quick grin so brief she almost missed it. "I can stay up for days on end if I have to, but if you're inviting me to join you…"

She snorted a laugh, and then sent a pulse of incandescent desire down their connection. He stumbled, inhaling, as his mind reeled from the volcanic heat of her need for him.

"Always," she said softly, squeezing his fingers.

"*Mein Gott*," he whispered in mock-horror. "What have I done to myself?"

To that, she laughed out loud.

* * *

Despite all the playful words and banter, however, Lina ended up sleeping alone for the remainder of the day. Paul took their signed marriage certificate and said that he had a bit more paperwork to do to ensure she was registered as his wife. Lina got the impression—both from his words and from the feel of his mind as he told her—that he was cutting a few bureaucratic corners and maybe calling in a favor or two in order to push the process through, but when he returned to his small apartment in the early evening, his mind radiated a kind of exhausted triumph.

"It's done," Paul said with a smile, making her look up from drying her hair. She'd awakened about an hour prior and had taken the opportunity to bathe. He walked into the bedroom where she sat with a towel wrapped around her and leaned down to deliver a scorchingly passionate kiss—despite his obvious fatigue.

"Wh-what?" Lina asked as she tried to gather her wits once he let her breathe again.

"It's done. You're officially registered as Mrs. Adalina Rutherford. The Army has your information logged into their records and is working with the Embassy to get you entry into the US. That shouldn't take more than a few days or so, and then we can head home."

Lina blinked at the word "home." Home was here! Or…well…in Berlin. When she was a girl, it had been Bremen. But certainly Germany. Never in a million years would she have used that word to describe some distant city in America. All of a sudden, she realized she didn't even have an idea as to *which* American city was "home."

Paul was hers and she, his. She knew, intimately, every line of his mental landscape…but in many ways, her husband was still a stranger.

"Tell me about your family," she said, causing him to glance up from where he'd been busily removing his shoes and preparing for his own cleansing ablutions.

"Not much to tell," he said. He looked at her for a moment before going back to his task. "My parents died when I was young; I was raised by my grandmother."

"And your sisters?"

"Hmm? Oh, yes. My twin died when we were twelve. There was an accident in a swimming hole."

"And your other sister?"

"Still alive."

"Where is she? Is she married? Does she have children?"

He looked up again and tilted his head to the side. She felt puzzled curiosity and an odd wariness flowing from his mind.

"She's married. She lives in a place called the Black Hills, out west in South Dakota. No children. Why the sudden interest, Lina?"

"You said we were going home, but I don't know where home is. Mine, such as I have, has been Berlin for the last few years, but that's closed to me now. I just realized that I know you, but I don't know anything about you, or your family, or your home."

"I grew up in Chicago," he said, standing up and pulling off his shirt. The sight of his bare chest with its lean musculature was almost enough to distract Lina from the conversation. Almost.

"Where's that?"

"In a state called Illinois, in the midwest. It's on the shores of a huge lake. It's one of our biggest cities, filled with all manner of people. I had a rough time growing up, especially after my sister died. I fell in with a rough crowd, did some things I'm not proud of. My grandmother set me straight, sent me to college. Then the war came, and I joined up, went to flight school, became a bombardier."

A horrible sinking feeling roiled through Lina's chest.

"It could have been you who killed my family," she whispered. "It could have been you who dropped those bombs."

"Where?"

"Bremen."

He shook his head, walked toward her, and reached out to take her hands. He drew her up to her feet and folded her into a gentle, but insistent embrace.

"It wasn't me," he said, kissing the top of her head. "I never did a mission over Bremen."

Lina let out a breath she hadn't realized she was holding and sagged against him, her cheek coming to rest on his bare chest.

"I'm sorry," she whispered. "We were on opposite sides during the war. I know that. It's just…if it had been you…"

"It wasn't," he said, kissing her again, "so let's not think about it. No sense borrowing trouble, sweetheart."

"You're right," she said, but deep inside her mind, that voice of doubt wondered. Would she someday meet the man who killed her family and destroyed her childhood? Would she know it if she did?

Would it matter?

To prevent herself from falling into that particular mental abyss, Lina kissed her husband back, which led them down a predictable, yet highly enjoyable path of mutual distraction that left them breathless and replete, and with barely enough time to get cleaned up and dressed before their dinner appointment.

"I almost forgot," Paul said as he walked into the bathroom and turned on the taps. "I found you a dress. It's in in the living room.

Hopefully it's not too big. I borrowed it from the general's wife. She's almost as thin as you."

"I'm sure it will be fine," Lina said, trying to stifle the sudden electric tingle of excitement that ran down her spine. It had been *ages* since she'd worn anything fancy. She'd never been a particularly vain woman, but once upon a time, she'd liked to dress up and look pretty for the other girls and boys in her school. As soon as Paul was busy washing himself, she slipped from the bed and padded on bare feet into the living room, where a midnight blue gown lay draped across the back of the sofa.

The gown itself was simply cut, with a high, wide waistband from which the skirt cascaded in satiny folds to the floor. The bodice featured a lower cut, heart-shaped neckline of pearl-grey silk. This was to be covered by a deep ocean blue short jacket—the same hue as the skirt, but covered all over in intricate beading that caught the light and scattered it in blue-black fire. A pair of black mid-length satin gloves and black leather pumps completed the ensemble.

Lina reached out a trembling hand and traced the line of beading on the jacket's hem. She could hardly imagine wearing something so beautiful, but all of a sudden, she *wanted* to, with a longing that surprised her with its vehemence. She carefully, reverently gathered the outfit's pieces up and carried them in to the bedroom so she could try them on.

"Lina?" Paul called out a short while later. "Are you still in—"

Lina turned away from the small mirror mounted over his chest of drawers and faced the bathroom door. He stood there with a towel wrapped around his waist, framed by the bright light behind him, staring at her with his mouth slightly ajar.

"Do I look all right?" she asked, her voice soft and tentative.

The wave of emotion that hit her through their connection actually made her stumble backward. Raw, primal lust carried with it an exquisite edge of something so poignant, so pure, it brought tears to her eyes. He wanted her. He desired her. She was all in his world, and he loved her beyond reason. Seeing her dressed this way, with her hair piled softly atop her head, leaving her long, slender neck bare, stirred things deep inside him he'd long thought dead and buried.

You make me better, he thought to her. *I'm not a good man, Lina. You make me want to be a good man.*

We are none of us angels, my love, she sent back, reaching her hand out toward his.

You look like one. He caught her fingers, then pressed a kiss into her palm, and on the inside of her wrist. *Let me get dressed, or we shall be late. The general's wife is going to be furious that you look so much more beautiful in that dress than she ever could.*

Wariness rose within Lina at that, but she pushed it away and concentrated on the feel of his lips on her skin. Women, she knew, could be catty and horrible, but she'd handled their jealousies before, and she could handle them again. As Paul had said earlier, no need to borrow trouble.

"Dress," she said. "I'll await you in the living room."

A few moments later Paul emerged from the bedroom, looking moderately splendid in his formal uniform. He offered her his arm, and they left the apartment to meet the general's driver downstairs at the bottom of the building.

"General DiNote is a damn good man," Paul said to her as they walked. "He's real happy we recovered Rolland and brought him back."

"Is that why he sent his driver to pick us up?"

Paul snorted a laugh. "Officially, probably. But the real reason is more than likely because Mrs. DiNote told him to. She's the kind of woman who's in the know about everything. She wanted to meet you, so she made sure you had a dress and a way to get to her dinner party."

"She sounds formidable."

"She is that, in spades."

Lina's unease about meeting Mrs. DiNote ratcheted up another notch, but she swallowed it down and locked it behind her cool, icy façade. She'd faced down criminals and ravening soldiers alike. One pampered American woman should be no trouble at all.

She straightened her shoulders, lifted her chin, and flatly refused to let her mind think about the only other American woman she'd ever met. This general's wife couldn't be Evelyn Adamsen. The name was wrong, for one, and for another, Lina would know if Adamsen were that close.

It had been over five years...but Lina knew she'd feel the proximity of the woman who'd ripped her world apart a second time and slaughtered the brothers and first love of her heart. There was too much between them. She would know.

Compared to Adamsen, facing down the formidable Mrs. DiNote should be no problem at all.

* * *

"Call me Jamie!" the general's wife said, joy in her voice as she grinned widely and wrapped her arms around Lina in an enveloping kind of hug. She squeezed Lina tightly, then let go to hold her at arm's length.

"My heavens! Don't you look beautiful? I love that dress on you! Chris, doesn't Mrs. Rutherford look simply ravishing?"

Jamie DiNote turned to look over her shoulder at her husband, who stood shaking Paul's hand. Major General Christopher DiNote was shorter than Paul, shorter than Lina herself, but he radiated confidence and competence, and he awarded his wife an easy grin.

"Almost as beautiful as you, my dear," he shot back, winking.

"Oh, good man," Jamie said, laughing and turning back to look up at Lina. "I have him well-trained, as you see. Welcome to our home, dear. We're *so* very glad you're here."

"Thank you," Lina managed to murmur. The DiNotes' easy welcome had surprised her. She'd been gearing herself up to do battle with a preening harpy of a woman, and instead found herself embraced like a sister and welcomed effusively—and in flawless German! Jamie must have noticed her wrong-footedness, because she laughed and slipped her arm through Lina's.

"I'm sorry, dear. I can be a bit much from time to time. I was just so thrilled to hear that Paul had found someone, and one of his contacts at that! I may be an old soldier's wife, but I confess to being a hopeless romantic on the inside. And to have it happen so fast! If it were anyone other than Paul, we'd worry that he'd been compromised, but he's the very model of a perfect operative."

"Your German is very good," Lina said, mostly to change the topic, but also because she was incredibly curious. "You speak like a native."

"Ah! Well, thank you for that," Jamie said. "I lived in Vienna for a few years when I was young…family connections there, you know. You pick things up. Come, I'll introduce you around to everyone."

This explanation felt a bit too flippant and pat for Lina's interrogator's instincts, but she could hardly begin questioning her hostess intensively whilst standing in her foyer. So she just smiled and let Jamie lead her through a set of double doors and into a parlor that contained several other ladies.

Paul?

It's all right, he said. *She's just taking you to meet the wives. I'll see you in a few minutes. The general wants to talk to me about something. Careful. Some of those ladies are real pieces of work.*

Paul! Lina tamped down hard on her urge to laugh.

You'll see what I mean.

Walking into the parlor felt like walking into a garden filled with poisonous flowers. Lina didn't know if it was due to her power or not, but for whatever reason, she felt various emotions emanating from the women who, one and all, turned to watch as Jamie DiNote led her into the room. Everything from simple curiosity, to catty skepticism, to outright hostility sizzled through the air at her, and Lina threw up another layer to her mental shields in sheer defense. Jamie glanced over at her, sympathy in her eyes, and gave her a wink.

"Buck up," she whispered in German. "They can't actually stab you."

"Jamie," a beautiful brunette simpered, walking forward with a supercilious smile and a mincing step in her too-tight emerald green silk. "Who is this lovely person?"

"Ladies, this is Lina Rutherford, Major Paul Rutherford's new bride," Jamie said in English.

An audible gasp rippled through the room, as surprise joined the other emotions swirling in the air. The woman in the green dress raised a hand to her chest. "Oh, my," she said, drawling her words out in a manner that made it harder for Lina to understand. "Mrs. *Paul Rutherford*, as I live and breathe. We never thought we'd see the day, did we, ladies?"

"Surprise," Jamie said, her words deadpan and dry. "Lina's been in Berlin since the war ended, and has just joined us from there this morning."

"Well! That must have been an adventure!" Green Dress said. "You'll have to tell us all about it during dinner, dear."

"I don't think so," Lina said, conscious of how clipped her English sounded. "It is not a story to be told over dinner."

Green Dress recoiled, her delicate arched eyebrows climbing up her forehead. "Well," she said again. It was clearly a favorite exclamation. "I'd never attempt to pry, of course! It's just, for you to come in here, as lovely as you are, just *dripping* mystery...and with that *precious* accent...Well. And then we learn that you're married to Major Mysterious himself! It's quite the event, isn't it, girls?" She turned around, her green satin skirts swishing, to nod at the other assembled women, who made various noises of agreement.

"Annette," Jamie said, her tone even drier at this blatant display of melodrama, "no need to make Lina uncomfortable. Let's not put her on the spot first thing, all right?"

"Of course not! The very idea," Annette said, her voice climbing another octave. "Well, I should hope I have better breeding than that!"

"I hope so, too," Lina said, causing the various women to gasp. Annette's eyes narrowed and she let out a hollow, obviously fake laugh. Jamie glanced quickly at Lina, merriment in her eyes.

"Shall we go find the men?" Jamie said into the shocked silence that followed. "I believe dinner will be served very soon, and I'd like a cocktail first. Lina?"

"Yes, please," Lina said and followed Jamie as she turned and left the room. She realized that Annette and the others waited a beat before following, and wondered about the reason for it.

"Oh!" Jamie said once they'd stepped out into the short hallway. She spoke under her breath in German, linking her arm through Lina's again and leaning close. "That was brilliant! Annette is such a vicious cow, it's nice to see someone put her in her place. She intimidates all the others, you see, because her husband is the next-highest-ranking officer here, blah, blah, blah. She hates me, of course, but I don't care. There's nothing she can do to *me*. Except isolate me, I suppose, but then, I'm a woman of many resources. I really don't need the society of simpering lilies like them."

"Then why invite them to your house?" Lina asked.

"Eh. It's expected, and it's part of my job as Christopher's wife. Don't worry for me, Lina, I've handled hundreds of catty women like Annette. It's just a treat to see someone else take her down a peg. So thank you for that."

"I didn't do anything in particular, I was just honest."

"Yes, and it's honesty that woman cannot abide. I'd warn you to watch yourself, but you've faced much worse than her, I'm sure," Jamie said. "I'm sorry to have to put you through that, but it's the way things are done, unfortunately."

"Does that mean they must always be done that way?"

"No," Jamie said, giving her an approving smile, "but one picks one's battles, no? Besides, sometimes it's entertaining. Just through here, dear. There are some people I think you'll be interested to meet."

She reached out and slid a heavy wooden pocket door back into the wall, revealing a long dining room with a wooden table set with fine china and glowing with candles set in intricate candelabras. Several gentlemen stood clustered about the fireplace at the far end, and they turned as Jamie and Lina walked in. Paul and General DiNote stood among them, as did a face Lina picked out of the crowd immediately.

"Doc!"

"Lina," Doc said, smiling a genuine, if tired, smile as she hurried across the room to him. "You look beautiful."

"How's Rolland?" she asked.

"Better now," he said, his smile growing. "His injuries were more extensive than we suspected. I have no idea how he managed the trip from Fürstenwalde, let alone the route you took by cart, but we got him here in time. In fact, I'd like to introduce you to someone, if you don't mind?"

"Of course not," she said while reaching her hand out to Paul as he stepped close to her side. She was only partially conscious of the movement; it was just her natural reaction to his proximity. Doc's eyes flitted down, then back up to her face, and his smile softened.

"I heard it's official. Congratulations."

"Thank you," Paul said, squeezing her fingers. Doc gave him a short nod and then turned to beckon someone forward.

"Mrs. Lina Rutherford, Paul, may I present Doctor Heinrich Krug? Doctor Krug is the surgeon whose expertise saved Rolland's life. Doctor, please meet the Rutherfords, who rescued your patient from the clutches of the Red Army."

Doctor Krug brought his feet together with a snap and gave them a short bow from the waist. "Major and Mrs. Rutherford, it's a pleasure to meet you," he said, his English barely accented. He had dark hair and light green eyes that looked out through rimless spectacles. His penetrating gaze lingered on Lina, and he narrowed his lids slightly.

"Forgive me, Madam," he said, "have we never met?"

"I don't believe so, Doctor," Lina said softly.

"But you are German, yes?"

"Yes," she said. "I was born in Bremen."

"And during the war?"

"I traveled," she said, her voice going tight. "Extensively."

"Ah," the doctor said, his lips curving up slightly. He gave her a little nod and let the subject drop. "Well, *enchanté*, as the French say. I'm pleased to report that your friend Thanhouser is resting comfortably. He sustained serious internal injuries, but we were able to get him into surgery in enough time to repair the worst of the damage. He'll have a long recovery, but he *will* recover."

"That's excellent news, Doctor," Paul said, reaching out to shake the man's hand. "When can we see him?"

"Perhaps tomorrow, perhaps the next day. Doctor Wholrab will let you know," Krug said, nodding at his colleague. "He'll continue in his role as your friend's primary doctor. I have other work to which I must return."

"Of course," Paul said, his tone chilling. Lina fought the urge to look up at him, but she extended a tendril of inquiry and found a sea of distaste seething in her husband's mind.

You feel this way about Doctor Krug? she asked as the man himself gave them a polite nod and turned to walk away.

That man is as close to evil as I've seen, Paul said, his vehemence almost physical. Lina tightened her fingers in his as confusion made her glance at their friend Doc, who was walking with Krug and speaking in an undertone about something.

Doctor Krug? Lina asked, still unsure. *He seemed perfectly pleasant, and Doc said he was the best surgeon in Europe...*

He is. I don't argue with his expertise. What nauseates me is the way he acquired it. He was a camp doctor at one of the Nazi death camps.

Death camps? Lina asked, her mind sharpening with scorn. *Work camps, yes. And yes, conditions were terrible...but 'death camps?' A bit melodramatic, no?*

Paul gripped her hand and pulled so she turned to face him. He took her other hand and locked his gaze onto hers with a painful intensity.

Lina, don't. If you love me at all, don't. I heard what Rolland told you at Dora, but he barely touched on the suffering those men endured. They were literally worked to death, so please don't diminish their pain by brushing it off. Conditions there were more than terrible; they were inhumane. They were evil, and they were nothing to the conditions in places like Birkenau. Those truly were 'death camps,' because their entire purpose was to exterminate the people unfortunate enough to be sent there. Unless monsters like Krug decided to use them in his experiments.

Experiments? Lina asked, as her spinning, careening mind seized on that one word. *What do you mean?*

Medical experiments. On living subjects. Who had no choice.

No, Lina said. *That's not possible...*

Volcanic anger burst forth in Paul's mind and scorched the lines of Lina's psyche. She stifled a gasp and let his fingers drop, taking a step back.

I assure you, Paul said, his words an icy contrast to the heat of his rage, *it's very much the truth. I've seen the photographs. That man, whom you find so pleasant, performed vivisections on men, women, and little children just to find out how our bodies work. He infected them with diseases just to watch how their immune systems work. He subjected them to toxic chemicals and freezing temperatures; he froze parts of their bodies off to see what would happen to aircrews at high altitudes. He committed atrocities in the name of research. That's why he's one of the most skilled surgeons in Europe.*

Lina felt the texture of her gloves on her lips and belatedly realized she'd covered her mouth in horror.

Wh-why is he here, then? she asked, hating how young and unsure her mind tone felt. *Why was he not imprisoned? Or hanged? Why—?*

Because the United States government wants his knowledge, Paul sent, every word edged in bitterness. *Because what he's learned can't be replicated. Because it's better for the American people if we have him and the Soviets do not.*

But—

But what?

But if he's done these things, should he not die? What you describe…that's not war. That's criminal!

Paul reached out and took hold of her hand again. He pulled her fingertips away from her lips and brought them to his own.

Lina, my love, where do we draw the line? Yes, he's a war criminal, but then, according to the law, so is Rolland. So are you!

I? I never hurt anyone! I only did my job!

Yes, you did your job. You used your powers to weed out resistance to Nazi rule and sent dissidents into captivity. Where do you think Krug got his victims, love? You're not evil, but these lovely hands of yours are far from clean.

Lina tried to pull away again, but Paul tightened his grip. Not enough to hurt, just enough that she couldn't disengage.

I love you, he said.

She tugged against his fingers again.

Lina, I love you. You said it yourself, none of us are angels here. I just…We cannot eliminate Krug's protections without also eliminating Rolland's, and more importantly, yours. Being my wife isn't enough to get you home where you're safe. Being a Confiscate asset might be. Just as with the Thanhouser girls.

Lina swallowed hard and closed her eyes, forcing herself to calm. Behind her barriers, she wept and raged that she was *nothing* like Krug. She'd never used human beings as laboratory animals! She'd never tortured anyone! She'd only ever done her duty! How was that different from the men who flew high over cities, unleashing fire and metal down on unsuspecting civilians below? They'd been at war!

But they'd lost.

That single thought crystalized in her mind, and stilled her storm of emotion. Anger and rage began to drain away, leaving only an emptied-out sort of feeling. In the end, none of it mattered. They'd lost. The world was torn apart, and now her task was simply to try to survive.

Paul squeezed her hand again.

I love you. Don't run away.

I'm not moving.

You know what I mean. I love you, Lina. I'm sorry I upset you, but I've always been honest with you.

I'm not like him. I only did my duty.

I know. Me too. Remember that, okay?

Lina blinked her eyes and turned to look at her husband's face. His handsome features creased in worry, but he summoned up a smile for her. Despite the fact that there were plenty of people around, Lina took a moment to reach up and lay the palm of her gloved hand against his cheek.

I will remember. We are none of us angels. I love you, too.

His smile deepened, reached up to his eyes, and he bent to press the lightest of kisses to her forehead.

Just then a chime announced it was time to eat, and Lina squared her shoulders and prepared to face the rest of the evening.

* * *

Of course she had to be seated next to Annette's husband, Colonel Cleverland. He was the commander of the local airfield, and a stone-faced man of few words. Which Lina could certainly understand, given the temperament of his wife. Indeed, if the woman's performance at dinner was any kind of indication as to her normal behavior, Lina was surprised the man ever spoke at all. He could hardly get a word in edgewise.

"Lina, my dear," Annette gushed as soon as the salad plates went down. "I'm so thrilled to get another chance to speak with you. You *must* tell me about how you and dear Rutherford met!"

"I don't think so," Lina said. "I was one of his contacts; I am not sure how much of the story can be told." Paul, sitting on her other side, had silently given her this helpful phrase as an out, and she felt a surge of amusement from him as she used it without hesitation.

"Ohhh," Annette said, her eyes going wide as she nodded in what Lina imagined was supposed to be a knowing and worldly-wise fashion. "I completely understand. I won't say another word, my dear. It's just that we're all so *fascinated*. You've made quite a catch, you know. Your husband is quite dashing, what with his war record and everything. Has he told you his stories?"

"Some of them."

"Yes, well, I imagine he's told you all the best ones. But then, maybe not, these dear men are so modest, are they not? They hate it when we women make a fuss." She gave her impassive husband a simpering look and a little giggle, which he ignored as he continued eating his salad. Lina felt a surge of pity for the man.

"Paul is very modest," Lina said when it became apparent that Annette expected some kind of reply.

"Isn't he just, though? I bet he didn't even tell you about being shot down in his bomber, did he? Or his daring escape through occupied Europe?"

A stab of alarm came from Paul, causing Lina to turn toward him.

"Mrs. Cleverland," Paul said, his tone dry and quelling, "there's no need to go into all that tonight."

"Oh, I'm so sorry, my dear," Annette said, her face assuming a look of mock horror, though Lina could see a glint of triumph in her eyes. "Perhaps you don't like talking about it. You lost friends in that crash, surely."

"We all lost friends in the war," Lina said, reaching out a hand to her husband. He took it and squeezed her fingers.

"Indeed," Annette said, her voice wavering. She gave a delicate sniff and dabbed at the corner of her eye with her napkin. Loathing rose up in Lina's throat like bile, and she inhaled slowly and took a sip of wine to keep from doing anything more drastic. Paul leaned forward and addressed some remark to Cleverland, but the man just grunted and continued eating. Annette scowled at him and began taking him to task in a low tone. She was making a bit of a scene, but Lina found she didn't mind. It was better than having the woman's attention centered on her.

She focused on her meal at that point, determined to keep her head down.

When can we leave? she asked Paul.

After dessert, he said. *I'm sorry, I should have plead fatigue and kept you away from here. It's just that the DiNotes are friends, and it could be helpful for you to know them. I didn't realize how miserable you'd be meeting everyone else.*

I am all right, she said. *I've done worse. At least they're not hitting me.*

Not physically, anyway, he responded with his usual dry humor. That made her snort softly in lieu of a smile, and she ducked her head lower to keep him from seeing the corners of her mouth lift.

The rest of the meal was unremarkable. Afterward, Jamie Di-Note's staff brought around whiskey and cigars for the men, and cordials for the women. Lina demurred, pleading fatigue.

"Well, of course you're tired," Jamie said, her tone as tart as the sorbet she'd served. "You just came in this morning! Rutherford, please, do take your lovely wife home and let her rest. Thank you for coming, my dear. You certainly added much joy to our party."

Paul nodded at Jamie and stood up, pulling Lina's chair back.

"Thank you, Mrs. DiNote," Lina said as she stood, "for your warm welcome. This evening has been an experience I'll not soon forget."

Jamie's barely-there wink told Lina that the general's wife fully understood the subtext of her comment. She realized rather suddenly that Paul was right. Jamie and her husband *were* friends, working on their behalf to help them reach their goals. The problem, of course, was that Lina wasn't sure just *what* her goal was. Paul had said he wanted to take her home, where it was safe…but would it be safe for her?

These thoughts tumbled around in Lina's head as they headed toward the cloakroom and the front door. To give herself a minute, Lina murmured a quick apology to Paul and ducked into the powder room that had been pointed out to her earlier. She looked at herself in the mirror, indulged in some mind-calming exercises, and squared her shoulders. Just as she reached for the door handle, however, it turned, and Annette Cleverland pulled it open.

"Oh! My gracious! Excuse me!" the woman said, raising a hand to her chest in surprise. Her eyes, however, showed only cold calculation and a spark of triumph.

"I was just finished," Lina said.

"Yes, well, I *am* sorry. But I can't regret one last opportunity to see your sweet face before you go, my dear. I really was *so* pleased to meet you this evening. I feel as if we shall really become the *best* of friends."

"That would be something."

"Wouldn't it just? You'll see, friendship with me has its perks. I know *all* the gossip, not that I like to indulge. But sometimes people have a right to know, don't you think? Like you, for example. If it were me, *I* would want to know about the mysterious woman who followed my husband all over Europe during the war. Was that one of the stories he told you?" Annette's smile grew nastier and nastier as she spoke, and she finally unsheathed the claws she'd clearly been dying to bury into Lina.

Lina couldn't help it. She laughed.

"Does that make you feel better?" she asked as Annette's expression faded from vicious pleasure to one of irritation.

"Does what make me feel better?"

"Saying hurtful things to people? Does it make you feel better about your own empty life? I don't know who my husband knew during the war. I don't care. He's mine now, forever and irrevocably. Nothing before that matters."

"You're nothing but a Nazi kraut bitch," Annette said, her voice dropping down into a low hiss. "He'll leave you within a month!"

"Doubtful," Lina said. "We're bonded in a way you can't begin to understand. Good evening, Mrs. Cleverland." She stepped toward Annette, and though the other woman was taller, and broader through the shoulders, she gave way and stepped back. Lina allowed herself a tiny smile as she walked past.

"Everything all right?" Paul asked when she rejoined him at the front door. He reached out a hand and Lina took it.

"Everything's fine," Lina said. "Let's go."

* * * * *

Chapter Eight –
Immigration

They remained in Oberursel for a little more than a month. During that time, Lina assisted Paul in "debriefing" the other "assets" gathered up as part of Operation Confiscate. Like Lina, each of these men had once been at the top of their profession, doing their work for the Reich and for Germany. Like Lina, each of them had come to the realization that serving the Americans was preferable to serving the Soviets. Both wartime enemies would coerce cooperation, but the Americans were at least polite about it. Most of the assets had families with them, and they'd formed quite the vibrant community, despite the armed guards and fence around the area.

Officially, the guards were there for the assets' protection, and no one ever called the families "hostages" out loud, but Lina wasn't inexperienced in the ways of coercion. The families would be protected. The assets would be hired. Everyone would be treated well, so long as the US Government got what it wanted...and the Soviets did not.

To a man, the assets found that an acceptable condition. Insufferable as the Americans were, they didn't tend to be vicious, like the Soviets. Rolland's experience demonstrated that with perfect eloquence.

269

He continued to heal under Doc's watchful eye. They were even able to reconstruct his hands, to a degree. Lina began visiting him daily, helping him translate his little notebook, and encouraging him in his physical rehabilitation exercises.

Lina even struck up a friendship with Jamie DiNote. The commanding general's wife had made it her personal mission to make Oberursel as comfortable as possible for the assets' families, and Lina found herself in the position of being able to act as a go-between.

"They're nervous talking to me, you see," Jamie said. "And who can blame them, with the war not five years done? But I need to know what's really going on with them if I'm to help, and they'll talk to you, Lina. They see you as one of them."

"Because I am," Lina said.

"Well," Jamie replied with her signature grin, "there is that."

But truth be told, Lina was glad to help. It gave her something to focus on other than the details she elicited from the assets, and it felt like putting something good into the world. Particularly when she was able to help the children with their wide, nervous eyes. It made her miss Johanna, Aleda, and Ginette, though. And that made her wonder if she should start thinking about her own children with Paul, someday.

All in all, though, it was a pleasant enough time. Lina would have quite enjoyed it, had it not been for the nightmares.

They started the night after the dinner party. In her sleep, Lina was walking through a snowy wood that tugged at her memory. She crept slowly forward, knowing it was imperative that she make no noise. She could barely see in the darkness, but a fire flickered through the trees not far away. She knew she couldn't look in that direction because it would ruin her night vision. She kept moving forward, sliding through the night and the trees until she could make out a lone figure up ahead. She drew her knife and continued, stepping so carefully, lest he turn and see her, and shoot her with the Mauser he carried—

Lina woke, gasping, sitting up in bed.

"The same dream?" Paul asked out loud, his voice thick with sleep.

"Yes," she said, reaching out to him. He opened his arms and welcomed her close. Through their link, Lina could feel his sleepy pleasure at the feeling of her nestling close.

"Wanna tell me about it this time?"

"No," she said. "No need. It's just a dream."

"You've had it for what, five weeks now?" Paul's voice strengthened as he awakened fully. "Don't you think you should talk about it? It might help."

"No," Lina said again, nestling her head into the hollow of her husband's shoulder. "I'm fine. It's just being here, talking to the assets. I'll be fine as soon as we leave tomorrow."

"Just like that?"

"We're starting a new life, are we not? Surely that must count for something."

Lina could feel Paul's doubt edging his thoughts, but he didn't push. Instead, he pulled her even closer and stroked her hair. The scent of his skin and the warmth of the bedcovers combined to soften her mind and relax her body enough so that she drifted back to sleep.

In the morning they woke and dressed, but instead of going to meet with the assets, they got into the DiNotes' shiny black car and took a short ride south across the river to Rhein-Main Air Base. The general's driver stopped to present his identification at the front gate, and once again Lina heard the low, almost subliminal buzz of aircraft engines in the distance.

"Have you ever flown on an airplane before?" Paul asked her as they pulled up to a large building labeled "Passenger Terminal." Lina shook her head, and Paul's smile turned grim.

"Well," he said, "you're about to get your fill of it. Try to sleep as much as you can; that's the best advice I can offer."

The car stopped, and the driver got out to open their door before proceeding to the rear of the car to pull out their luggage. Neither of them had much, and Lina thanked him with a smile as he handed her the small valise. He nodded acknowledgment, and that was that. She and Paul turned and went into the terminal.

Over the next two days, Lina remembered Paul's advice and tried her best to take it to heart. Unfortunately for her, air travel wasn't exactly comfortable. The aircraft were primarily designed to haul military cargo, and passenger seats were small, webbed affairs that offered nothing in the way of support. It was cramped, the constant stench of fuel gave her a headache, and the sensation of movement made her feel sick to her stomach, especially when there was turbulence. So Lina laid her head on Paul's shoulder and spent the majority of the flight to London with her eyes squeezed shut, willing herself to sleep.

After London, they flew to Ireland, then Newfoundland, and then finally to New York City. None of the flight experiences were any more agreeable, and Lina felt that she could have wept with exhaustion once they finally stepped off the last airplane. It was late in the night, and Paul got them a car from the airport to a hotel, where he checked them in.

Lina fell into the bed, reveling in the feeling of being able to stretch out and really, truly rest. Her eyes drifted closed, and sleep reached up to claim her mind as a single thought remained.

She was in America. The belly of the beast.

What a strange world this had become.

* * *

Lina slept for at least twelve hours and woke up ravenous in a room she didn't recognize. Only Paul's light snores beside her kept her from panicking as she sat up and looked around at the completely unfamiliar furnishings. It was daytime, judging by the stream of light coming between the two heavy drapes that shrouded the window. A small table stood at the foot of the bed, set with covered dishes. An open door beyond that hinted at the presence of a bathroom. She looked down and found her own valise beside the bed.

A hotel. Their hotel. Paul had brought them here after they'd landed and processed in. She barely remembered going through immigration. They'd questioned her about the marriage, hadn't they?

Whatever they'd done, it didn't matter nearly as much as the way her stomach rumbled. She flipped the blankets back and slipped out of the bed. She was still wearing her traveling clothes. She'd been too tired to even undress.

She padded in her stocking feet over to the table and lifted the cover off one of the dishes. Toast and sausages, and something that might have been eggs? She grabbed a sausage link and popped it into her mouth, closing her eyes in bliss at the taste, even cold. Hunger truly was the best sauce.

She ate all the sausages and bread on that plate, leaving the might-be-eggs for further investigation. That took the edge off of her hunger and left her feeling dirty and rumpled. Paul still slept, so she might as well use the time to her advantage.

Lina grabbed her valise and headed for the bathroom. A switch near the door turned on the electric light and sent Lina's eyebrows up in surprise. The bathroom was positively *luxurious*! The marble vanity counter and white porcelain bathtub shone, and she could see her reflection in the polished fixtures. She fiddled with the bath faucet experimentally and made another discovery—this bathtub had an overhead shower! Steam began to billow out as hot water sluiced down from the overhead nozzle. Lina reached out to let the water run over her fingers, then stripped out of her wrinkled clothes, kicked them to the side, and stepped over the edge of the tub and into the deliciously hot stream.

The water pounded down on her head and shoulders like a masseuse's fingers. She tilted her head back, shaking her head to wet all of her hair. A small trio of bottles sat on the back lip of the tub. She didn't recognize all the English words on the label, but it smelled nice and felt like shampoo, so she worked it into her scalp and through her tresses.

The shower felt so good she almost didn't want to leave it, but eventually her fingertips got wrinkled and plump, and her skin had turned bright red from the heat of the spray. She turned the water off and grabbed one of the hotel's fluffy white towels.

By the time she got herself dried off and dressed, Paul was awake, and he met her eyes with a smile as she emerged from the bathroom.

"I see you found the shower."

"Are all American hotels this nice?" she asked.

"Just the Ritz-Carlton," he said with a smile. "I wanted to bring you somewhere nice."

"Why?" she asked as she walked toward him. "This must have cost a fortune."

"Money I've got," he said. "I thought you'd enjoy a little luxury. Since this is the closest thing we've had to a honeymoon...yet."

"It's lovely," she said, "but it seems impractical. Surely it's better to keep a little by? For emergencies?"

Paul smiled at her and got out of bed, then walked over to fold her into a hug. She inhaled, drawing in the scent of his skin and reveling in the way his embrace always made her feel protected.

"My grandmother died a few years ago," he said into her hair. "I didn't know it when she was alive, but she was a rich woman, and very smart with her money. She left me everything she had. She was a lady through and through, and she would've wanted my bride to have the best. Don't worry, Lina. We have more than enough set by for emergencies."

Lina wanted to protest that he never knew. That her family had been rich once, too. But in the end, even their money hadn't been enough to save them, and after the war, it was all worthless anyway. Paul spoke with the easy confidence of someone whose home had never been threatened by war. She envied him that.

"All right," she said. "So what will we do now, then?"

He kissed her briefly, then let her go and gave her a little smile. His eyes took on that dark gleam that meant he was thinking of sex, and she couldn't help but laugh.

"After that?"

"Well," he said, "I thought I'd take a shower, and then we'll go out and get something to eat. I ordered room service before I went to bed, but I know that won't be enough for you for long."

"Then?"

"Then we'll check out and buy tickets west. I promised you I'd take you to Isa and the girls. You still want to see them, right?"

"Oh, yes!" she said, a sudden hope burning painfully in her chest. "More than anything!"

"Well, that's what we'll do. It's a long trip, but you'll get to see some of your new country while we're at it."

My new country. She shut her barriers down before Paul could feel her shock at the thought. Was that what this was? Was she to become an American now? After all that had happened, after all the Americans had taken from her? Could she just turn her coat and be one of them...for a man?

She shoved those thoughts away and locked a mental door on them as Paul took her hand and pulled her back toward the bed. She could figure it out later. For now, she had other, more important things to do.

* * *

America was massive.

Lina had known, intellectually, that it was a big place, but she'd never realized just exactly *how* big it was. They'd boarded a train in Manhattan three days ago, and Lina sensed no end in sight. No matter which direction she stared out the train's windows, she could see only field after field of summer crops, stretching off to an achingly distant horizon. There had been mountains and lakes and cities a day or so ago, but just now Lina felt like a tiny speck lost in a rippling sea of grass.

"How did people cross these plains before there were trains?" Lina asked, turning her attention to Paul at her side. "On horseback? Could it be possible? There's nothing here!"

"There's nothing here *now*," Paul said. "The Plains Indians lived here for thousands of years, though. Once upon a time, vast herds of buffalo roamed all throughout here. Entire tribes would follow the herds and live off their meat and such."

"And now?" Lina asked, turning back to look out the window, trying to imagine a vast herd of animals inhabiting such a desolate place.

"Now it's mostly farmland," Paul said. "The Indians are mostly gone, or have been moved to reservations. The buffalo have all but died out."

"What happened? Disease?"

"Overhunting. Buffalo skins are valuable, and you can kill a lot more of them with a rifle from a train than you can with a bow and arrow from horseback." Lina turned back to look at him, wondering if this was more of his dry humor, but he just shrugged and tilted his head in such a way that she knew it was the naked truth.

"That's horrible," she murmured.

"That's progress," he answered, and this time she could hear the sarcasm in his words. She felt him reach out and take her hand, twining their fingers together. "None of us are angels, remember."

"Of course," she said. "It's just...with all this space, it seems odd that people can't coexist."

"Land is like any other resource, my love. There's always someone who wants more of it."

She nodded, looking out at the waving grasses once more.

"Where are we going again?" she asked after a few moments, ready to change the subject.

"To see my sister. Isa and the Thanhouser girls are staying with her while she tutors the girls."

"No, I knew that," Lina said, scowling up at him before giving him a smile. "I meant the name of the place. I've forgotten."

"Oh, Rapid City, in the state of South Dakota."

"That seems a strange name for a city in the midst of this sea of grass."

"Well, Rapid's on the edge of the Black Hills, so it's not quite like this everywhere. There's a small river that runs through the town. That's what it's named after."

"And these Black Hills? Are they truly black?"

"From a distance. They're covered in pine trees, which are so dark green they look black. It's pretty country, actually. I think you'll like it."

"Anything would be better than this," Lina said, gesturing to the window. Paul let out a short, sharp laugh.

"Ah, Lina," he said. "You don't understand! That's part of why we won the war—both wars. The one in 1918, as well. Those crops you see? That's all food. No matter what happens, America can feed herself and her allies. You have to admit, that's no mean feat."

"Yes," she said, swaying as the train rocked them back and forth. "Germany would have given much to say the same. You're like the

Russians in that respect. You always have your endless fields to fall back upon."

Paul didn't say anything to that, simply wrapped his arm around her shoulders and pulled her back to lean against him. Lina let her eyes fall closed, and her mind drift. The motion of the train and the rhythm of the sounds it made lulled her toward sleep.

...once more she stepped through the snow-covered trees, stalking the German soldier. No matter how much her mind screamed at her to stop, she continued gliding silently forward. Her hand drew her knife, her arm went up and plunged downward, driving into the joint between the neck and shoulder...

Lina sat up, gaspi—no, retching. To her immense shame and embarrassment, she leaned forward and emptied the contents of her stomach onto the carpeted floor of the train car.

"Lina!" Paul said, sitting up and reaching to support her upper body as she continued to heave until tears ran thick down her face. A steward appeared next to their seats, offering towels and a wet cloth, which Paul laid over the back of her neck.

"I'm so sorry," she whimpered as soon as she could speak. Her voice remained thick and broken. "I don't—I don't know why—"

"Shh, Lina, it's all right," Paul said, using another cloth to wipe her chin clean.

"It's no problem, Madam," the train steward said as he bent to clean up the mess she'd made. "Motion sickness happens all the time. When you're ready, I'll reseat you both, and we'll get this cleaned up in no time."

* * *

Finally, finally, they arrived in Rapid City.

Lina felt dazed with fatigue. Every time she closed her eyes, her brain had her stalking through the snowy wood. Between that and the motion sickness from the train's sway, she didn't dare sleep, no matter how much Paul begged her to try. She could feel his worry simmering down their link, but she couldn't stand the thought of facing the dream or the nausea once again.

The midmorning sun slanted through the train's windows by the time the conductor walked through, announcing their imminent arrival. Relief poured over Lina, along with an eagerness to leave this benighted train behind forever. She didn't care if she had to *walk* back to New York City. She wasn't getting on another American train, ever. Clearly they'd done something different over here, because taking the train had never bothered her in Europe.

"Lina?" Paul asked, his voice uncharacteristically tentative.

"I'm fine," she said, a bit more waspishly than she'd intended. "I just need to get off this train."

"All right," he said. "I just—well. It can wait. Let's get you off, and we'll find a place for you to rest."

She wanted to snap back at him that she didn't need to rest, but she obviously did, so she held her tongue. The train slowed and jolted to a stop, and Lina pushed herself up to her feet and followed Paul as he stepped out into the aisle, then down the stairs and onto the platform.

"Thank you for traveling with us, ma'am," the steward who'd helped them earlier said as they passed. Lina gave him a wan smile and hurried on ahead, driven by her need to be on solid ground once more.

The platform seethed with people. Glad cries of welcome and homecoming rose all around, and everywhere Lina looked, she saw people embracing, patting each other on the back, shaking hands, weeping. Despite her grinding fatigue and the lingering nausea, a warm feeling spread through her as she watched all the joyful reunions.

"Paul!" a woman's voice called out behind them, gladness ringing through the tone. Lina turned with her husband to see a dark-haired woman rushing toward them, her arms stretched wide in welcome. "We thought we'd surprise you—"

The bottom dropped out of Lina's stomach as she got a good look at the tall woman's face. Screams started in the back of her mind and came roaring to the forefront. A red haze—red as the blood on the floor of a snow-covered tent—crowded in from the edges of her vision. She couldn't breathe, couldn't speak past the pain that wrapped around her throat and squeezed with pitiless, life-destroying anger—

"Evie, No!" Paul yelled, but it was too late. The brunette woman's face creased in confusion and hurt. Then she turned her eyes to Lina.

Lina struck.

Josef's face, and Kristoff's, Hans' and Willi's and Werner's... they all appeared in Lina's mind's eye as she took all the pain, all the anguish she'd buried from that night so long ago and forged it into a needle-pointed weapon of destruction. Lina *pulled* everything she had, everything she could touch, everything she could grab from Paul's psyche, and used it to propel her sword of rage and hatred forward. Just as she'd done once before in a Berlin cellar, she lashed out to rend, to break, to destroy...

Evelyn Adamsen staggered backward, her hands going to her mouth. Somehow, she threw up a defense, but it was incomplete and weak. Lina's rage was too powerful. She couldn't turn it aside, couldn't dispel it. Lina struck again and again, hammering her pain and fear into the other woman's psyche, cracking her barriers, exposing the depths of her mind—

Something twisted, and a door long-forgotten opened in Lina's mind as Evelyn Adamsen reopened the link between them.

Agony like a storm howled in, engulfing Lina in a whirling maelstrom of fear and pain and confusion. She couldn't breathe, couldn't think, couldn't focus on anything except a single pinprick of heat, a tiny burn etched on the inside of her arm...the curve of a letter...a focus for a psychic pathway...

No! Evelyn's will hit her like a sledgehammer to the chest. The maelstrom deepened, howling louder in her mind. She was lost in the storm, adrift and helpless while the waves of pain and fear crashed over her, driving her under...

This is mine! Lina screamed into the storm. *I made this! This is mine to trap and hold you! And you will not take it from me the way you took everything else!*

She flexed her will, and the storm stuttered. The inferno inside her built, spilling out along the lines of her psyche, driving back the wind and the stinging, scouring rain.

You were trying to kill me! Evelyn shouted. *You were trying to drive me mad!*

I was doing my JOB! Lina's rage erupted, throwing out a heat so intense as to flash the rain to steam. The wind continued to howl around her, but it only whipped her flames higher, feeding the agony and intensity of pain she'd hidden deep inside for five long years. *You took everything from me! You took the man I loved! You took my brothers! You took my parents, and my little sisters! You took my purpose and my place in the world, and left me a broken thing! You rent my world asunder! You should have died in that tent, not me! NEVER ME!*

With those last words, the flames of Lina's revenge seared out and ignited the wind of the maelstrom itself. Hurricane became firestorm, and everywhere the rage touched, it burnt, crisped, cauterized.

On a train platform in Rapid City, South Dakota, Adalina Sucherin finally had her revenge as she and her greatest enemy cried out with one voice and fell, simultaneously, to the ground.

* * *

The slide of metal on metal penetrated through the lovely fog that wreathed Lina's mind and pulled her slowly to the surface.

Despite the weight of her eyelids, she managed to crack them open in time to see a white-clad woman bending to open a curtain a second before she felt the gentle warmth of sunlight bathing her face.

"Ready for another bottle?" the nurse said and turned to look at something out of Lina's field of vision. She jiggled something, and a sudden, sharp pain in the back of Lina's hand brought her mind the rest of the way out of the fog and threw everything into sharp focus.

"Bottle of what?" Lina asked. Or tried to ask, anyway. Her voice sounded rusty and raw, as if she'd been gargling with a slurry of metal shavings. The nurse started and turned to peer at Lina's face.

"Well!" the woman said in a cheery voice, a smile breaking open on her face. "Look at that. Back with us now, are you, Mrs. Rutherford? And how are you feeling?"

"Sore," Lina said. "All over."

"Yes, I imagine you do. Seizures can take people like that sometimes. When the muscles lock up and such. But otherwise?"

"I feel fine," she said. "What happened?"

"Well, my dear, just as I said. You had a seizure out at the train station. But not to worry, Dr. Mickey checked you out, and you're right as rain now. No harm to the baby at all."

"Baby?"

The nurse's eyes went wide. "Oh! You...you didn't know? Mrs. Rutherford, you're expecting a child. Dr. Mickey said you're between four and six weeks along."

Lina blinked rapidly as her mind tried to wrap around this information. There was something she was forgetting, something important, but all she could focus on was the idea of a child. A child!

"Why don't I send your husband in?" the nurse said, her voice gentle. "Congratulations."

Lina heard the door open and close, only to open again a moment later. She turned her head to look past the half-open curtain and saw Paul standing silhouetted in the doorway.

"Lina?"

He sounded worse than she did. His smooth, dark voice, always so confident and assured, sounded broken and tense. She watched him take one unsure step toward the bed, then another. As he came closer, she could see the deep lines of worry and fatigue etched into his proud, handsome face. Without thinking about it or meaning to do so, she reached up toward him.

Paul let out a sound like a sob and fell forward onto his knees next to the bed. He wrapped his hands around hers and pressed her knuckles to his lips, and Lina felt the wetness of tears on his cheeks.

"Oh, God. My Lina, I'm so sorry," he whispered. "I didn't—I didn't know how to—"

Memory came swirling back. The train. The nightmares. The nausea. The platform.

Evelyn...

Evelyn. For the first time since waking up surrounded by the dead bodies of her brothers and her love, Lina could think the American psychic's name and feel nothing. No rage, no pain, no fear...nothing. And not because she was locking her emotions away in a box...there *were* no emotions. They were just...gone. Burnt out. Expended.

"Does she live?" Lina asked.

Paul nodded, his eyes dark with pain. "Barely."

"Why didn't you tell me?"

"God, Lina, I wanted to! I was going to tell you on the train, but then you were so sick, and I just wanted to get you somewhere you could rest. I had no idea she'd come to surprise me!"

"How do you know her? Is she really your sister?"

"In every way that matters. I was her bombardier in the war. When *Pretty Cass* got shot down, and you and your men captured her, I...helped rescue them, after she..." he trailed off.

"You killed my men," Lina whispered. "Stalked them in the snow, between the trees."

"Yes," he said. "How did you...?"

"That was my nightmare. But it wasn't a dream. It was your memory."

Paul stared at her, silent for a long moment. Then he pressed his lips to her hand again and bent his head to rest on the edge of her hospital bed.

"What else?" Lina asked.

"That's it. I helped Evie, Sean, and Abram escape. We thought you were dead; we thought Wolffs had killed you. Then we escaped through Belgium and France over the Pyrenees to Spain."

"I chased you."

"I know," he said, lifting his head. "You nearly caught us at Bonaparte Beach."

"I wanted her dead. I wanted you all dead."

Paul looked at her, his dark eyes shiny with tears.

"I love you," he said in that broken parody of his usual voice. "I loved you in Berlin, when you were so strong in the face of torture. I loved you in Treplin, when I thought I'd lost you. I loved you in Erik's cabin, when you became my wife. I love you now. My life is yours. If you need to take it for my sins…it's yours. Do with it what you will."

Lina laced her fingers through his and reached out. The connection leapt into being between the two of them, like a puppy jumping up to meet its returning master. She felt her deep, cool reserves of power like a mirror-still, fathomless pond in her mind. She tapped into that power and began slowly feeding it along the lines of their connection like a caress, filling him full of herself. He shivered as the pathways of his psyche began to stretch, began to strain under the weight of all that energy. She waited for him to cry out, to pull away…

But he didn't. He simply met her eyes and dropped the last of his barriers, leaving his mind, his innermost being entirely exposed and vulnerable to her touch. She spread her deadliest self all along the pathways of his essence and paused, vibrating with power, poised on the edge of destruction, waiting for him to flinch.

I love you.

His thought dropped like a stone into the deep, still well of her power. A tiny ripple appeared on the surface of that pool and began to spread, leaving memory after memory in its wake:

His haughty face, backing her into a corner in Berlin.

His hands, white-knuckled on the steering wheel as he rocketed away from the security headquarters.

His eyes, dark with fury at what had been done to her.

His grin, lightning-quick at their improbable plan to rescue Rolland.

His hands again, trembling with desire, limned in moonlight as they touched her bare skin.

His lips, softness overlying steel as he kissed her in front of the chaplain.

His tears, streaking down his cheeks in relief at the sight of her awake.

His love. His heart-rending, aching love. So complete that he couldn't live without her. Would rather let himself be destroyed than live without her.

I love you too, enemy of my enemy, her mind whispered, *partner of my life, father of my child. We are none of us angels here.*

Paul drew in a deep, shuddering breath and lurched upward to press his lips to hers.

You are, he replied as he lifted up and looked into her eyes. *You're carrying our baby? You must be an angel.*

Angel of death, perhaps, she said, and was rewarded with a short, dry laugh from him.

An angel nonetheless. You really forgive me? I tore your world asunder!

But then you gave it back to me, she said. *Then you made it whole again.*

* * * * *

Epilogue

"**A**re you sure about this?" the red-haired man named Sean asked Paul for the fortieth time. Sean hadn't aged much in the five years since Lina had last seen him, but since he wasn't bleeding from a dozen minor injuries and beaten to a pulp, she almost hadn't recognized him at first. He knew her right away, though, and hadn't stopped staring daggers at her since she'd walked into his wife's hospital room.

"Sean," Paul said, "I love Evie, too, remember? I know it's hard, but please, you have to trust me. This might be our only chance to get her back."

Sean shifted in his chair next to the hospital bed, where his wife lay unresponsive. Then he turned, and for the first time, his furious blue eyes looked right at Lina.

"If you hurt her," he said in a low tone, "if you do a single thing to harm her, I'll find out about it, and I will kill you where you stand."

"Sean—" Paul started to say, his tone taking on a warning note, but Lina held up her hand and nodded.

"That's a fair condition," Lina said, and felt, more than saw her husband turn to stare at her in incredulity. Before Paul could say or do anything else, Lina walked forward and placed her hand on Evelyn's wrist, reaching out with her mind as she did so.

Once more the disused door in her mind creaked open. Only this time, there was no storm on the other side.

Evelyn? Lina called out down the lines of the link between them. The thought bounced back at her like an echo, but no response came from Evelyn herself. *Evelyn Adamsen, you must wake now. You are needed.*

Still nothing. Lina pulled back into her own body and pursed her lips, then nodded at Paul. Her husband swallowed hard, then stepped away to the door of the hospital room. He opened it, and three small, slight figures followed him in. The smallest, Johanna, smiled up at Lina and placed her tiny hand in Lina's outstretched one. Her oldest sister Ginette followed suit, giving each of the men a grave nod. Last came Aleda, the middle sister, the one with the strongest and most obvious psychic power. She joined her hands and her mind to her sisters and Lina, and together the four of them reached out to Evelyn once more.

Evelyn. Evie. Come back. Your family needs you.

A flurry of images rushed past Lina's mind's eye, surging through her mind down the link to the girls' minds. A blonde woman smiling a cheeky smile. A surge of fear as a wisp of cloud crossed in front of the nose of an aircraft in flight. A dizzying spin of ground and sky. A black mountain peak, looking tall and impossibly hard to cross. An overwhelming sense of gladness at the act of stepping off a boat. The sun shining through Sean's hair, turning it copper in the late afternoon light. A surge of pride as a door opened on a small, neat two-story house near the mountains...

...an interlocking love, so deep and constant that it couldn't be broken. Not even when the connection stretched for hundreds, thousands of miles. Not even when an ocean lay between nodes in the network...

Lina.

Evie.

What are you doing here?

I'm trying to bring you home. We're trying to bring you home.

Why?

Because…because your husband hasn't eaten for days. Because Abram and Mary are arriving tonight from California. Because Paul's worried about you.

Why do you care? You hate me.

Hated you.

Hated?

Lina took a deep breath, mindful of the Thanhouser girls' presence in their network.

Evie, you destroyed me, but I survived. My world was broken, but Paul helped me put it back together. The two of you are part of each other. I think you have been since the war. If I love him, I can't deny that. I can't deny that I love him, and so…

So?

So it's done. You destroyed me. I came back. I destroyed you. Now it's time for you to come back.

Just like that?

Just like that. If you're strong enough.

Pride flashed through Evie's mind, ricocheting back at Lina and the girls.

I'm the strongest there is.

Then prove it. Come back from where I sent you. If you can.

You're a bitch, Lina Sucherin.

Lina Rutherford, and watch your language, please. There are children present.

Lina felt a great heave and a wrench. On the hospital bed, Evie opened her eyes, looked around at her husband, her students, her brother, and her enemy…and started to laugh.

ABOUT THE AUTHOR

Kacey Ezell is an active duty USAF instructor pilot with 2500+ hours in the UH-1N Huey and Mi-171 helicopters. When not teaching young pilots to beat the air into submission, she writes sci-fi/fantasy/horror/noir/alternate history fiction. Her first novel, MINDS OF MEN, was a Dragon Award Finalist for Best Alternate History. She's contributed to multiple Baen anthologies and has twice been selected for inclusion in the Year's Best Military and Adventure Science Fiction compilation. In 2018, her story "Family Over Blood" won the Year's Best Military and Adventure Science Fiction Readers' Choice Award. In addition to writing for Baen, she has published several novels and short stories with independent publisher Chris Kennedy Publishing. She is married with two daughters. You can find out more and join her mailing list at www.kaceyezell.net.

* * * * *

Connect with Kacey Ezell Online

Website: www.kaceyezell.net

Amazon: https://www.amazon.com/Kacey-Ezell/e/B0195040QU/

Facebook: https://www.facebook.com/AuthorKaceyEzell/

Twitter: @Sevillalost

The following is an

Excerpt from Book One of the Salvage Title Trilogy:

Salvage Title

Kevin Steverson

Available Now from Theogony Books

eBook, Paperback, and Audio Book

Excerpt from "Salvage Title:"

The first thing Clip did was get power to the door and the access panel. Two of his power cells did the trick once he had them wired to the container. He then pulled out his slate and connected it. It lit up, and his fingers flew across it. It took him a few minutes to establish a link, then he programmed it to search for the combination to the access panel.

"Is it from a human ship?" Harmon asked, curious.

"I don't think so, but it doesn't matter; ones and zeros are still ones and zeros when it comes to computers. It's universal. I mean, there are some things you have to know to get other races' computers to run right, but it's not that hard," Clip said.

Harmon shook his head. *Riiigghht,* he thought. He knew better. Clip's intelligence test results were completely off the charts. Clip opted to go to work at Rinto's right after secondary school because there was nothing for him to learn at the colleges and universities on either Tretra or Joth. He could have received academic scholarships for advanced degrees on a number of nearby systems. He could have even gone all the way to Earth and attended the University of Georgia if he wanted. The problem was getting there. The schools would have provided free tuition if he could just have paid to get there.

Secondary school had been rough on Clip. He was a small guy that made excellent grades without trying. It would have been worse if Harmon hadn't let everyone know that Clip was his brother. They lived in the same foster center, so it was mostly true. The first day of school, Harmon had laid down the law—if you messed with Clip, you messed up.

299

At the age of fourteen, he beat three seniors senseless for attempting to put Clip in a trash container. One of them was a Yalteen, a member of a race of large humanoids from two systems over. It wasn't a fair fight—they should have brought more people with them. Harmon hated bullies.

After the suspension ended, the school's Warball coach came to see him. He started that season as a freshman and worked on using it to earn a scholarship to the academy. By the time he graduated, he was six feet two inches with two hundred and twenty pounds of muscle. He got the scholarship and a shot at going into space. It was the longest time he'd ever spent away from his foster brother, but he couldn't turn it down.

Clip stayed on Joth and went to work for Rinto. He figured it was a job that would get him access to all kinds of technical stuff, servos, motors, and maybe even some alien computers. The first week he was there, he tweaked the equipment and increased the plant's recycled steel production by 12 percent. Rinto was eternally grateful, as it put him solidly into the profit column instead of toeing the line between profit and loss. When Harmon came back to the planet after the academy, Rinto hired him on the spot on Clip's recommendation. After he saw Harmon operate the grappler and got to know him, he was glad he did.

A steady beeping brought Harmon back to the present. Clip's program had succeeded in unlocking the container. "Right on!" Clip exclaimed. He was always using expressions hundreds or more years out of style. "Let's see what we have; I hope this one isn't empty, too." Last month they'd come across a smaller vault, but it had been empty.

Harmon stepped up and wedged his hands into the small opening the door had made when it disengaged the locks. There wasn't enough power in the small cells Clip used to open it any further. He put his weight into it, and the door opened enough for them to get inside. Before they went in, Harmon placed a piece of pipe in the doorway so it couldn't close and lock on them, baking them alive before anyone realized they were missing.

Daylight shone in through the doorway, and they both froze in place; the weapons vault was full.

* * * * *

Get "Salvage Title" now at:
https://www.amazon.com/dp/B07H8Q3HBV.

Find out more about Kevin Steverson and "Salvage Title" at:
http://chriskennedypublishing.com/.

* * * * *

The following is an
Excerpt from Book One of the Earth Song Cycle:

Overture

Mark Wandrey

Now Available from Theogony Books

eBook and Paperback

Excerpt from "Overture:"

Dawn was still an hour away as Mindy Channely opened the roof access and stared in surprise at the crowd already assembled there. "Authorized Personnel Only" was printed in bold red letters on the door through which she and her husband, Jake, slipped onto the wide roof.

A few people standing nearby took notice of their arrival. Most had no reaction, a few nodded, and a couple waved tentatively. Mindy looked over the skyline of Portland and instinctively oriented herself before glancing to the east. The sky had an unnatural glow that had been growing steadily for hours, and as they watched, scintillating streamers of blue, white, and green radiated over the mountains like a strange, concentrated aurora borealis.

"You almost missed it," one man said. She let the door close, but saw someone had left a brick to keep it from closing completely. Mindy turned and saw the man who had spoken wore a security guard uniform. The easy access to the building made more sense.

"Ain't no one missin' this!" a drunk man slurred.

"We figured most people fled to the hills over the past week," Jake replied.

"I guess we were wrong," Mindy said.

"Might as well enjoy the show," the guard said and offered them a huge, hand-rolled cigarette that didn't smell like tobacco. She waved it off, and the two men shrugged before taking a puff.

"Here it comes!" someone yelled. Mindy looked to the east. There was a bright light coming over the Cascade Mountains, so intense it was like looking at a welder's torch. Asteroid LM-245 hit the atmosphere at over 300 miles per second. It seemed to move faster and faster, from east to west, and the people lifted their hands to shield their eyes from the blinding light. It looked like a blazing comet or a science fiction laser blast.

"Maybe it will just pass over," someone said in a voice full of hope.

Mindy shook her head. She'd studied the asteroid's track many times.

In a matter of a few seconds, it shot by and fell toward the western horizon, disappearing below the mountains between Portland and the ocean. Out of view of the city, it slammed into the ocean.

The impact was unimaginable. The air around the hypersonic projectile turned to superheated plasma, creating a shockwave that generated 10 times the energy of the largest nuclear weapon ever detonated as it hit the ocean's surface.

The kinetic energy was more than 1,000 megatons; however, the object didn't slow as it flashed through a half mile of ocean and into the sea bed, then into the mantel, and beyond.

On the surface, the blast effect appeared as a thermal flash brighter than the sun. Everyone on the rooftop watched with wide-eyed terror as the Tualatin Mountains between Portland and the Pacific Ocean were outlined in blinding light. As the light began to dissipate, the outline of the mountains blurred as a dense bank of smoke climbed from the western range.

The flash had incinerated everything on the other side.

The physical blast, travelling much faster than any normal atmospheric shockwave, hit the mountains and tore them from the bedrock, adding them to the rolling wave of destruction traveling east at several thousand miles per hour. The people on the rooftops of Portland only had two seconds before the entire city was wiped away.

Ten seconds later, the asteroid reached the core of the planet, and another dozen seconds after that, the Earth's fate was sealed.

* * * * *

Get "Overture" now at:
https://www.amazon.com/dp/B077YMLRHM/

Find out about Mark Wandrey and the Earth Song Cycle at:
https://chriskennedypublishing.com/

* * * * *

The following is an

Excerpt from Book One of the Revelations Cycle:

Cartwright's Cavaliers

Mark Wandrey

Available Now Seventh Seal Press

eBook, Paperback, and Audio Book

Excerpt from "Cartwright's Cavaliers:"

The last two operational tanks were trapped on their chosen path. Faced with destroyed vehicles front and back, they cut sideways to the edge of the dry river bed they'd been moving along and found several large boulders to maneuver around that allowed them to present a hull-down defensive position. Their troopers rallied on that position. It was starting to look like they'd dig in when *Phoenix 1* screamed over and strafed them with dual streams of railgun rounds. A split second later, *Phoenix 2* followed on a parallel path. Jim was just cheering the air attack when he saw it. The sixth damned tank, and it was a heavy.

"I got that last tank," Jim said over the command net.

"Observe and stand by," Murdock said.

"We'll have these in hand shortly," Buddha agreed, his transmission interspersed with the thudding of his CASPer firing its magnetic accelerator cannon. "We can be there in a few minutes."

Jim examined his battlespace. The tank was massive. It had to be one of the fusion-powered beasts he'd read about. Which meant shields and energy weapons. It was heading down the same gap the APC had taken, so it was heading right towards the APC and Second Squad, and fast.

"Shit," he said.

"Jim," Hargrave said, "we're in position. What are you doing?"

"Leading," Jim said as he jumped out from the rock wall.

# # # # #

Get "Cartwright's Cavaliers" now at:
https://www.amazon.com/dp/B077YMLRHM/

Find out about Mark Wandrey and the Earth Song Cycle at:
https://chriskennedypublishing.com/

* * * * *

Made in the USA
Las Vegas, NV
21 March 2023

69428365R00174